"A real staggerer by a man who is both a poetic dreamer and a competent scientist."

—Gilbert Highet

The coming of the Overlords was the most important and impressive event in Earth's history. These visitors from outer space brought peace and prosperity with them.

What more could the human race want?

But soon the change began . . .

The aliens started by subverting the children, pulling them away from their human heritage.

And that was only the beginning . . .

When the Overlords made their announcement, they had taken the first step in the elimination of the human race!

Also by Arthur C. Clarke
published by Ballantine Books:

EARTHLIGHT

EXPEDITION TO EARTH

IMPERIAL EARTH

PRELUDE TO SPACE

REACH FOR TOMORROW

RENDEZVOUS WITH RAMA

TALES FROM THE "WHITE HART"

Childhood's End

Arthur C. Clarke

A Del Rey Book

BALLANTINE BOOKS • NEW YORK

*The opinions expressed
in this book are not
those of the author.*

A Del Rey Book
Published by Ballantine Books

Library of Congress Catalog Card Number: 53-10419

ISBN 0-345-31558-8

Manufactured in the United States of America

First Ballantine Books Edition: August 1953
Forty-Eighth Printing: January 1984

First Special Printing: November 1974

Cover art by Stanislaw Fernandes

Childhood's
End

Prologue

1

THE VOLCANO that had reared Taratua up from the Pacific depths had been sleeping now for half a million years. Yet in a little while, thought Reinhold, the island would be bathed with fires fiercer than any that had attended its birth. He glanced towards the launching site, and his gaze climbed the pyramid of scaffolding that still surrounded the "Columbus." Two hundred feet above the ground, the ship's prow was catching the last rays of the descending sun. This was one of the last nights it would ever know: soon it would be floating in the eternal sunshine of space.

It was quiet here beneath the palms, high up on the rocky spine of the island. The only sound from the Project was the occasional yammering of an air compressor or the faint shout of a workman. Reinhold had grown fond of these clustered palms; almost every evening he had come here to survey his little empire. It saddened him to think that they would be blasted to atoms when the "Columbus" rose in flame and fury to the stars.

A mile beyond the reef, the "James Forrestal" had switched on her searchlights and was sweeping the dark waters. The sun had now vanished completely, and the swift tropical night was racing in from the east. Reinhold wondered, a little sardonically, if the carrier expected to find Russian submarines so close to shore.

The thought of Russia turned his mind, as it always did, to Konrad and that morning in the cataclysmic spring of 1945. More than thirty years had passed, but the memory of those last days when the Reich was crumbling beneath the waves from the East and from the West had never faded. He could still see Konrad's tired blue eyes, and the golden stubble on his chin, as they shook hands and parted in that ruined Prussian village, while the refugees streamed endlessly past. It was a parting that symbolized everything that had since happened to the world—the cleavage between East and West. For Konrad chose the road to Moscow. Reinhold had thought him a fool, but now he was not so sure.

For thirty years he had assumed that Konrad was dead. It was only a week ago that Colonel Sandmeyer, of Technical Intelligence, had given him the news. He didn't like Sandmeyer, and he was sure the feeling was mutual. But neither let that interfere with business.

"Mr. Hoffmann," the Colonel had begun, in his best official manner, "I've just had some alarming information from Washington. It's top secret, of course, but we've decided to break it to the engineering staff so that they'll realize the necessity for speed." He paused for effect, but the gesture was wasted on Reinhold. Somehow, he already knew what was coming.

"The Russians are nearly level with us. They've got some kind of atomic drive—it may even be more efficient than ours, and they're building a ship on the shores of Lake Baikal. We don't know how far they've got, but Intelligence believes it may be launched this year. You know what *that* means."

Yes, thought Reinhold, I know. The race is on—and we may not win it.

"Do you know who's running their team?" he had asked, not really expecting an answer. To his surprise, Colonel Sandmeyer had pushed across a typewritten sheet and there at its head was the name: Konrad Schneider.

"You knew a lot of these men at Peenemünde, didn't you?" said the Colonel. "That may give us some insight into their methods. I'd like you to let me have notes on as many of them as you can—their specialties, the bright ideas they had, and so on. I know it's asking a lot after all this time—but see what you can do."

"Konrad Schneider is the only one who matters," Reinhold had answered. "He was brilliant—the others are just competent engineers. Heaven only knows what he's done in thirty years. Remember—he's probably seen all our results and we haven't seen any of his. That gives him a decided advantage."

He hadn't meant this as a criticism of Intelligence, but for a moment it seemed as if Sandmeyer was going to be offended. Then the Colonel shrugged his shoulders.

"It works both ways—you've told me that yourself. Our free exchange of information means swifter progress, even if we do give away a few secrets. The Russian research departments probably don't know what their own people are doing half the time. We'll show them that Democracy can get to the moon first."

Democracy—Nuts! thought Reinhold, but knew better than to say it. One Konrad Schneider was worth a million names on an electoral roll. And what had Konrad done by this time, with all the resources of the U.S.S.R. behind him? Perhaps, even now, his ship was already outward bound from Earth. . . .

The sun which had deserted Taratua was still high above Lake Baikal when Konrad Schneider and the Assistant Commissar for Nuclear Science walked slowly back from the motor test rig. Their ears were still throbbing painfully, though the last thunderous echoes had died out across the lake ten minutes before.

"Why the long face?" asked Grigorievitch suddenly. "You should be happy now. In another month we'll be on our way, and the Yankees will be choking themselves with rage."

"You're an optimist, as usual," said Schneider. "Even though the motor works, it's not as easy as that. True, I can't see any serious obstacles now—but I'm worried about the reports from Taratua. I've told you how good Hoffmann is, and he's got billions of dollars behind him. Those photographs of his ship aren't very clear, but it looks as if it's not far from completion. And we know he tested his motor five weeks ago."

"Don't worry," laughed Grigorievitch. *"They're* the ones who are going to have the big surprise. Remember—they don't know a thing about us."

Schneider wondered if that was true, but decided it was much safer to express no doubts. That might start Grigorievitch's mind exploring far too many tortuous channels, and if there had been a leak, he would find it hard enough to clear himself.

The guard saluted as he re-entered the administration building. There were nearly as many soldiers here, he thought grimly, as technicians. But that was how the Russians did things, and as long as they kept out of his way he had no complaints. On the whole—with exasperating exceptions—events had turned out very much as he had hoped. Only the future could tell if he or Reinhold had made the better choice.

He was already at work on his final report when the sound of shouting voices disturbed him. For a moment he sat motionless at his desk, wondering what conceivable event could have disturbed the rigid discipline of the camp. Then he walked to the window—and for the first time in his life he knew despair.

The stars were all around him as Reinhold descended the little hill. Out at sea, the "Forrestal" was still sweeping the water with her fingers of light, while further along the beach the scaffolding round the "Columbus" had transformed itself into an illuminated Christmas tree. Only the projecting prow of the ship lay like a dark shadow across the stars.

A radio was blaring dance music from the living quarters, and unconsciously Reinhold's feet accelerated to the rhythm. He had almost reached the narrow road along the edge of the sands when some premonition, some half-glimpsed movement, made him stop. Puzzled, he glanced from land to sea and back again: it was some little time before he thought of looking at the sky.

Then Reinhold Hoffmann knew, as did Konrad Schneider at this same moment, that he had lost his race. And he knew that he had lost it, not by the few weeks or months that he had feared, but by millennia. The huge and silent shadows driving across the stars, more miles above his head than he dared to guess, were as far beyond his little "Columbus" as it surpassed the log canoes of paleolithic man. For a moment that seemed to last forever, Reinhold watched, as all the world was watching, while the great ships descended in their overwhelming majesty—until at last he could hear the faint scream of their passage through the thin air of the stratosphere.

He felt no regrets as the work of a lifetime was swept away. He had labored to take man to the stars, and, in the moment of success, the stars—the aloof, indifferent stars—had come to him. This was the moment when history held its breath, and the present sheared asunder from the past as an iceberg splits from its frozen, parent cliffs, and goes sailing out to sea in lonely pride. All that the past ages had achieved was as nothing now: only one thought echoed and re-echoed through Reinhold's brain:

The human race was no longer alone.

1

Earth and the Overlords

~~~~~~

2

THE SECRETARY-GENERAL of the United Nations stood motionless by the great window, staring down at the crawling traffic on Forty-third Street. He sometimes wondered if it was a good thing for any man to work at such an altitude above his fellow humans. Detachment was all very well, but it could change so easily to indifference. Or was he merely trying to rationalize his dislike of skyscrapers, still unabated after twenty years in New York?

He heard the door open behind him, but did not turn his head as Pieter Van Ryberg came into the room. There was the inevitable pause as Pieter looked disapprovingly at the thermostat, for it was a standing joke that the Secretary-General liked living in an icebox. Stormgren waited until his assistant joined him at the window, then tore his gaze away from the familiar yet always fascinating panorama below.

"They're late," he said. "Wainwright should have been here five minutes ago."

"I've just heard from the police. He's got quite a procession with him, and it's snarled up the traffic. He should be here any moment now."

13

Van Ryberg paused, then added abruptly, "Are you *still* sure it's a good idea to see him?"

"I'm afraid it's a little late to back out of it now. After all, I've agreed—though as you know it was never my idea in the first place."

Stormgren had walked to his desk and was fidgeting with his famous uranium paperweight. He was not nervous—merely undecided. He was also glad that Wainwright was late, for that would give him a slight moral advantage when the interview opened. Such trivialities played a greater part in human affairs than anyone who set much store on logic and reason might wish.

"Here they are!" said Van Ryberg suddenly, pressing his face against the window. "They're coming along the Avenue—a good three thousand, I'd say."

Stormgren picked up his notebook and rejoined his assistant. Half a mile away, a small but determined crowd was moving slowly toward the Secretariat Building. It carried banners that were indecipherable at this distance, but Stormgren knew their message well enough. Presently he could hear, rising above the sound of the traffic, the ominous rhythm of chanting voices. He felt a sudden wave of disgust sweep over him. Surely the world had had enough of marching mobs and angry slogans!

The crowd had now come abreast of the building; it must know that he was watching, for here and there fists were being shaken, rather self-consciously, in the air. They were not defying him, though the gesture was doubtless meant for Stormgren to see. As pygmies may threaten a giant, so those angry fists were directed against the sky fifty kilometers above his head—against the gleaming silver cloud that was the flagship of the Overlord fleet.

And very probably, thought Stormgren, Karellen was watching the whole thing and enjoying himself hugely, for this meeting would never have taken place except at the Supervisor's instigation.

This was the first time that Stormgren had ever met the head of the Freedom League. He had ceased to wonder if the action was wise, for Karellen's plans were often too subtle for merely human understanding. At the worst,

Stormgren did not see that any positive harm could be done. If he had refused to see Wainwright, the league would have used the fact as ammunition against him.

Alexander Wainwright was a tall, handsome man in his late forties. He was, Stormgren knew, completely honest, and therefore doubly dangerous. Yet his obvious sincerity made it hard to dislike him, whatever views one might have about the cause for which he stood—and about some of the followers he had attracted.

Stormgren wasted no time after Van Ryberg's brief and somewhat strained introductions.

"I suppose," he began, "the chief object of your visit is to register a formal protest against the Federation scheme. Am I correct?"

Wainwright nodded gravely.

"That is my main purpose, Mr. Secretary. As you know, for the last five years we have tried to awaken the human race to the danger that confronts it. The task has been a difficult one, for the majority of people seem content to let the Overlords run the world as they please. Nevertheless, more than five million patriots, in every country, have signed our petition."

"That is not a very impressive figure out of two and a half billion."

"It is a figure that cannot be ignored. And for every person who has signed, there are many who feel grave doubts about the wisdom, not to mention the rightness, of this Federation plan. Even Supervisor Karellen, for all his powers, cannot wipe out a thousand years of history at the stroke of a pen."

"What does anyone know of Karellen's powers?" retorted Stormgren. "When I was a boy, the Federation of Europe was a dream—but when I grew to manhood it had become reality. And *that* was before the arrival of the Overlords. Karellen is merely finishing the work we had begun."

"Europe was a cultural and geographic entity. The world is not—that is the difference."

"To the Overlords," replied Stormgren sarcastically, "the Earth probably is a great deal smaller than Europe seemed to our fathers—and their outlook, I submit, is more mature than ours."

"I do not necessarily quarrel with Federation as an *ultimate* objective—though many of my supporters might not agree. But it must come from within—not be super-imposed from without. We must work out our own destiny. There must be no more interference in human affairs!"

Stormgren sighed. All this he had heard a hundred times before, and he knew that he could only give the old answer that the Freedom League had refused to accept. He had faith in Karellen, and they had not. That was the fundamental difference, and there was nothing he could do about it. Luckily, there was nothing that the Freedom League could do, either.

"Let me ask you a few questions," he said. "Can you deny that the Overlords have brought security, peace, and prosperity to the world?"

"That is true. But they have taken our liberty. Man does not live—"

"—by bread alone. Yes, I know—but this is the first age in which every man was sure of getting even that. In any case, what freedom have we lost compared with that which the Overlords have given us for the first time in human history?"

"Freedom to control our own lives, under God's guidance."

At last, thought Stormgren, we've got to the point. Basically, the conflict is a religious one, however much it may be disguised. Wainwright never let you forget he was a clergyman. Though he no longer wore a clerical collar, somehow one always got the impression it was still there.

"Last month," pointed out Stormgren, "a hundred bishops, cardinals, and rabbis signed a joint declaration pledging their support for the Supervisor's policy. The world's religions are against you."

Wainwright shook his head in angry denial.

"Many of the leaders are blind; they have been corrupted by the Overlords. When they realize the danger, it may be too late. Humanity will have lost its initiative and become a subject race."

There was silence for a moment. Then Stormgren replied.

"In three days I will be meeting the Supervisor again. I will explain your objections to him, since it is my duty to represent the views of the world. But it will alter nothing—I can assure you of that."

"There is one other point," said Wainwright slowly. "We have many objections to the Overlords—but above all we detest their secretiveness. You are the only human being who has ever spoken with Karellen, and even *you* have never seen him! Is it surprising that we doubt his motives?"

"Despite all that he has done for humanity?"

"Yes—despite that. I do not know which we resent more—Karellen's omnipotence, or his secrecy. If he has nothing to hide, why will he never reveal himself? Next time you speak with the Supervisor, Mr. Stormgren, ask him that!"

Stormgren was silent. There was nothing he could say to this—nothing, at any rate, that would convince the other. He sometimes wondered if he had really convinced himself.

It was, of course, only a very small operation from their point of view, but to Earth it was the biggest thing that had ever happened. There had been no warning when the great ships came pouring out of the unknown depths of space. Countless times this day had been described in fiction, but no one had really believed that it would ever come. Now it had dawned at last; the gleaming, silent shapes hanging over every land were the symbol of a science man could not hope to match for centuries. For six days they had floated motionless above his cities, giving no hint that they knew of his existence. But none was needed; not by chance alone could those mighty ships have come to rest so precisely over New York, London, Paris, Moscow, Rome, Cape Town, Tokyo, Canberra. . . .

Even before the ending of those heart-freezing days, some men had guessed the truth. This was not a first tentative contact by a race which knew nothing of man. Within those silent, unmoving ships, master psychologists were studying humanity's reactions. When the curve of tension had reached its peak, they would act.

And on the sixth day, Karellen, Supervisor for Earth, made himself known to the world in a broadcast that blanketed every radio frequency. He spoke in English so perfect that the controversy it began was to rage across the Atlantic for a generation. But the context of the speech was more staggering even than its delivery. By any standards, it was a work of superlative genius, showing a complete and absolute mastery of human affairs. There could be no doubt that its scholarship and virtuosity, its tantalizing glimpses of knowledge still untapped, were deliberately designed to convince mankind that it was in the presence of overwhelming intellectual power. When Karellen had finished, the nations of Earth knew that their days of precarious sovereignty had ended. Local, internal governments would still retain their powers, but in the wider field of international affairs the supreme decisions had passed from human hands. Argument—protests—all were futile.

It was hardly to be expected that all the nations of the world would submit tamely to such a limitation of their powers. Yet active resistance presented baffling difficulties, for the destruction of the Overlord's ships, even if it could be achieved, would annihilate the cities beneath them. Nevertheless, one major power had made the attempt. Perhaps those responsible hoped to kill two birds with one atomic missile, for their target was floating above the capital of an adjoining and unfriendly nation.

As the great ship's image had expanded on the television screen in the secret control room, the little group of officers and technicians must have been torn by many emotions. If they succeeded, what action would the remaining ships take? Could they also be destroyed, leaving humanity to go its own way once more? Or would Karellen wreak some frightful vengeance upon those who had attacked him?

The screen became suddenly blank as the missile destroyed itself on impact, and the picture switched immediately to an airborne camera many miles away. In the fraction of a second that had elapsed, the fireball should already have formed and should be filling the sky with its solar flame.

Yet nothing whatsoever had happened. The great ship floated unharmed, bathed in the raw sunlight at the edge of space. Not only had the bomb failed to touch it, but no one could ever decide what had happened to the missile. Moreover, Karellen took no action against those responsible, nor even indicated that he had known of the attack. He ignored them contemptuously, leaving them to worry over a vengeance that never came. It was a more effective, and more demoralizing, treatment than any punitive action could have been. The government responsible collapsed in mutual recrimination a few weeks later.

There had also been some passive resistance to the policy of the Overlords. Usually, Karellen had been able to deal with it by letting those concerned have their own way, until they had discovered that they were only hurting themselves by their refusal to co-operate. Only once had he taken any direct action against a recalcitrant government.

For more than a hundred years the Republic of South Africa had been the center of racial strife. Men of good will on both sides had tried to build a bridge, but in vain —fears and prejudices were too deeply ingrained to permit any co-operation. Successive governments had differed only in the degree of their intolerance; the land was poisoned with the hate and the aftermath of civil war.

When it became clear that no attempt would be made to end discrimination, Karellen gave his warning. It merely named a date and time—no more. There was apprehension, but little fear or panic, for no one believed that the Overlords would take any violent or destructive action which would involve innocent and guilty alike.

Nor did they. All that happened was that as the sun passed the meridian at Cape Town it went out. There remained visible merely a pale, purple ghost, giving no heat or light. Somehow, out in space, the light of the sun had been polarized by two crossed fields so that no radiation could pass. The area affected was five hundred kilometers across, and perfectly circular.

The demonstration lasted thirty minutes. It was sufficient; the next day the government of South Africa announced that full civil rights would be restored to the white minority.

Apart from such isolated incidents, the human race had accepted the Overlords as part of the natural order of things. In a surprisingly short time, the initial shock had worn off, and the world went about its business again. The greatest change a suddenly-awakened Rip Van Winkle would have noticed was a hushed expectancy, a mental glancing-over-the-shoulder, as mankind waited for the Overlords to show themselves and to step down from their gleaming ships.

Five years later, it was still waiting. That, thought Stormgren, was the cause of all the trouble.

There was the usual circle of sight-seers, cameras at the ready, as Stormgren's car drove on to the landing field. The Secretary-General exchanged a few final words with his assistant, collected his brief case, and walked through the ring of spectators.

Karellen never kept him waiting for long. There was a sudden "Oh!" from the crowd, and a silver bubble expanded with breath-taking speed in the sky above. A gust of air tore at Stormgren's clothes as the tiny ship came to rest fifty meters away, floating delicately a few centimeters above the ground, as if it feared contamination with Earth. As he walked slowly forward, Stormgren saw that familiar puckering of the seamless metallic hull, and in a moment the opening that had so baffled the world's best scientists appeared before him. He stepped through it into the ship's single, softly-lit room. The entrance sealed itself as if it had never been, shutting out all sound and sight.

It opened again five minutes later. There had been no sensation of movement, but Stormgren knew that he was now fifty kilometers above the earth, deep in the heart of Karellen's ship. He was in the world of the Overlords; all around him, they were going about their mysterious business. He had come nearer to them than had any other man; yet he knew no more of their physical nature than did any of the millions on the world below.

The little conference room at the end of the short connecting corridor was unfurnished, apart from the single chair and the table beneath the vision screen. As was intended, it told absolutely nothing of the creatures who had built it. The vision screen was empty now, as it had always been. Sometimes in his dreams Stormgren had imagined that it had suddenly flashed into life, revealing the secret that tormented all the world. But the dream had never come true; behind that rectangle of darkness lay utter mystery. Yet there also lay power and wisdom—and, perhaps most of all, an immense and humorous affection for the little creatures crawling on the planet beneath.

From the hidden grille came that calm, never-hurried voice that Stormgren knew so well though the world had heard it only once in history. Its depth and resonance gave the single clue that existed to Karellen's physical nature, for it left an overwhelming impression of sheer *size*. Karellen was large—perhaps much larger than a man. It was true that some scientists, after analyzing the record of his only speech, had suggested that the voice was that of a machine. This was something that Stormgren could never believe.

"Yes, Rikki, I was listening to your little interview. What did you make of Mr. Wainwright?"

"He's an honest man, even if many of his supporters aren't. What are we going to do about him? The league itself isn't dangerous, but some of its extremists are openly advocating violence. I've been wondering if I should put a guard on my house. But I hope it isn't necessary."

Karellen evaded the point in the annoying way he sometimes had.

"The details of the World Federation have been out for a month now. Has there been a substantial increase in the seven percent who don't approve of me, or the twelve percent who Don't Know?"

"Not yet. But that's of no importance: what *does* worry

me is a general feeling, even among your supporters, that it's time this secrecy came to an end."

Karellen's sigh was technically perfect, yet somehow lacked conviction.

"That's your feeling too, isn't it?"

The question was so rhetorical that Stormgren did not bother to answer it.

"I wonder if you really appreciate," he continued earnestly, "how difficult this state of affairs makes my job?"

"It doesn't exactly help mine," replied Karellen with some spirit. "I wish people would stop thinking of me as a dictator, and remember I'm only a civil servant trying to administer a colonial policy in whose shaping I had no hand."

That, thought Stormgren, was quite an engaging description. He wondered just how much truth it held.

"Can't you at least give us *some* reason for your concealment? Because we don't understand it, it annoys us and gives rise to endless rumors."

Karellen gave that rich, deep laugh of his, just too resonant to be altogether human.

"What am I supposed to be now? Does the robot theory still hold the field? I'd rather be a mass of electron tubes than a thing like a centipede—oh, yes, I've seen that cartoon in yesterday's *Chicago Tribune!* I'm thinking of requesting the original."

Stormgren pursed his lips primly. There were times, he thought, when Karellen took his duties too lightly.

"This is *serious*," he said reprovingly.

"My dear Rikki," Karellen retorted, "it's only by *not* taking the human race seriously that I retain what fragments of my once considerable mental powers I still possess!"

Despite himself, Stormgren smiled.

"That doesn't help me a great deal, does it? I have to go down there and convince my fellow men that, although you won't show yourself, you've got nothing to hide. It's not an easy job. Curiosity is one of the most dominant of human characteristics. You can't defy it forever."

"Of all the problems that faced us when we came to

Earth, this was the most difficult," admitted Karellen. "You have trusted our wisdom in other matters—surely you can trust us in this!"

"*I* trust you," said Stormgren, "but Wainwright doesn't, nor do his supporters. Can you really blame them if they put a bad interpretation on your unwillingness to show yourselves?"

There was silence for a moment. Then Stormgren heard that faint sound (was it a *crackling?*) that might have been caused by the Supervisor moving his body slightly.

"You know why Wainwright and his kind fear me, don't you?" asked Karellen. His voice was somber now, like a great organ rolling its notes from a high cathedral nave. "You will find men like him in all the world's religions. They know that we represent reason and science, and, however confident they may be in their beliefs, they fear that we will overthrow their gods. Not necessarily through any deliberate act, but in a subtler fashion. Science can destroy religion by ignoring it as well as by disproving its tenets. No one ever demonstrated, so far as I am aware, the nonexistence of Zeus or Thor, but they have few followers now. The Wainwrights fear, too, that we know the truth about the origins of their faiths. How long, they wonder, have we been observing humanity? Have we watched Mohammed begin the hegira, or Moses giving the Jews their laws? Do we know all that is false in the stories they believe?"

"And *do* you?" whispered Stormgren, half to himself.

"That, Rikki, is the fear that torments them, even though they will never admit it openly. Believe me, it gives us no pleasure to destroy men's faiths, but *all* the world's religions cannot be right, and they know it. Sooner or later man has to learn the truth: but that time is not yet. As for our secrecy, which you are correct in saying aggravates our problems—that is a matter beyond my control. I regret the need for this concealment as much as you do, but the reasons are sufficient. However, I will try to get a statement from my—superiors—which may satisfy you and perhaps placate the Freedom League.

Now, please, can we return to the agenda and start recording again?"

"Well?" asked Van Ryberg anxiously. "Did you have any luck?"

"I don't know," Stormgren replied wearily as he threw the files down on his desk and collapsed into the seat. "Karellen's consulting *his* superiors now, whoever or whatever they may be. He won't make any promises."

"Listen," said Pieter abruptly, "I've just thought of something. What reason have we for believing that there is anyone beyond Karellen? Suppose *all* the Overlords, as we've christened them, are right here on Earth in these ships of theirs? They may have nowhere else to go and are hiding the fact from us."

"It's an ingenious theory," grinned Stormgren. "But it clashes with what little I know—or think I know—about Karellen's background."

"And how much is that?"

"Well, he often refers to his position here as something temporary, hindering him from getting on with his real work, which I think is some form of mathematics. Once I quoted Acton's comment about power corrupting, and absolute power corrupting absolutely. I wanted to see how he'd react to *that*. He gave that cavernous laugh of his, and said: 'There's no danger of that happening to me. In the first case, the sooner I finish my work here, the sooner I can get back to where I belong, a good many light-years from here. And secondly, I don't have absolute power, by any means. I'm just—Supervisor.' Of course, he may have been misleading me. I can never be sure of that."

"He's immortal, isn't he?"

"Yes, by our standards, though there's something in the future he seems to fear. I can't imagine what it is. And that's really all I know about him."

"It isn't very conclusive. My theory is that his little fleet's lost in space and is looking for a new home. He doesn't want us to know how few he and his comrades are. Perhaps all those other ships are automatic, and there's no one in any of them. They're just an imposing façade."

"You," said Stormgren, "have been reading too much science-fiction."

Van Ryberg grinned, a little sheepishly.

"The 'Invasion From Space' didn't turn out quite as expected, did it? My theory would certainly explain why Karellen never shows himself. He doesn't want us to learn that there aren't any more Overlords."

Stormgren shook his head in amused disagreement.

"Your explanation, as usual, is much too ingenious to be true. Though we can only infer its existence, there must be a great civilization behind the Supervisor—and one that's known about man for a very long time. Karellen himself must have been studying us for centuries. Look at his command of English, for example. He taught *me* how to speak it idiomatically!"

"Have you ever discovered *anything* he doesn't know?"

"Oh yes, quite often—but only on trivial points. I think he has an absolutely perfect memory, but there are some things he hasn't bothered to learn. For instance, English is the only language he understands completely, though in the last two years he's picked up a good deal of Finnish just to tease me. And one doesn't learn Finnish in a hurry! He can quote great slabs of the *Kalevala,* whereas I'm ashamed to say I know only a few lines. He also knows the biographies of all living statesmen, and sometimes I can identify the references he's used. His knowledge of history and science seems complete—you know how much we've already learned from him. Yet, taken one at a time, I don't think his mental gifts are quite outside the range of human achievement. But no one man could possibly do *all* the things he does."

"That's more or less what I've decided already," agreed Van Ryberg. "We can argue round Karellen forever, but in the end we always come back to the same question: Why the devil won't he show himself? Until he does, I'll go on theorizing and the Freedom League will go on fulminating."

He cocked a rebellious eye at the ceiling.

"One dark night, Mr. Supervisor, I hope some reporter takes a rocket up to your ship and climbs in through the back door with a camera. What a scoop *that* would be!"

If Karellen was listening, he gave no sign. But, of course, he never did.

In the first year of their coming, the advent of the Overlords had made less difference to the pattern of human life than might have been expected. Their shadow was everywhere, but it was an unobtrusive shadow. Though there were few great cities on Earth where men could not see one of the silver ships glittering against the zenith, after a little while they were taken as much for granted as the sun, moon, or clouds. Most men were probably only dimly aware that their steadily rising standards of living were due to the Overlords. When they stopped to think of it—which was seldom—they realized that those silent ships had brought peace to all the world for the first time in history, and were duly grateful.

But these were negative and unspectacular benefits, accepted and soon forgotten. The Overlords remained aloof, hiding their faces from mankind. Karellen could command respect and admiration; he could win nothing deeper so long as he pursued his present policy. It was hard not to feel resentment against these Olympians who spoke to man only over the radioteleprinter circuits at United Nations Headquarters. What took place between Karellen and Stormgren was never publicly revealed, and sometimes Stormgren himself wondered why the Supervisor found these interviews necessary. Perhaps he felt the need of direct contact with one human being at least; perhaps he realized that Stormgren needed this form of personal support. If this was the explanation, the Secretary-General appreciated it; he did not mind if the Freedom League referred to him contemptuously as "Karellen's office boy."

The Overlords had never had any dealings with individual states and governments. They had taken the United Nations Organization as they found it, had given instructions for installing the necessary radio equipment, and had issued their orders through the mouth of the Secretary-

General. The Soviet delegate had quite correctly pointed out, at considerable length and upon innumerable occasions, that this was not in accordance with the Charter. Karellen did not seem to worry.

It was amazing that so many abuses, follies, and evils could be dispelled by those messages from the sky. With the arrival of the Overlords, nations knew that they need no longer fear each other, and they guessed—even before the experiment was made—that their existing weapons were certainly impotent against a civilization that could bridge the stars. So at once the greatest single obstacle to the happiness of mankind had been removed.

The Overlords seemed largely indifferent to forms of government, provided that they were not oppressive or corrupt. Earth still possessed democracies, monarchies, benevolent dictatorships, communism, and capitalism. This was a source of great surprise to many simple souls who were quite convinced that theirs was the only possible way of life. Others believed that Karellen was merely waiting to introduce a system which would sweep away all existing forms of society, and so had not bothered with minor political reforms. But this, like all other speculations concerning the Overlords, was pure guesswork. No one knew their motives: and no one knew toward what future they were shepherding mankind.

3

STORMGREN WAS SLEEPING badly these nights, which was strange, since soon he would be putting aside the cares of office forever. He had served mankind for forty years, and its masters for five, and few men could look back upon a life that had seen so many of its ambitions achieved. Perhaps that was the trouble: in the years of retirement, however many they might be, he would have no further goals to give any zest to life. Since Martha had died and the children had established their own families, his ties with the world seemed to have weakened. It might be, too, that he was beginning to identify himself with the Overlords and thus to become detached from humanity.

This was another of those restless nights when his brain went on turning like a machine whose governor had failed. He knew better than to woo sleep any further, and reluctantly climbed out of bed. Throwing on his dressing gown, he strolled out on to the roof garden of his modest flat. There was not one of his direct subordinates who did not possess much more luxurious quarters, but this place was ample for Stormgren's needs. He had reached the position where neither personal possessions nor official ceremony could add anything to his stature.

The night was warm, almost oppressive, but the sky was clear and a brilliant moon hung low in the southwest. Ten kilometers away, the lights of New York glowed on the skyline like a dawn frozen in the act of breaking.

Stormgren raised his eyes above the sleeping city, climbing again the heights that he alone of living men had scaled. Far away though it was, he could see the hull of Karellen's ship glinting in the moonlight. He wondered what the Supervisor was doing, for he did not believe that the Overlords ever slept.

High above, a meteor thrust its shining spear through the dome of the sky. The luminous trail glowed faintly for a while; then it died away, leaving only the stars. The reminder was brutal: in a hundred years, Karellen would still be leading mankind towards the goal that he alone could see, but four months from now another man would be Secretary-General. That in itself Stormgren was far from minding, but it meant that little time was left if he ever hoped to learn what lay behind that darkened screen.

Only in the last few days had he dared to admit that the Overlords' secretiveness was beginning to obsess him. Until recently, his faith in Karellen had kept him free from doubts; but now, he thought a little wryly, the protests of the Freedom League were beginning to have their effect upon him. It was true that the propaganda about man's enslavement was no more than propaganda. Few people seriously believed it, or really wished for a return to the old days. Men had grown accustomed to Karellen's imperceptible rule, but they were becoming impatient to know who ruled them. And how could they be blamed?

Though it was much the largest, the Freedom League was only one of the organizations that opposed Karellen— and, consequently, the humans who co-operated with the Overlords. The objections and policies of these groups varied enormously: some took the religious viewpoint, while others were merely expressing a sense of inferiority. They felt, with good reason, much as a cultured Indian of the nineteenth century must have done as he contemplated the British Raj. The invaders had brought peace and prosperity to Earth—but who knew what the cost might be? History was not reassuring; even the most peaceable of contacts between races at very different cultural levels had often resulted in the obliteration of the more backward society. Nations, as well as individuals, could lose their spirit when confronted by a challenge which they could not meet. And the civilization of the Overlords, veiled in mystery though it might be, was the greatest challenge man had ever faced.

There was a faint "click" from the facsimile machine in the adjoining room as it ejected the hourly summary sent out by Central News. Stormgren wandered indoors and ruffled halfheartedly through the sheets. On the other side of the world, the Freedom League had inspired a not-very original headline. "IS MAN RULED BY MONSTERS?" asked the paper, and went on to quote: "Addressing a meeting in Madras today, Dr. C. V. Krishnan, President of the Eastern Division of the Freedom League, said, 'The explanation of the Overlords' behavior is quite simple. Their physical form is so alien and so repulsive that they dare not show themselves to humanity. I challenge the Supervisor to deny this.' "

Stormgren threw down the sheet in disgust. Even if the charge were true, would it really matter? The idea was an old one, but it had never worried him. He did not believe that there was any biological form, however strange, which he could not accept in time and, perhaps, even find beautiful. The mind, not the body, was all that mattered. If only he could convince Karellen of this, the Overlords might change their policy. It was certain that they could not be half as hideous as the imaginative drawings that had filled the papers soon after their coming to Earth!

Yet it was not, Stormgren knew, entirely consideration for his successor that made him anxious to see the end of this state of affairs. He was honest enough to admit that, in the final analysis, his main motive was simple human curiosity. He had grown to know Karellen as a person, and he would never be satisfied until he had also discovered what kind of creature he might be.

When Stormgren failed to arrive at his usual hour next morning, Pieter Van Ryberg was surprised and a little annoyed. Though the Secretary-General often made a number of calls before reaching his own office, he invariably left word that he was doing so. This morning, to make matters worse, there had been several urgent messages for Stormgren. Van Ryberg rang half a dozen departments trying to locate him, then gave it up in disgust.

By noon he had become alarmed and sent a car to Stormgren's house. Ten minutes later he was startled by the scream of a siren, and a police patrol came racing up Roosevelt Drive. The news agencies must have had friends in that vehicle, for even as Van Ryberg watched it approach, the radio was telling the world that he was no longer merely Assistant, but Acting-Secretary-General of the United Nations.

Had Van Ryberg had fewer troubles on his hands, he would have found it entertaining to study the press reactions to Stormgren's disappearance. For the past month, the world's papers had divided themselves into two sharply defined groups. The Western press, on the whole, approved of Karellen's plan to make all men citizens of the world. The Eastern countries, on the other hand, were undergoing violent but largely synthetic spasms of national pride. Some of them had been independent for little more than a generation, and felt that they had been cheated out of their gains. Criticism of the Overlords was widespread and energetic: after an initial period of extreme caution, the press had quickly found that it could be as rude to Karellen as it liked and nothing would happen. Now it was excelling itself.

Most of these attacks, though very vocal, were not representative of the great mass of the people. Along the frontiers that would soon be gone forever the guards had been doubled, but the soldiers eyed each other with a still inarticulate friendliness. The politicians and the generals might storm and rave, but the silently waiting millions felt that, none too soon, a long and bloody chapter of history was coming to an end.

And now Stormgren had gone, no one knew where. The tumult suddenly subsided as the world realized that it had lost the only man through whom the Overlords, for their own strange reasons, would speak to Earth. A paralysis seemed to descend upon press and radio commentators, but in the silence could be heard the voice of the Freedom League, anxiously protesting its innocence.

It was utterly dark when Stormgren awoke. For a moment he was too sleepy to realize how strange that was. Then, as full consciousness dawned, he sat up with a start and felt for the switch beside his bed.

In the darkness his hand encountered a bare stone wall, cold to the touch. He froze instantly, mind and body paralyzed by the impact of the unexpected. Then, scarcely believing his senses, he kneeled on the bed and began to explore with his finger tips that shockingly unfamiliar wall.

He had been doing this only for a moment when there was a sudden "click" and a section of the darkness slid aside. He caught a glimpse of a man silhouetted against a dimly lit background; then the door closed again and the darkness returned. It happened so swiftly that he had no chance to see anything of the room in which he was lying.

An instant later, he was dazzled by the light of a powerful electric torch. The beam flickered across his face, held him steadily for a moment, then dipped to illuminate the whole bed, which was, he now saw, nothing more than a mattress supported on rough planks.

Out of the darkness a soft voice spoke to him in excellent English, but with an accent which Stormgren could not at first identify.

"Ah, Mr. Secretary, I'm glad to see you're awake. I hope you feel *quite* all right."

There was something about the last sentence that caught Stormgren's attention, so that the angry questions he had been about to ask died upon his lips. He stared back into the darkness, then replied calmly, "How long have I been unconscious?"

The other chuckled.

"Several days. We were promised there'd be no after-effects. I'm glad to see it's true."

Partly to gain time, partly to test his own reactions, Stormgren swung his legs over the side of the bed. He was still wearing his nightclothes, but they were badly crumpled and seemed to have gathered considerable dirt. As he moved he felt a slight dizziness—not enough to be unpleasant but sufficient to convince him that he had indeed been drugged.

He turned towards the light.

"Where am I?" he said sharply. "Does Wainwright know about this?"

"Now, don't get excited," replied the shadowy figure. "We won't talk about that sort of thing yet. I guess you're pretty hungry. Get dressed and come along to dinner."

The oval of light slipped across the room and for the first time Stormgren had an idea of its dimensions. It was scarcely a room at all, for the walls seemed bare rock, roughly smoothed into shape. He realized that he was underground, possibly at a great depth. And if he had been unconscious for several days, he might be anywhere on Earth.

The torchlight illuminated a pile of clothes draped over a packing case.

"This should be enough for you," said the voice from the darkness. "Laundry's rather a problem here, so we grabbed a couple of your suits and half a dozen shirts."

"That," said Stormgren without humor, "was very considerate of you."

"We're sorry about the absence of furniture and electric light. This place is convenient in some ways, but it rather lacks amenities."

"Convenient for what?" asked Stormgren as he climbed into a shirt. The feel of the familiar cloth beneath his fingers was strangely reassuring.

"Just—convenient," said the voice. "And by the way, since we're likely to spend a good deal of time together, you'd better call me Joe."

"Despite your nationality," retorted Stormgren, "—you're Polish, aren't you?—I think I could pronounce your real name. It won't be worse than many Finnish ones."

There was a slight pause and the light flickered for an instant.

"Well, I should have expected it," said Joe resignedly. "You must have plenty of practice at this sort of thing."

"It's a useful hobby for a man in my position. At a guess I should say you were brought up in the United States but didn't leave Poland until . . ."

"That," said Joe firmly, "is quite enough. As you seem to have finished dressing—thank you."

The door opened as Stormgren walked towards it, feeling mildly elated by his small victory. As Joe stood aside to let him pass, he wondered if his captor was armed. Almost certainly he would be, and in any case he would have friends around.

The corridor was dimly lit by oil lamps at intervals, and for the first time Stormgren could see Joe clearly. He was a man of about fifty, and must have weighed well over two hundred pounds. Everything about him was outsize, from the stained battle-dress that might have come from any of half a dozen armed forces, to the startlingly large signet ring on his left hand. A man built on this scale probably would not bother to carry a gun. It should not be difficult to trace him, thought Stormgren, if he ever got out of this place. He was a little depressed to realize that Joe must also be perfectly well aware of this fact.

The walls around them, though occasionally faced with concrete, were mostly bare rock. It was clear to Stormgren that he was in some disused mine, and he could think of few more effective prisons. Until now the fact of his kidnapping had failed to worry him greatly. He had felt that, whatever happened, the immense resources of the Overlords would soon locate and rescue him. Now he was not so sure. He had already been gone several days—and nothing had happened. There must be a limit even to Karellen's power, and if he were indeed buried in some remote continent, all the science of the Overlords might be unable to trace him.

There were two other men sitting at the table in the bare, dimly lit room. They looked up with interest, and more than a little respect, as Stormgren entered. One of them pushed across a bundle of sandwiches which Stormgren accepted eagerly. Though he felt extremely hungry, he could have done with a more interesting meal, but it was very obvious that his captors had dined no better.

As he ate, he glanced quickly at the three men around him. Joe was by far the most outstanding character, and not merely in the matter of physical bulk. The others were clearly his assistants—nondescript individuals, whose origins Stormgren would be able to place when he heard them talk.

Some wine had been produced in a not-too-aseptic glass, and Stormgren washed down the last of the sandwiches. Feeling now more fully in command of the situation, he turned to the huge Pole.

"Well," he said evenly, "perhaps you'll tell me what all this is about, and just what you hope to get out of it."

Joe cleared his throat.

"I'd like to make one thing straight," he said. "This has nothing to do with Wainwright. He'll be as surprised as anyone."

Stormgren had half expected this, though he wondered why Joe was confirming his suspicions. He had long suspected the existence of an extremist movement inside—or on the frontiers of—the Freedom League.

"As a matter of interest," he said, "how did you kidnap me?"

He hardly expected a reply to this, and was somewhat taken aback by the other's readiness—even eagerness—to answer.

"It was all rather like a Hollywood thriller," said Joe cheerfully. "We weren't sure if Karellen kept a watch on you, so we took somewhat elaborate precautions. You were knocked out by gas in the air conditioner—that was easy. Then we carried you out into the car—no trouble at all. All this, I might say, wasn't done by any of our people. We hired—er— professionals for the job. Karellen may get them—in fact, he's supposed to—but he'll be no wiser. When it left your house, the car drove into a long road tunnel not a thousand kilometers from New York. It came out again on schedule at the opposite end, still carrying a drugged man extraordinarily like the Secretary-General. Quite a while later a large truck loaded with metal cases emerged in the opposite direction and drove to a certain airfield where the cases were loaded aboard a freighter on perfectly legitimate business. I'm sure tho owners of those cases would be horrified to know how we employed them.

"Meanwhile the car that had actually done the job continued elaborate evasive action towards the Canadian border. Perhaps Karellen's caught it by now; I don't know or care. As you'll see—I do hope you appreciate my frankness—our whole plan depended on one thing. We're pretty sure that Karellen can see and hear everything that happens on the surface of the earth—but unless he uses magic, not science, he can't see *underneath* it. So he won't know about the transfer in the tunnel—at least until it's too late. Naturally we've taken a risk, but there were also one or two other safeguards I won't go into now. We may want to use them again, and it would be a pity to give them away."

Joe had related the whole story with such obvious gusto that Stormgren could hardly help smiling. Yet he also felt very disturbed. The plan was an ingenious one, and it was quite possible that Karellen had been deceived. Stormgren was not even certain that the Overlord kept any form of protective surveillance over him. Nor, clearly, was Joe. Perhaps that was why he had been so frank—he wanted to test Stormgren's reactions. Well, he would try to appear confident, whatever his real feelings might be.

"You must be a lot of fools," said Stormgren scornfully, "if you think you can trick the Overlords as easily as this. In any case, what conceivable good will it do?"

Joe offered him a cigarette, which Stormgren refused, then lit one himself and sat on the edge of the table. There was an ominous creaking and he jumped off hastily.

"Our motives," he began, "should be pretty obvious. We've found argument useless, so we have to take other measures. There have been underground movements before, and even Karellen, whatever powers he's got, won't find it easy to deal with us. We're out to fight for our independence. Don't misunderstand me. There'll be nothing violent—at first, anyway—but the Overlords have to use human agents, and we can make it mighty uncomfortable for them."

Starting with me, I suppose, thought Stormgren. He wondered if the other had given him more than a fraction of the whole story. Did they really think that these gangster methods would influence Karellen in the slightest? On the other hand, it was quite true that a well-organized resistance movement could make life very difficult. For Joe had put his finger on the one weak spot in the Overlords' rule. Ultimately, all their orders were carried out by human agents. If these were terrorized into disobedience, the whole system might collapse. It was only a faint possibility, for Stormgren felt confident that Karellen would soon find some solution.

"What do you intend to do with me?" asked Stormgren at length. "Am I a hostage, or what?"

"Don't worry—we'll look after you. We expect some visitors in a few days, and until then we'll entertain you as well as we can."

He added some words in his own language, and one of the others produced a brand-new pack of cards.

"We got these especially for you," explained Joe. "I

read in *Time* the other day that you were a good poker player." His voice suddenly became grave. "I hope there's plenty of cash in your wallet," he said anxiously. "We never thought of looking. After all, we can hardly accept checks."

Quite overcome, Stormgren stared blankly at his captors. Then, as the true humor of the situation sank into his mind, it suddenly seemed to him that all the cares and worries of office had lifted from his shoulders. From now on, it was Van Ryberg's show. Whatever happened, there was absolutely nothing he could do about it—and now these fantastic criminals were anxiously waiting to play poker with him.

Abruptly, he threw back his head and laughed as he had not done for years.

There was no doubt, thought Van Ryberg morosely, that Wainwright was telling the truth. He might have his suspicions, but he did not know who had kidnapped Stormgren. Nor did he approve of the kidnapping itself. Van Ryberg had a shrewd idea that for some time extremists in the Freedom League had been putting pressure on Wainwright to make him adopt a more active policy. Now they were taking matters into their own hands.

The kidnapping had been beautifully organized, there was no doubt of that. Stormgren might be anywhere on Earth, and there seemed little hope of tracing him. Yet something must be done, Van Ryberg decided, and done quickly. Despite the jests he had so often made, his real feeling towards Karellen was one of overwhelming awe. The thought of approaching the Supervisor directly filled him with dismay, but there seemed no alternative.

The communications section occupied the entire top floor of the great building. Lines of facsimile machines, some silent, some clicking busily, stretched away into the distance. Through them poured endless streams of statistics: production figures, census returns, and all the bookkeeping of a world economic system. Somewhere up in Karellen's ship must lie the equivalent of this great room —and Van Ryberg wondered, with a tingling of the spine, what shapes moved to and fro collecting the messages that Earth was sending to the Overlords.

But today he was not interested in these machines and the routine business they handled. He walked to the little private room that only Stormgren was supposed to enter. At his instructions, the lock had been forced and the Chief Communications Officer was waiting there for him.

"It's an ordinary teleprinter—standard typewriter keyboard," he was told. "There's a facsimile machine as well if you want to send any pictures or tabular information, but you said you wouldn't be needing that."

Van Ryberg nodded absently. "That's all. Thanks," he said. "I don't expect to be here very long. Then get the place locked up again and give me all the keys."

He waited until the Communications Officer had left, and then sat down at the machine. It was, he knew, very seldom used, since nearly all business between Karellen and Stormgren was dealt with at their weekly meetings. Since this was something of an emergency circuit, he expected a fairly quick reply.

After a moment's hesitation, he began to tap out his message with unpracticed fingers. The machine purred away quietly and the words gleamed for a few seconds on the darkened screen. Then he leaned back and waited for the answer.

Scarcely a minute later the machine started to whirr again. Not for the first time, Van Ryberg wondered if the Supervisor ever slept.

The message was as brief as it was unhelpful.

NO INFORMATION. LEAVE MATTERS ENTIRELY TO YOUR DISCRETION. K.

Rather bitterly, and without any satisfaction at all, Van Ryberg realized how much greatness had been thrust upon him.

During the past three days Stormgren had analyzed his captors with some thoroughness. Joe was the only one of any importance: the others were nonentities—the riffraff one would expect any illegal movement to gather round itself. The ideals of the Freedom League meant nothing to them: their only concern was earning a living with the minimum of work.

Joe was an altogether more complex individual, though sometimes he reminded Stormgren of an overgrown baby. Their interminable poker games were punctuated with violent political arguments, and it soon became obvious to Stormgren that the big Pole had never thought seriously about the causes for which he was fighting. Emotion and extreme conservatism clouded all his judgments. His country's long struggle for independence had conditioned him so completely that he still lived in the past. He was a picturesque survival, one of those who had no use for an ordered way of life. When his type vanished, if it ever did, the world would be a safer but less interesting place.

There was now little doubt, as far as Stormgren was concerned, that Karellen had failed to locate him. He had tried to bluff, but his captors were unconvinced. He was fairly certain that they had been holding him here to see if Karellen would act, and now that nothing had happened they could proceed with their plans.

Stormgren was not surprised when, a few days later, Joe told him to expect visitors. For some time the little group had shown increasing nervousness, and the prisoner guessed that the leaders of the movement, having seen that the coast was clear, were at last coming to collect him.

They were already waiting, gathered round the rickety table, when Joe waved him politely into the living room. Stormgren was amused to note that his jailer was now wearing, very ostentatiously, a huge pistol that had never been in evidence before. The two thugs had vanished, and even Joe seemed somewhat restrained. Stormgren could see at once that he was now confronted by men of a much higher caliber, and the group opposite him reminded him strongly of a picture he had once seen of Lenin and his associates in the first days of the Russian Revolution. There was the same intellectual force, iron determination, and ruthlessness in these six men. Joe and his kind were harmless; here were the real brains behind the organization.

With a curt nod, Stormgren moved over to the only vacant seat and tried to look self-possessed. As he approached, the elderly, thickset man on the far side of the table leaned forward and stared at him with piercing gray eyes. They made Stormgren so uncomfortable that he spoke first—something he had not intended to do.

"I suppose you've come to discuss terms. What's my ransom?"

He noticed that in the background someone was taking down his words in a shorthand notebook. It was all very businesslike.

The leader replied in a musical Welsh accent.

"You could put it that way, Mr. Secretary-General. But we're interested in information, not cash."

So that was it, thought Stormgren. He was a prisoner of war, and this was his interrogation.

"You know what our motives are," continued the other in his softly lilting voice. "Call us a resistance movement, if you like. We believe that sooner or later Earth will have to fight for its independence—but we realize that the struggle can only be by indirect methods such as sabotage and disobedience. We kidnapped you, partly to show Karellen that we mean business and are well organized, but largely because you are the only man who can tell us anything of the Overlords. You're a reasonable man, Mr. Stormgren. Give us your co-operation, and you can have your freedom."

"Exactly what do you wish to know?" asked Stormgren cautiously.

Those extraordinary eyes seemed to search his mind to its depths; they were unlike any that Stormgren had ever seen in his life. Then the singsong voice replied:

"Do you know who, or what, the Overlords really are?"

Stormgren almost smiled.

"Believe me," he said, "I'm quite as anxious as you to discover that."

"Then you'll answer our questions?"

"I make no promises. But I may."

There was a slight sigh of relief from Joe, and a rustle of anticipation ran round the room.

"We have a general idea," continued the other, "of the circumstances in which you meet Karellen. But perhaps you would describe them carefully, leaving out nothing of importance."

That was harmless enough, thought Stormgren. He had done it many times before, and it would give the appearance of co-operation. There were acute minds here, and perhaps they could uncover something new. They were welcome to any fresh information they could extract from him—so long as they shared it. That it could harm Karellen in any way he did not for a moment believe.

Stormgren felt in his pockets and produced a pencil and an old envelope. Sketching rapidly while he spoke, he began:

"You know, of course, that a small flying machine, with no obvious means of propulsion, calls for me at regular intervals and takes me up to Karellen's ship. It enters the hull—and you've doubtless seen the telescopic films that have been taken of *that* operation. The door opens again—if you can call it a door—and I go into a small room with a table, a chair, and a vision screen. The layout is something like this."

He pushed the plan across to the old Welshman, but the strange eyes never turned towards it. They were still fixed on Stormgren's face, and as he watched them something seemed to change in their depths. The room had become completely silent, but behind him he heard Joe take a sudden indrawn breath.

Puzzled and annoyed, Stormgren stared back at the other, and as he did so, understanding slowly dawned. In his confusion, he crumpled the envelope into a ball of paper and ground it underfoot.

He knew now why those gray eyes had affected him so strangely. The man opposite him was blind.

Van Ryberg had made no further attempts to contact Karellen. Much of his department's work—the forwarding of statistical information, the abstracting of the world's press, and the like—had continued automatically. In Paris the lawyers were still wrangling over the proposed World

Constitution, but that was none of his business for the moment. It was a fortnight before the Supervisor wanted the final draft; if it was not ready by then, no doubt Karellen would take what action he thought fit.

And there was still no news of Stormgren.

Van Ryberg was dictating when the "Emergency Only" telephone started to ring. He grabbed the receiver and listened with mounting astonishment, then threw it down and rushed to the open window. In the distance, cries of amazement were rising from the streets, and traffic was slowing to a halt.

It was true: Karellen's ship, that never-changing symbol of the Overlords, was no longer in the sky. He searched the heavens as far as he could see, and found no trace of it. Then, suddenly, it seemed as if night had swiftly fallen. Coming down from the north, its shadowed underbelly black as a thundercloud, the great ship was racing low over the towers of New York. Involuntarily, Van Ryberg shrank away from the onrushing monster. He had always known how huge the ships of the Overlords really were—but it was one thing to see them far away in space, and quite another to watch them passing overhead like demon-driven clouds.

In the darkness of that partial eclipse, he watched until the ship and its monstrous shadow had vanished into the south. There was no sound, not even the whisper of air, and Van Ryberg realized that despite its apparent nearness the ship had passed at least a kilometer above his head. Then the building shuddered once as the shock wave struck it, and from somewhere came the tinkling of broken glass as a window blew inwards.

In the office behind him all the telephones had started to ring, but Van Ryberg did not move. He remained leaning against the window ledge, still staring into the south, paralyzed by the presence of illimitable power.

As Stormgren talked, it seemed to him that his mind was operating on two levels simultaneously. On the one hand he was trying to defy the men who had captured him, yet on the other he was hoping that they might help him unravel Karellen's secret. It was a dangerous game, yet to his surprise he was enjoying it.

The blind Welshman had conducted most of the interrogation. It was fascinating to watch that agile mind trying one opening after another, testing and rejecting all the theories that Stormgren himself had abandoned long ago. Presently he leaned back with a sigh.

"We're getting nowhere," he said resignedly. "We want more facts, and that means action, not argument." The sightless eyes seemed to stare thoughtfully at Stormgren. For a moment he tapped nervously on the table—it was the first sign of uncertainty Stormgren had noticed. Then he continued:

"I'm a little surprised, Mr. Secretary, that you've never made any effort to learn more about the Overlords."

"What do you suggest?" asked Stormgren coldly, trying to disguise his interest. "I've told you that there's only one way out of the room in which I have my talks with Karellen—and that leads straight back to Earth."

"It might be possible," mused the other, "to devise instruments which could teach us something. I'm no scientist, but we can look into the matter. If we give you your freedom, would you be willing to assist with such a plan?"

"Once and for all," said Stormgren angrily, "let me make my position perfectly clear. Karellen is working for a united world, and I'll do nothing to help his enemies. What his ultimate plans may be, I don't know, but I believe that they are good."

"What real proof have we of that?"

"*All* his actions, ever since his ships appeared in our skies. I defy you to mention one act that, in the ultimate analysis, hasn't been beneficial." Stormgren paused for a moment, letting his mind run back through the past years. Then he smiled.

"If you want a single proof of the essential—how shall I put it—*benevolence* of the Overlords, think of that cruelty-to-animals order which they made within a month of their arrival. If I had had any doubts about Karellen before, that banished them—even though that order has caused me more trouble than anything else he's ever done!"

That was scarcely an exaggeration, Stormgren thought. The whole incident had been an extraordinary one, the first revelation of the Overlords' hatred of cruelty. That, and their passion for justice and order, seemed to be the dominant emotions in their lives—as far as one could judge them by their actions.

And it was the only time Karellen had shown anger, or at least the appearance of anger. "You may kill one another if you wish," the message had gone, "and that is a matter between you and your own laws. But if you slay, except for food or in self-defense, the beasts that share your world with you—then you may be answerable to me."

No one knew exactly how comprehensive this ban was supposed to be, or what Karellen would do to enforce it. They had not long to wait.

The Plaza de Toros was full when the matadors and their attendants began their processional entry. Everything seemed normal; the brilliant sunlight blazed harshly on the traditional costumes, the great crowd greeted its favorites as it had a hundred times before. Yet here and there faces were turned anxiously towards the sky, to the aloof silver shape fifty kilometers above Madrid.

Then the picadors had taken up their places and the bull had come snorting out into the arena. The skinny horses, nostrils wide with terror, had wheeled in the sunlight as their riders forced them to meet their enemy. The first lance flashed—made contact—and at that moment came a sound that had never been heard on earth before.

It was the sound of ten thousand people screaming with the pain of the same wound—ten thousand people who, when they had recovered from the shock, found themselves completely unharmed. But that was the end of that bullfight, and indeed of all bullfighting, for the news spread rapidly. It is worth recording that the *aficionados* were so shaken that only one in ten asked for his money back, and also that the London *Daily Mirror* made matters much worse by suggesting that the Spaniards adopt cricket as a new national sport.

"You may be correct," the old Welshman replied. "Possibly the motives of the Overlords are good—according to their standards, which may sometimes be the same as ours. But they are interlopers—we never asked them to come here and turn our world upside down, destroying ideals—yes, and nations—that generations of men have fought to protect."

"I come from a small nation that had to fight for its liberties," retorted Stormgren. "Yet I am for Karellen. You may annoy him, you may even delay the achievement of his aims, but it will make no difference in the end. Doubtless you are sincere in believing as you do. I can understand your fear that the traditions and cultures of little countries will be overwhelmed when the world state arrives. But you are wrong; it is useless to cling to the past. Even before the Overlords came to Earth, the sovereign state was dying. They have merely hastened its end: no one can save it now—and no one should try."

There was no answer. The man opposite neither moved nor spoke. He sat with lips half open, his eyes now lifeless as well as blind. Around him the others were equally motionless, frozen in strained, unnatural attitudes. With a gasp of pure horror, Stormgren rose to his feet and backed away towards the door. As he did so the silence was suddenly broken.

"That was a nice speech, Rikki: thank you. Now I think we can go."

Stormgren spun on his heels and stared into the shadowed corridor. Floating there at eye level was a small, featureless sphere—the source, no doubt, of whatever mysterious force the Overlords had brought into action. It was hard to be certain, but Stormgren imagined that he could hear a faint humming, as of a hive of bees on a drowsy summer day.

"Karellen! Thank God! But what have you done?"

"Don't worry: they're all right. You can call it a paralysis, but it's much subtler than that. They're simply living a few thousand times more slowly than normal. When we've gone they'll never know what happened."

"You'll leave them here until the police come?"

"No. I've a much better plan. I'm letting them go."

Stormgren felt a surprising sense of relief. He gave a last, valedictory glance at the little room and its frozen occupants. Joe was standing on one foot, staring very stupidly at nothing. Suddenly Stormgren laughed and fumbled in his pockets.

"Thanks for the hospitality, Joe," he said. "I think I'll leave a souvenir."

He ruffled through the scraps of paper until he had found the figures he wanted. Then, on a reasonably clean sheet, he wrote carefully:

"BANK OF MANHATTAN
*Pay Joe the sum of One Hundred Thirty-Five
Dollars and Fifty Cents (135.50)*
R. Stormgren."

As he laid the strip of paper beside the Pole, Karellen's voice inquired:

"Exactly *what* are you doing?"

"We Stormgrens always pay our debts. The other two cheated, but Joe played fair. At least, I never caught him cheating."

He felt very gay and lightheaded, and quite forty years younger, as he walked to the door. The metal sphere moved aside to let him pass. He assumed that it was some kind of robot, and it explained how Karellen had been able to reach him through the unknown layers of rock overhead.

"Go straight ahead for a hundred meters," said the sphere, speaking in Karellen's voice. "Then turn to the left until I give you further instructions."

He strode forward eagerly, though he realized that there was no need for hurry. The sphere remained hanging in the corridor, presumably covering his retreat.

A minute later he came across a second sphere, waiting for him at a branch in the corridor.

"You've half a kilometer to go," it said. "Keep to the left until we meet again."

Six times he encountered the spheres on his way to the open. At first he wondered if, somehow, the robot was managing to keep ahead of him; then he guessed that there must be a chain of the machines maintaining a complete circuit down into the depths of the mine. At the entrance, a group of guards formed a piece of improbable statuary, watched over by yet another of the ubiquitous spheres. On the hillside a few meters away lay the little flying machine in which Stormgren had made all his journeys to Karellen.

He stood for a moment blinking in the sunlight. Then he saw the ruined mining machinery around him, and beyond that a derelict railway stretching down the mountainside. Several kilometers away a dense forest lapped at the base of the mountain, and very far off Stormgren could see the gleam of water from a great lake. He guessed that he was somewhere in South America, though it was not easy to say exactly what gave him that impression.

As he climbed into the little flying machine, Stormgren had a last glimpse of the mine entrance and the men frozen around it. Then the door sealed behind him and with a sigh of relief he sank back upon the familiar couch.

For a while he waited until he had recovered his breath; then he uttered a single, heartfelt syllable:

"Well??"

"I'm sorry I couldn't rescue you before. But you see how very important it was to wait until all the leaders had gathered here."

"Do you mean to say," spluttered Stormgren, "that you knew where I was all the time? If I thought——"

"Don't be too hasty," answered Karellen, "at least, let me finish explaining."

"Very good," said Stormgren darkly. "I'm listening." He was beginning to suspect that he had been no more than bait in an elaborate trap.

"I've had a—perhaps 'tracer' is the best word for it— on you for some time," began Karellen. "Though your late friends were correct in thinking that I couldn't follow you underground, I was able to keep track until they brought you to the mine. That transfer in the tunnel was ingenious, but when the first car ceased to react it gave the plan away and I soon located you again. Then it was merely a matter of waiting. I knew that once they were certain I'd lost you, the leaders would come here and I'd be able to trap them all."

"But you're letting them go!"

"Until now," said Karellen, "I had no way of telling who of the two and a half billion men on this planet were the real heads of the organization. Now that they're located, I can trace their movements anywhere on Earth, and can watch their actions in detail if I want to. That's far better than locking them up. If they make any moves, they'll betray their remaining comrades. They're effectively neutralized, and they know it. Your rescue will be completely inexplicable to them, for you must have vanished before their eyes."

That rich laugh echoed round the tiny room.

"In some ways the whole affair was a comedy, but it had a serious purpose. I'm not merely concerned with the few score men in this organization—I have to think of the moral effect on other groups that exist elsewhere."

Stormgren was silent for a while. He was not altogether satisfied, but he could see Karellen's point of view, and some of his anger had evaporated.

"It's a pity to do it in my last few weeks of office," he said finally, "but from now on I'm going to have a guard on my house. Pieter can be kidnaped next time. How has he managed, by the way?"

"I've watched him carefully this last week, and have deliberately avoided helping him. On the whole he's done very well—but he's not the man to take your place."

"That's lucky for him," said Stormgren, still somewhat aggrieved. "And by the way, have you had any word yet from your superiors—about showing yourself to us? I'm sure now that it's the strongest argument your enemies have. Again and again they told me: 'We'll never trust the Overlords until we can see them.' "

Karellen sighed.

"No. I have heard nothing. But I know what the answer must be."

Stormgren did not press the matter. Once he might have done so, but now for the first time the faint shadow of a plan was beginning to take shape in his mind. The words of his interrogator passed again through his memory. Yes, perhaps instruments could be devised. . . .

What he had refused to do under duress, he might yet attempt of his own free will.

4

IT WOULD NEVER HAVE OCCURRED to Stormgren, even a few days before, that he could seriously have considered the action he was planning now. This ridiculously melodramatic kidnapping, which in retrospect seemed like a third-rate TV drama, probably had a great deal to do with his new outlook. It was the first time in his life that Stormgren had ever been exposed to violent physical action, as opposed to the verbal battles of the conference room. The virus must have entered his bloodstream; or else he was merely approaching second childhood more quickly than he had supposed.

Sheer curiosity was also a powerful motive, and so was a determination to get his own back for the trick that had been played upon him. It was perfectly obvious now that Karellen had used him as bait, and even if this had been for the best of reasons, Stormgren did not feel inclined to forgive the Supervisor at once.

Pierre Duval showed no surprise when Stormgren walked unannounced into his office. They were old friends and there was nothing unusual in the Secretary-General paying a personal visit to the Chief of the Science

Bureau. Certainly Karellen would not think it odd, if by any chance he—or one of his underlings—turned his instruments of surveillance upon this spot.

For a while the two men talked business and exchanged political gossip; then, rather hesitantly, Stormgren came to the point. As his visitor talked, the old Frenchman leaned back in his chair and his eyebrows rose steadily, millimeter by millimeter, until they were almost entangled in his forelock. Once or twice he seemed about to speak, but each time thought better of it.

When Stormgren had finished, the scientist looked nervously around the room.

"Do you think he's listening?" he said.

"I don't believe he can. He's got what he calls a tracer on me, for my protection. But it doesn't work underground, which is one reason why I came down to this dungeon of yours. It's supposed to be shielded from all forms of radiation, isn't it? Karellen's no magician. He knows where I am, but that's all."

"I hope you're right. Apart from that, won't there be trouble when he discovers what you're trying to do? Because he will, you know."

"I'll take that risk. Besides, we understand each other rather well."

The physicist toyed with his pencil and stared into space for a while.

"It's a very pretty problem. I like it," he said simply. Then he dived into a drawer and produced an enormous writing pad, quite the biggest that Stormgren had ever seen.

"Right," he began, scribbling furiously in what seemed to be some private shorthand. "Let me make sure I have all the facts. Tell me everything you can about the room in which you have your interviews. Don't omit any detail, however trivial it seems."

"There isn't much to describe. It's made of metal, and is about eight meters square and four high. The vision screen is about a meter on a side and there's a desk immediately beneath it—here, it will be quicker if I draw it for you."

Rapidly Stormgren sketched the little room he knew so well, and pushed the drawing over to Duval. As he did so, he recalled, with a slight shiver, the last time he had done this sort of thing. He wondered what had happened to the blind Welshman and his confederates, and how they had reacted to his abrupt departure.

The Frenchman studied the drawing with a puckered brow.

"And that's all you can tell me?"

"Yes."

Duval snorted in disgust.

"What about lighting? Do you sit in total darkness? And how about ventilation, heating—"

Stormgren smiled at the characteristic outburst.

"The whole ceiling is luminous, and as far as I can tell the air comes through the speaker grille. I don't know how it leaves; perhaps the stream reverses at intervals, but I haven't noticed it. There's no sign of any heater, but the room is always at normal temperature."

"Meaning, I suppose, that the water vapor has frozen out, but not the carbon dioxide."

Stormgren did his best to smile at the well-worn joke.

"I think I've told you everything," he concluded. "As for the machine that takes me up to Karellen's ship, the room in which I travel is as featureless as an elevator cage. Apart from the couch and table, it might very well be one."

There was silence for several minutes while the physicist embroidered his writing pad with meticulous and microsopic doodles. As he watched, Stormgren wondered why it was that a man like Duval—whose mind was incomparably more brilliant than his own—had never made a greater mark in the world of science. He remembered an unkind and probably inaccurate comment of a friend in the U.S. State Department. "The French produce the best second-raters in the world." Duval was the sort of man who supported that statement.

The physicist nodded to himself in satisfaction, leaned forward and pointed his pencil at Stormgren.

"What makes you think, Rikki," he asked, "that Karellen's vision screen, as you call it, really is what it pretends to be?"

"I've always taken it for granted; it looks exactly like one. What else would it be, anyway?"

"When you say that it *looks* like a vision screen, you mean, don't you, that it looks like one of *ours?*"

"Of course."

"I find that suspicious in itself. I'm sure the Overlords' own apparatus won't use anything as crude as an actual physical screen—they'll probably materialize images directly in space. But why should Karellen bother to use a TV system, anyway? The simplest solution is always best. Doesn't it seem far more probable that your 'vision screen' is really *nothing more complicated than a sheet of one-way glass?"*

Stormgren was so annoyed with himself that for a moment he sat in silence, retracing the past. From the beginning, he had never challenged Karellen's story—yet now he came to look back, when had the Supervisor ever told him that he was using a TV system? He had simply taken it for granted: the whole thing had been a piece of psychological trickery, and he had been completely deceived. Always assuming, of course, that Duval's theory *was* correct. But he was jumping to conclusions again; no one had proved anything yet.

"If you're right," he said, "all I have to do is to smash the glass—"

Duval sighed.

"These unscientific laymen! Do you think it'll be made of anything you could smash without explosives? And if you succeeded, do you imagine that Karellen is likely to breathe the same air that we do? Won't it be nice for both of you if he flourishes in an atmosphere of chlorine?"

Stormgren felt a little foolish. He should have thought of that.

"Well, what *do* you suggest?" he asked with some exasperation.

"I want to think it over. First of all we've got to find if my theory is correct, and if so learn something about the material of that screen. I'll put a couple of my men on the job. By the way, I suppose you carry a brief case when you visit the Supervisor? Is it the one you've got there?"

"Yes."

"It should be big enough. We don't want to attract attention by changing it for another, particularly if Karellen's grown used to it."

"What do you want me to do?" asked Stormgren. "Carry a concealed X-ray set?"

The physicist grinned.

"I don't know yet, but we'll think of something. I'll let you know what it is in about two weeks."

He gave a little laugh.

"Do you know what all this reminds me of?"

"Yes," said Stormgren promptly, "the time you were building illegal radio sets during the German occupation."

Duval looked disappointed.

"Well, I suppose I *have* mentioned that once or twice before. But there's one other thing—"

"What's that?"

"When you are caught, *I* didn't know what you wanted the gear for."

"What, after all the fuss you once made about the scientist's social responsibility for his inventions? Really, Pierre, I'm ashamed of you!"

Stormgren laid down the thick folder of typescript with a sigh of relief.

"Thank heavens *that's* settled at last," he said. "It's strange to think that these few hundred pages hold the future of mankind. The World State! I never thought I would see it in my lifetime!"

He dropped the file into his brief case, the back of which was no more than ten centimeters from the dark rectangle of the screen. From time to time his fingers played across the locks in a half-conscious, nervous reaction, but he had no intention of pressing the concealed switch until the meeting was over. There was a chance that something might go wrong; though Duval had sworn that Karellen would detect nothing, one could never be sure.

"Now, you said you'd some news for me," Stormgren continued, with scarcely concealed eagerness. "Is it about—"

"Yes," said Karellen. "I received a decision a few hours ago."

What did he mean by that? wondered Stormgren. Surely it was not possible for the Supervisor to have communicated with his distant home, across the unknown numbers of light-years that separated him from his base. Or perhaps—this was Van Ryberg's theory—he had merely been consulting some vast computing machine which could predict the outcome of any political action.

"I don't think," continued Karellen, "that the Freedom League and its associates will be very satisfied, but it should help to reduce the tension. We won't record this, by the way.

"You've often told me, Rikki, that no matter how unlike you we are physically, the human race would soon grow accustomed to us. That shows a lack of imagination on your part. It would probably be true in your case, but you must remember that most of the world is still uneducated by any reasonable standards, and is riddled with prejudices and superstitions that may take decades to eradicate.

"You will grant that we know something of human psychology. We know rather accurately what would happen if we revealed ourselves to the world in its present state of development. I can't go into details, even with you, so you must accept my analysis on trust. We can, however, make this definite promise, which should give you some satisfaction. *In fifty years—two generations from now—we will come down from our ships and humanity will at last see us as we are.*"

Stormgren was silent for a while, absorbing the Supervisor's words. He felt little of the satisfaction that Karellen's statement would once have given him. Indeed, he was somewhat confused by his partial success, and for a moment his resolution faltered. The truth would come with the passage of time: all his plotting was unnecessary and perhaps unwise. If he still went ahead, it would be only for the selfish reason that he would not be alive in fifty years.

Karellen must have seen his irresolution, for he continued:

"I'm sorry if this disappoints you, but at least the political problems of the near future won't be your responsibility. Perhaps you still think that our fears are unfounded—but believe me we've had convincing proofs of the danger of any other course."

Stormgren leaned forward, breathing heavily.

"So you *have* been seen by Man!"

"I didn't say that," Karellen answered promptly. *"Your* world isn't the only planet we've supervised."

Stormgren was not to be shaken off so easily.

"There have been many legends suggesting that Earth has been visited in the past by other races."

"I know: I've read the Historical Research Section's report. It makes Earth look like the crossroads of the Universe."

"There may have been visits about which you know nothing," said Stormgren, still angling hopefully. "Though since you must have been observing us for thousands of years, I suppose that's rather unlikely."

"I suppose it is," replied Karellen, in his most unhelpful manner. And at that moment Stormgren made up his mind.

"Karellen," he said abruptly, "I'll draft out the statement and send it up to you for approval. But I reserve the right to continue pestering you, and if I see any opportunity, I'll do my best to learn your secret."

"I'm perfectly well aware of that," replied the Supervisor, with a slight chuckle.

"And you don't mind?"

"Not in the least—though I draw the line at nuclear weapons, poison gas, or anything else that might strain our friendship."

Stormgren wondered what, if anything, Karellen had guessed. Behind the Supervisor's banter he had recognized a note of understanding, perhaps—who could tell? —even of encouragement.

"I'm glad to know it," Stormgren replied in as level a voice as he could manage. He rose to his feet, bringing down the cover on his case as he did so. His thumb slid along the catch.

"I'll draft that statement at once," he repeated, "and send it up on the teletype later today."

While he was speaking, he pressed the button—and knew that all his fears had been groundless. Karellen's senses were no subtler than Man's. The Supervisor could have detected nothing, for there was no change in his voice as he said good-by and spoke the familiar code-words that opened the door of the chamber.

Yet Stormgren still felt like a shoplifter leaving a department store under the eyes of the store detective, and breathed a sigh of relief when the smooth wall had sealed itself behind him.

"I admit," said Van Ryberg, "that some of my theories haven't been very successful. But tell me what you think of this one."

"Must I?" sighed Stormgren.

Pieter didn't seem to notice.

"It isn't really my idea," he said modestly. "I got it from a story of Chesterton's. Suppose the Overlords are hiding the fact that they've got nothing to hide?"

"That sounds just a little complicated to me," said Stormgren, beginning to take a slight interest.

"What I mean is this," Van Ryberg continued eagerly. "*I* think that physically they're human beings like us. They realize that we'll tolerate being ruled by creatures we imagine to be—well, alien and superintelligent. But the human race being what it is, it just won't be bossed around by creatures of the same species."

"Very ingenious, like all your theories," said Stormgren. "I wish you'd give them opus numbers so that I could keep up with them. The objections to this one—"

But at that moment Alexander Wainwright was shown in.

Stormgren wondered what he was thinking. He wondered, too, if Wainwright had made any contact with the men who had kidnaped him. He doubted it, for he believed Wainwright's disapproval of violence to be perfectly genuine. The extremists in his movement had discredited themselves thoroughly, and it would be a long time before the world heard of them again.

The head of the Freedom League listened carefully while the draft was read to him. Stormgren hoped he appreciated this gesture, which had been Karellen's idea. Not for another twelve hours would the rest of the world know of the promise that had been made to its grandchildren.

"Fifty years," said Wainwright thoughtfully. "That is a long time to wait."

"For mankind, perhaps, but not for Karellen," Stormgren answered. Only now was he beginning to realize the neatness of the Overlords' solution. It had given them the breathing space they believed they needed, and it had cut the ground from beneath the Freedom League's feet. He did not imagine that the League would capitulate, but its position would be seriously weakened. Certainly Wainwright realized this as well.

"In fifty years," he said bitterly, "the damage will be done. Those who remembered our independence will be dead; humanity will have forgotten its heritage."

Words—empty words, thought Stormgren. The words for which men had once fought and died, and for which they would never die or fight again. And the world would be better for it.

As he watched Wainwright leave, Stormgren wondered how much trouble the Freedom League would still cause in the years that lay ahead. Yet that, he thought with a lifting of his spirits, was a problem for his successor.

There were some things that only time could cure. Evil men could be destroyed, but nothing could be done with good men who were deluded.

"Here's your case," said Duval. "It's as good as new."

"Thanks," Stormgren answered, inspecting it carefully none the less. "Now perhaps you'll tell me what it was all about, and what we are going to do next."

The physicist seemed more interested in his own thoughts.

"What I can't understand," he said, "is the ease with which we've got away with it. Now if I'd been Kar—"

"But you're not. Get to the point, man. What *did* we discover?"

"Ah me, these excitable, highly strung Nordic races!" sighed Duval. "What we did was to make a type of low powered radar set. Besides radio waves of very high frequency, it used far infrared—all waves, in fact, which we were sure no creature could possibly see, however weird an eye it had."

"How could you be sure of that?" asked Stormgren, becoming intrigued by the technical problem in spite of himself.

"Well—we couldn't be *quite* sure," admitted Duval reluctantly. "But Karellen views you under normal lighting, doesn't he? So his eyes must be approximately similar to ours in spectral range. Anyway, it worked. We've proved that there *is* a large room behind that screen of yours. The screen is about three centimeters thick, and the space behind it is at least ten meters across. We couldn't detect any echo from the far wall, but we hardly expected to with the low power which was all we dared use. However, we did get *this*."

He pushed across a piece of photographic paper on which was a single wavy line. In one spot was a kink like the autograph of a mild earthquake.

"See that little kink?"

"Yes: what is it?"

"Only Karellen."

"Good Lord! Are you sure?"

"It's a pretty safe guess. He's sitting, or standing, or whatever it is he does, about two meters on the other side of the screen. If the resolution had been a bit better, we might even have calculated his size."

Stormgren's feelings were very mixed as he stared at that scarcely visible inflection of the trace. Until now, there had been no proof that Karellen even had a material body. The evidence was still indirect, but he accepted it without question.

"The other thing we had to do," said Duval, "was to calculate the transmission of the screen to ordinary light. We think we've got a reasonable idea of that—anyway it doesn't matter if we're out even by a factor of ten. You'll realize, of course, that there's no such thing as a truly one-way glass. It's simply a matter of arranging the lights. Karellen sits in a darkened room: you are illuminated—that's all." Duval chuckled. "Well, we're going to change that!"

With the air of a conjurer producing a whole litter of white rabbits, he reached into his desk and pulled out an overgrown flashlight. The end flared out into a wide nozzle, so that the whole device looked rather like a blunderbuss.

Duval grinned.

"It's not as dangerous as it looks. All you have to do is to ram the nozzle against the screen and press the trigger. It gives out a very powerful beam lasting ten seconds, and in that time you'll be able to swing it round the room and get a good view. All the light will go through the screen and it will floodlight your friend beautifully."

"It won't hurt Karellen?"

"Not if you aim low and sweep upwards. That will give his eyes time to adapt—I suppose he has reflexes like ours, and we don't want to blind him."

Stormgren looked at the weapon doubtfully and hefted it in his hand. For the last few weeks his conscience had been pricking him. Karellen had always treated him with unmistakable affection, despite his occasional devastating frankness, and now that their time together was drawing to its close he did not wish to do anything that might spoil that relationship. But the Supervisor had received due warning, and Stormgren had the conviction that if the choice had been his, Karellen would long ago have shown himself. Now the decision would be made for him: when their last meeting came to its end, Stormgren would gaze upon Karellen's face.

If, of course, Karellen had a face.

The nervousness that Stormgren had first felt had long since passed away. Karellen was doing almost all the talking, weaving the intricate sentences which he was prone to use. Once this had seemed to Stormgren the most wonderful and certainly the most unexpected of all Karellen's gifts. Now it no longer appeared quite so marvelous, for he knew that like most of the Supervisor's abilities it was the result of sheer intellectual power and not of any special talent.

Karellen had time for any amount of literary compositions when he slowed his thoughts down to the pace of human speech.

"There is no need for you or your successor to worry unduly about the Freedom League, even when it has recovered from its present despondency. It has been very quiet for the past month, and, though it will revive again, it will not be a danger for some years. Indeed, since it is always valuable to know what your opponents are doing, the League is a very useful institution. Should it ever get into financial difficulties I might even have to subsidize it."

Stormgren had often found it difficult to tell when Karellen was joking. He kept his face impassive and continued to listen.

"Very soon the League will lose another of its arguments. There has been a good deal of criticism, all somewhat childish, of the special position you have held for the past few years. I found it very valuable in the early days of my administration, but now that the world is moving along the lines that I planned, it can cease. In future, all my dealings with Earth will be indirect and the office of Secretary-General can revert to something resembling its original form.

"During the next fifty years there will be many crises, but they will pass. The pattern of the future is clear enough, and one day all these difficulties will be forgotten—even to a race with memories as long as yours."

The last words were spoken with such peculiar emphasis that Stormgren immediately froze in his seat. Karellen, he was sure, never made accidental slips: even his indiscretions were calculated to many decimal places. But there was no time to ask questions—which certainly would not be answered—before the Supervisor had changed the subject again.

"You have often asked me about our long-term plans," he continued. "The foundation of the World State is, of course, only the first step. You will live to see its completion—but the change will be so imperceptible that few will notice it when it comes. After that there will be a period of slow consolidation while your race becomes prepared for us. And then will come the day which we have promised. I am sorry you will not be there."

Stormgren's eyes were open, but his gaze was fixed far beyond the dark barrier of the screen. He was looking into the future, imagining the day that he would never see, when the great ships of the Overlords came down at last to Earth and were thrown open to the waiting world.

"On that day," continued Karellen, "the human race will experience what can only be called a psychological discontinuity. But no permanent harm will be done: the men of that age will be more stable than their grandfathers. We will always have been part of their lives, and when they meet us we will not seem so—strange—as we would do to you."

Stormgren had never known Karellen in so contemplative a mood, but this gave him no surprise. He did not believe that he had ever seen more than a few facets of the Supervisor's personality: the real Karellen was unknown and perhaps unknowable to human beings. And once again Stormgren had the feeling that the Supervisor's real interests were elsewhere, and that he ruled Earth with only a fraction of his mind, as effortlessly as a master of three-dimensional chess might play a game of checkers.

"And after that?" asked Stormgren softly.

"*Then* we can begin our real work."

"I have often wondered what that might be. Tidying

up our world and civilizing the human race is only a means—you must have an end as well. Will we ever be able to come out into space and see your universe—perhaps even help you in your tasks?"

"You can put it that way," said Karellen—and now his voice held a clear yet inexplicable note of sadness that left Stormgren strangely perturbed.

"But suppose, after all, your experiment fails with Man? We have known such things in our own dealings with primitive human races. Surely you have had your failures too?"

"Yes," said Karellen, so softly that Stormgren could scarcely hear him. "We have had our failures."

"And what do you do then?"

"We wait—and try again."

There was a pause lasting perhaps five seconds. When Karellen spoke again, his words were so unexpected that for a moment Stormgren did not react.

"Good-by, Rikki!"

Karellen had tricked him—probably it was already too late. Stormgren's paralysis lasted only a moment. Then with a single swift, well-practiced movement, he whipped out the flash gun and jammed it against the glass.

The pine trees came almost to the edge of the lake, leaving along its border only a narrow strip of grass a few meters wide. Every evening when it was warm enough Stormgren, despite his ninety years, would walk briskly along this strip to the landing stage, watch the sunlight die upon the water, and then return to the house before the chill night wind came up from the forest. The simple ritual gave him much contentment, and he would continue it as long as he had the strength.

Far away over the lake something was coming in from the west, flying low and fast. Aircraft were uncommon in these parts, unless one counted the transpolar lines which must be passing overhead every hour of the day and night. But there was never any sign of their presence, save an occasional vapor trail high against the blue of the stratosphere. This machine was a small helicopter, and it was coming towards him with obvious determination. Stormgren glanced along the beach and saw that there was no chance of escape. Then he shrugged his shoulders and sat down on the wooden bench at the head of the jetty.

The reporter was so deferential that Stormgren found it surprising. He had almost forgotten that he was not only an elder statesman but, outside his own country, almost a mythical figure.

"Mr. Stormgren," the intruder began, "I'm very sorry to bother you, but I wonder if you'd care to comment on something we've just heard about the Overlords."

Stormgren frowned slightly. After all these years, he still shared Karellen's dislike for that word.

"I do not think," he said, "that I can add a great deal to what has been written elsewhere."

The reporter was watching him with a curious intentness.

"I thought that you might. A rather strange story has just come to our notice. It seems that, nearly thirty years ago, one of the Science Bureau's technicians made some remarkable equipment for you. We wondered if you could tell us anything about it."

For a moment Stormgren was silent, his mind going back into the past. He was not surprised that the secret had been discovered. Indeed, it was surprising that it had been kept so long.

He rose to his feet and began to walk back along the jetty, the reporter following a few paces behind.

"The story," he said, "contains a certain amount of truth. On my last visit to Karellen's ship I took some apparatus with me, in the hope that I might be able to see the Supervisor. It was rather a foolish thing to do but— well, I was only sixty at the time."

He chuckled to himself and then continued.

"It's not much of a story to have brought you all this way. You see, it didn't work."

"You saw nothing?"

"No, nothing at all. I'm afraid you'll have to wait—but after all, there are only twenty years to go!"

Twenty years to go. Yes, Karellen had been right. By then the world would be ready, as it had not been when he had spoken that same lie to Duval thirty years ago.

Karellen had trusted him, and Stormgren had not betrayed his faith. He was as sure as he could be of anything that the Supervisor had known his plan from the beginning, and had foreseen every moment of its final act.

Why else had that enormous chair been already empty when the circle of light blazed upon it? In the same moment he had started to swing the beam, fearing that he was too late. The metal door, twice as high as a man, was closing swiftly when he first caught sight of it—closing swiftly, yet not quite swiftly enough.

Yes, Karellen had trusted him, had not wished him to go down into the long evening of his life haunted by a mystery he could never solve. Karellen dared not defy the unknown powers above him (were *they* of that same race also?), but he had done all that he could. If he had disobeyed them, they could never prove it. It was the final proof, Stormgren knew, of Karellen's affection for him. Though it might be the affection of a man for a devoted and intelligent dog, it was none the less sincere for that, and Stormgren's life had given him few greater satisfactions.

"We have had our failures."

Yes, Karellen, that was true: and were *you* the one who failed, before the dawn of human history? It must have been a failure indeed, thought Stormgren, for its echoes to roll down all the ages, to haunt the childhood of every race of man. Even in fifty years, could you overcome the power of all the myths and legends of the world?

Yet Stormgren knew there would be no second failure. When the two races met again, the Overlords would have won the trust and friendship of mankind, and not even the shock of recognition could undo that work. They would go together into the future, and the unknown tragedy that must have darkened the past would be lost forever down the dim corridors of prehistoric time.

And Stormgren hoped that when Karellen was free to walk once more on Earth, he would one day come to these northern forests, and stand beside the grave of the first man ever to be his friend.

II

The Golden Age

5

"THIS IS THE DAY!" whispered the radios in a hundred tongues. "This is the day!" said the headlines of a thousand newspapers. "This is the day!" thought the cameramen as they checked and rechecked the equipment gathered round the vast empty space upon which Karellen's ship would be descending.

There was only the single ship now, hanging above New York. Indeed, as the world had just discovered, the ships above man's other cities had never existed. The day before, the great fleet of the Overlords had dissolved into nothingness, fading like mist beneath the morning sun.

The supply ships, coming and going far out in space, had been real enough; but the silver clouds that had hung for a lifetime over the capitals of Earth had been an illusion. How it had been done, no one could tell, but it seemed that every one of those ships had been nothing more than an image of Karellen's own vessel. Yet it had been far more than a matter of playing with light, for radar had also been deceived and there were still men alive who swore that they had heard the shriek of torn air as the fleet came in through the skies of Earth.

It was not important: all that mattered was that Karellen no longer felt the need for this display of force. He had thrown away his psychological weapons.

"The ship is moving!" came the word, flashed instantly to every corner of the planet. "It is heading westward!"

At less than a thousand kilometers an hour, falling slowly down from the empty heights of the stratosphere, the ship moved out to the great plains and to its second rendezvous with history. It settled down obediently before the waiting cameras and the packed thousands of spectators, so few of whom could see as much as the millions gathered round their TV sets.

The ground should have cracked and trembled beneath that tremendous weight, but the vessel was still in the grip of whatever forces drove it among the stars. It kissed the earth as gently as a falling snowflake.

The curving wall twenty meters above the ground seemed to flow and shimmer: where there had been a smooth and shining surface, a great opening had appeared. Nothing was visible within it, even to the questing eyes of the camera. It was as dark and shadowed as the entrance to a cave.

Out of the orifice, a wide, glittering gangway extruded itself and drove purposefully towards the ground. It seemed a solid sheet of metal with handrails along either side. There were no steps; it was steep and smooth as a toboggan slide and, one would have thought, equally impossible to ascend or descend in any ordinary manner.

The world was watching that dark portal, within which nothing had yet stirred. Then the seldom-heard yet unforgettable voice of Karellen floated softly down from some hidden source. His message could scarcely have been more unexpected.

"There are some children by the foot of the gangway. I would like two of them to come up and meet me."

There was silence for a moment. Then a boy and a girl broke from the crowd and walked, with complete lack of self-consciousness, towards the gangway and into history. Others followed, but stopped when Karellen's chuckle came from the ship.

"Two will be enough."

Eagerly anticipating the adventure, the children—they could not have been more than six years old—jumped on to the metal slide. Then the first miracle happened.

Waving cheerfully to the crowds beneath, and to their anxious parents—who, too late, had probably remembered the legend of the Pied Piper—the children began swiftly ascending the steep slope. Yet their legs were motionless, and soon it was clear also that their bodies were tilted at right angles to that peculiar gangway. It possessed a private gravity of its own, one which could ignore that of Earth. The children were still enjoying this novel experience, and wondering what was drawing them upwards, when they disappeared into the ship.

A vast silence lay over the whole world for the space of twenty seconds—though, afterward, no one could believe that the time had been so short. Then the darkness of the great opening seemed to move forward, and Karellen came forth into the sunlight. The boy was sitting on his left arm, the girl on his right. They were both too busy playing with Karellen's wings to take any notice of the watching multitude.

It was a tribute to the Overlords' psychology, and to their careful years of preparation, that only a few people fainted. Yet there could have been fewer still, anywhere in the world, who did not feel the ancient terror brush for one awful instant against their minds before reason banished it forever.

There was no mistake. The leathery wings, the little horns, the barbed tail—all were there. The most terrible of all legends had come to life, out of the unknown past. Yet now it stood smiling, in ebon majesty, with the sunlight gleaming upon its tremendous body, and with a human child resting trustfully on either arm.

6

FIFTY YEARS is ample time in which to change a world and its people almost beyond recognition. All that is required for the task are a sound knowledge of social engineering, a clear sight of the intended goal—and power.

These things the Overlords possessed. Though their goal was hidden, their knowledge was obvious—and so was their power.

That power took many forms, few of them realized by the peoples whose destinies the Overlords now ruled. The might enshrined in their great ships had been clear enough for every eye to see. But behind that display of sleeping force were other and much subtler weapons.

"All political problems," Karellen had once told Stormgren, "can be solved by the correct application of power."

"That sounds a rather cynical remark," Stormgren had replied doubtfully. "It's a little too much like 'Might is Right'. In our own past, the use of power has been notably unsuccessful in solving anything."

"The operative word is *correct*. You have never possessed real power, or the knowledge necessary to apply it. As in all problems, there are efficient and inefficient approaches. Suppose, for example, that one of your nations, led by some fanatical ruler, tried to revolt against me. The highly inefficient answer to such a threat would be some billions of horsepower in the shape of atomic bombs. If I used enough bombs, the solution would be complete and final. It would also, as I remarked, be inefficient—even if it possessed no other defects."

"And the efficient solution?"

"That requires about as much power as a small radio transmitter—and rather similar skills to operate. For it's the *application* of the power, not its amount, that matters. How long do you think Hitler's career as dictator of Germany would have lasted, if wherever he went a voice was talking quietly in his ear? Or if a steady musical note, loud enough to drown all other sounds and to prevent sleep, filled his brain night and day? Nothing brutal, you appreciate. Yet, in the final analysis, just as irresistible as a tritium bomb."

"I see," said Stormgren, "and there would be no place to hide?"

"No place where I could not send my—ah—devices if I felt sufficiently strongly about it. And that is why I shall never have to use really drastic methods to maintain my position."

The great ships, then, had never been more than symbols, and now the world knew that all save one had been phantoms. Yet, by their mere presence, they had changed the history of Earth. Now their task was done, and their achievement lingered behind them to go echoing down the centuries.

Karellen's calculations had been accurate. The shock of revulsion had passed swiftly, though there were many who prided themselves on their freedom from superstition yet would never be able to face one of the Overlords. There was something strange here, something beyond all reason or logic. In the Middle Ages, people believed in the Devil and feared him. But this was the twenty-first century: could it be that, after all, there was such a thing as racial memory?

It was, of course, universally assumed that the Overlords, or beings of the same species, had come into violent conflict with ancient man. The meeting must have lain in the remote past, for it had left no traces in recorded history. Here was another puzzle, and Karellen would give no help in its solution.

The Overlords, though they had now shown themselves to man, seldom left their one remaining ship. Perhaps they found it physically uncomfortable on Earth, for their size, and the existence of their wings, indicated that they came from a world of much lower gravity. They were never seen without a belt adorned with complex mechanisms which, it was generally believed, controlled their weight and enabled them to communicate with each other. Direct sunlight was painful to them, and they never stayed in it for more than a few seconds. When they had to go into the open for any length of time, they wore dark glasses which gave them a somewhat incongruous appearance. Though they seemed able to breathe terrestrial air, they sometimes carried small cylinders of gas from which they refreshed themselves occasionally.

Perhaps these purely physical problems accounted for their aloofness. Only a small fraction of the human race had ever actually met an Overlord in the flesh, and no one could guess how many of them were aboard Karellen's ship. No more than five had ever been seen together at one time, but there might be hundreds, even thousands, of them aboard that tremendous vessel.

In many ways, the appearance of the Overlords had raised more problems than it had solved. Their origin was still unknown, their biology a source of endless speculation. On many matters they would give information freely, but on others their behavior could only be described as secretive. On the whole, however, this did not annoy anyone except the scientists. The average man, though he might prefer not to meet the Overlords, was grateful to them for what they had done to his world.

By the standards of all earlier ages, it was Utopia. Ignorance, disease, poverty, and fear had virtually ceased to exist. The memory of war was fading into the past as a nightmare vanishes with the dawn; soon it would lie outside the experience of all living men.

With the energies of mankind directed into constructive channels, the face of the world had been remade. It was, almost literally, a new world. The cities that had been good enough for earlier generations had been rebuilt— or deserted and left as museum specimens when they had ceased to serve any useful purpose. Many cities had already been abandoned in this manner, for the whole pattern of industry and commerce had changed completely. Production had become largely automatic: the robot factories poured forth consumer goods in such unending streams that all the ordinary necessities of life were virtually free. Men worked for the sake of the luxuries they desired: or they did not work at all.

It was One World. The old names of the old countries were still used, but they were no more than convenient postal divisions. There was no one on earth who could not speak English, who could not read, who was not within range of a television set, who could not visit the other side of the planet within twenty-four hours. . . .

Crime had practically vanished. It had become both unnecessary and impossible. When no one lacks anything, there is no point in stealing. Moreover, all potential criminals knew that there could be no escape from the surveillance of the Overlords. In the early days of their rule, they had intervened so effectively on behalf of law and order that the lesson had never been forgotten.

Crimes of passion, though not quite extinct, were almost unheard of. Now that so many of its psychological problems had been removed, humanity was far saner and less irrational. And what earlier ages would have called vice was now no more than eccentricity—or, at the worst, bad manners.

One of the most noticeable changes had been a slowing down of the mad tempo that had so characterized the twentieth century. Life was more leisurely than it had been for generations. It therefore had less zest for the few, but more tranquility for the many. Western man had relearned—what the rest of the world had never forgotten—that there was nothing sinful in leisure as long as it did not degenerate into mere sloth.

Whatever problems the future might bring, time did not yet hang heavy on humanity's hands. Education was now much more thorough and much more protracted. Few people left college before twenty—and that was merely the first stage, since they normally returned again at twenty-five for at least three more years, after travel and experience had broadened their minds. Even then, they would probably take refresher courses at intervals for the remainder of their lives in the subjects that particularly interested them.

This extension of human apprenticeship so far past the beginning of physical maturity had given rise to many social changes. Some of these had been necessary for generations, but earlier periods had refused to face the challenge—or had pretended that it did not exist. In particular, the patterns of sexual *mores*—insofar as there had ever been one pattern —had altered radically. It had been virtually shattered by two inventions, which were, ironically enough, of purely human origin and owed nothing to the Overlords.

The first was a completely reliable oral contraceptive: the second was an equally infallible method—as certain as fingerprinting, and based on a very detailed analysis of the blood—of identifying the father of any child. The effect of these two inventions upon human society could only be described as devastating, and they had swept away the last remnants of the Puritan aberration.

Another great change was the extreme mobility of the new society. Thanks to the perfection of air transport, everyone was free to go anywhere at a moment's notice. There was more room in the skies than there had ever been on the roads, and the twenty-first century had repeated, on a larger scale, the great American achievement of putting a nation on wheels. It had given wings to the world.

Though not literally. The ordinary private flyer or aircar had no wings at all, or indeed any visible control surfaces. Even the clumsy rotor blades of the old helicopters had been banished. Yet Man had not discovered anti-gravity: only the Overlords possessed that ultimate secret. His aircars were propelled by forces which the Wright brothers would have understood. Jet reaction, used both directly and in the more subtle form of boundary layer control, drove his flyers forward and held them in the air. As no laws or edicts of the Overlords could have done, the ubiquitous little aircars had washed away the last barriers between the different tribes of mankind.

Profounder things had also passed. It was a completely secular age. Of the faiths that had existed before the coming of the Overlords, only a form of purified Buddhism—perhaps the most austere of all religions—still survived. The creeds that had been based upon miracles and revelations had collapsed utterly. With the rise of education, they had already been slowly dissolving, but for a while the Overlords had taken no sides in the matter. Though Karellen was often asked to express his views on religion, all that he would say was that a man's beliefs were his own affair, so long as they did not interfere with the liberty of others.

Perhaps the old faiths would have lingered for generations yet, had it not been for human curiosity. It was known that the Overlords had access to the past, and more than once historians had appealed to Karellen to settle some ancient controversy. It may have been that he had grown tired of such questions, but it is more likely that he knew perfectly well what the outcome of his generosity would be. . . .

The instrument he handed over on permanent loan to the World History Foundation was nothing more than a television receiver with an elaborate set of controls for determining co-ordinates in time and space. It must have been linked somehow to a far more complex machine, operating on principles that no one could imagine, aboard Karellen's ship. One had merely to adjust the controls, and a window into the past was opened up. Almost the whole of human history for the past five thousand years became accessible in an instant. Earlier than that the machine would not go, and there were baffling blanks all down the ages. They might have had some natural cause, or they might be due to deliberate censorship by the Overlords.

Though it had always been obvious to any rational mind that *all* the world's religious writings could not be true, the shock was nevertheless profound. Here was a revelation which no one could doubt or deny: here, seen by some unknown magic of Overlord science, were the true beginnings of all the world's great faiths. Most of them were noble and inspiring—but that was not enough. Within a few days, all mankind's multitudinous messiahs had lost their divinity. Beneath the fierce and passionless light of truth, faiths that had sustained millions for twice a thousand years vanished like morning dew. All the good and all the evil they had wrought were swept suddenly into the past, and could touch the minds of men no more.

Humanity had lost its ancient gods: now it was old enough to have no need for new ones.

Though few realized it as yet, the fall of religion had been paralleled by a decline in science. There were plenty of technologists, but few original workers extending the frontiers of human knowledge. Curiosity remained, and the leisure to indulge in it, but the heart had been taken out of fundamental scientific research. It seemed futile to spend a lifetime searching for secrets that the Overlords had probably uncovered ages before.

This decline had been partly disguised by an enormous efflorescence of the descriptive sciences such as zoology, botany, and observational astronomy. There had never been so many amateur scientists gathering facts for their own amusement—but there were few theoreticians correlating these facts.

The end of strife and conflict of all kinds had also meant the virtual end of creative art. There were myriads of performers, amateur and professional, yet there had been no really outstanding new works of literature, music, painting, or sculpture for a generation. The world was still living on the glories of a past that could never return.

No one worried except a few philosophers. The race was too intent upon savoring its new-found freedom to look beyond the pleasures of the present. Utopia was here at last: its novelty had not yet been assailed by the supreme enemy of all Utopias—boredom.

Perhaps the Overlords had the answer to that, as they had to all other problems. No one knew—any more than they knew, a lifetime after their arrival, what their ultimate purpose might be. Mankind had grown to trust them, and to accept without question the superhuman altruism

that had kept Karellen and his companions so long ex-
iled from their homes.

If, indeed, it was altruism. For there were still some
who wondered if the policies of the Overlords would
always coincide with the true welfare of humanity.

7

WHEN RUPERT BOYCE sent out the invitations for his
party, the total mileage involved was impressive. To list
only the first dozen guests, there were: the Fosters from
Adelaide, the Shoenbergers from Haiti, the Farrans from
Stalingrad, the Moravias from Cincinnati, the Ivankos
from Paris, and the Sullivans from the general vicinity of
Easter Island, but approximately four kilometers down
on the ocean bed. It was a considerable compliment to
Rupert that although thirty guests had been invited, over
forty turned up. Only the Krauses let him down, and that
was simply because they forgot about the International
Date Line and arrived twenty-four hours late.

By noon an imposing collection of flyers had accumulated in the park, and the later arrivals would have quite
a distance to walk once they had found somewhere to
land. The assembled vehicles ranged from one-man Flit-
terbugs to family Cadillacs which were more like airborne palaces than sensible flying machines. In this age,
however, nothing could be deduced concerning the social
status of the guests from their modes of transport.

"It's a very *ugly* house," said Jean Morrel as the Mete-
or spiralled down. "It looks rather like a box that somebody's stepped on."

George Greggson, who had an old-fashioned dislike of
automatic landings, readjusted the rate-of-descent control
before answering.

"It's hardly fair to judge the place from *this* angle," he replied, sensibly enough. "From ground level it may look quite different."

George selected a landing place and they floated to rest between another Meteor and something that neither of them could identify. It looked very fast and, Jean thought, very uncomfortable. One of Rupert's technical friends, she decided, had probably built it himself. She had an idea that there was a law against that sort of thing.

The heat hit them like a blast from a blowtorch as they stepped out of the flyer. It seemed to suck the moisture from their bodies, and George almost imagined that he could feel his skin cracking. It was partly their own fault, of course. They had left Alaska three hours before, and should have remembered to adjust the cabin temperature accordingly.

"What a place to live!" gasped Jean. "I thought this climate was supposed to be controlled."

"So it is," replied George. "This was all desert once—and look at it now. Come on—it'll be all right indoors!"

Rupert's voice, slightly larger than life, boomed cheerfully in their ears. Their host was standing beside the flyer, a glass in each hand, looking down at them with a roguish expression. He looked down at them for the simple reason that he was about twelve feet tall: he was also semitransparent. One could see right through him without much difficulty.

"This is a fine trick to play on your guests!" protested George. He grabbed at the drinks, which he could just reach. His hand, of course, went right through them. "I hope you've got something more substantial for us when we reach the house!"

"Don't worry!" laughed Rupert. "Just give your order now, and it'll be ready by the time you arrive."

"Two large beers, cooled in liquid air," said George promptly. "We'll be right there."

Rupert nodded, put down one of his glasses on an invisible table, adjusted an equally invisible control, and promptly vanished from sight.

"Well!" said Jean. "That's the first time I've seen one

of those gadgets in action. How did Rupert get hold of it? I thought only the Overlords had them."

"Have you ever known Rupert *not* get anything he wanted?" replied George. "That's just the toy for him. He can sit comfortably in his studio and go wandering round half of Africa. No heat, no bugs, no exertion—and the icebox always in reach. I wonder what Stanley and Livingstone would have thought?"

The sun put an end to further conversation until they had reached the house. As they approached the front door (which was not very easy to distinguish from the rest of the glass wall facing them) it swung automatically open with a fanfare of trumpets. Jean guessed, correctly, that she would be heartily sick of that fanfare before the day was through.

The current Mrs. Boyce greeted them in the delicious coolness of the hall. She was, if the truth be known, the main reason for the good turnout of guests. Perhaps half of them would have come in any case to see Rupert's new house: the waverers had been decided by the reports of Rupert's new wife.

There was only one adjective that adequately described her. She was distracting. Even in a world where beauty was almost commonplace, men would turn their heads when she entered the room. She was, George guessed, about one quarter Negro. Her features were practically Grecian and her hair was long and lustrous. Only the dark, rich texture of her skin—the overworked word "chocolate" was the only one that described it—revealed her mixed ancestry.

"You're Jean and George, aren't you?" she said, holding out her hand. "I'm so pleased to meet you. Rupert is doing something complicated with the drinks—come along and meet everybody."

Her voice was a rich contralto that sent little shivers running up and down George's back, as if someone was playing on his spine like a flute. He looked nervously at Jean, who had managed to force a somewhat artificial smile, and finally recovered his voice.

"It's—it's very nice to meet you," he said lamely. "We've been looking forward to this party."

"Rupert *always* gives such nice parties," put in Jean. By the way she accented the "always," one knew perfectly well she was thinking, Every time he gets married. George flushed slightly and gave Jean a glance of reproof, but there was no sign that their hostess noticed the barb. She was friendliness itself as she ushered them into the main lounge, already half packed with a representative collection of Rupert's numerous friends. Rupert himself was sitting at the console of what seemed to be a television engineer's control unit: it was, George assumed, the device that had projected his image out to meet them. He was busily demonstrating it by surprising two more arrivals as they descended into the parking place, but paused just long enough to greet Jean and George and to apologize for having given their drinks to somebody else.

"You'll find plenty more over there," he said, waving one hand vaguely behind him while he adjusted controls with the other. "Just make yourself at home. You know most of the people here—Maia will introduce you to the rest. Good of you to come."

"Good of you to invite us," said Jean, without much conviction. George had already departed towards the bar and she made her way after him, occasionally exchanging greetings with someone she recognized. About three-quarters of those present were perfect strangers, which was the normal state of affairs at one of Rupert's parties.

"Let's explore," she said to George when they had refreshed themselves and waved to everyone they knew. "I want to look at the house."

George, with a barely concealed backward look at Maia Boyce, followed after her. There was a faraway look in his eyes that Jean didn't like in the least. It was such a nuisance that men were fundamentally polygamous. On the other hand, if they weren't . . . Yes, perhaps it was better this way, after all.

George quickly came back to normal as they investigated the wonders of Rupert's new abode. The house seemed very large for two people, but this was just as well in view of the frequent overloads it would have to handle. There were two stories, the upper considerably larger so that it overhung and provided shade around the ground floor. The degree of mechanization was considerable, and the kitchen closely resembled the cockpit of an airliner.

"Poor Ruby!" said Jean. "She would have loved this place."

"From what I've heard," replied George, who had no great sympathy for the last Mrs. Boyce, "she's perfectly happy with her Australian boy-friend."

This was such common knowledge that Jean could hardly contradict it, so she changed the subject.

"She's awfully pretty, isn't she?"

George was sufficiently alert to avoid the trap.

"Oh, I suppose so," he replied indifferently. "That is, of course, if one likes brunettes."

"Which you don't, I take it," said Jean sweetly.

"Don't be jealous, dear," chuckled George, stroking her platinum hair. "Let's go and look at the library. What floor do you think *that* will be on?"

"It must be up here: there's no more room down below. Besides, that fits in with the general design. All the living, eating, sleeping, and so on's relegated to the ground floor. This is the fun and games department—though I still think it's a crazy idea having a swimming pool upstairs."

"I guess there's some reason for it," said George, opening a door experimentally. "Rupert must have had skilled advice when he built this place. I'm sure he couldn't have done it himself."

"You're probably right. If he had, there'd have been rooms without doors, and stairways leading nowhere. In fact, I'd be afraid to step inside a house that Rupert had designed all by himself."

"Here we are," said George, with the pride of a navigator making landfall, "the fabulous Boyce collection in its new home. I wonder just how many of them Rupert has really read."

The library ran the whole width of the house, but was

virtually divided into half a dozen small rooms by the great bookcases extending across it. These held, if George remembered correctly, some fifteen thousand volumes—almost everything of importance that had ever been published on the nebulous subjects of magic, psychic research, divining, telepathy, and the whole range of elusive phenomena lumped in the category of paraphysics. It was a very peculiar hobby for anyone to have in this age of reason. Presumably it was simply Rupert's particular form of escapism.

George noticed the smell the moment he entered the room. It was faint but penetrating, not so much unpleasant as puzzling. Jean had observed it too: her forehead was wrinkled in the effort of identification. Acetic acid, thought George—that's the nearest thing to it. But it's got something else as well. . . .

The library terminated in a small open space just large enough for a table, two chairs and some cushions. This, presumably, was where Rupert did most of his reading. Someone was reading there now, in an unnaturally dim light.

Jean gave a little gasp and clutched at George's hand. Her reaction was, perhaps, excusable. It was one thing to watch a television picture, quite another to meet the reality. George, who was seldom surprised by anything, rose to the occasion at once.

"I hope we haven't disturbed you, Sir," he said politely. "We'd no idea that there was anyone here. Rupert never told us . . ."

The Overlord put down the book, looked at them closely, then commenced reading again. There was nothing impolite about the action, coming as it did from a being who could read, talk, and probably do several other things at the same time. Nevertheless, to human observers the spectacle was disturbingly schizophrenic.

"My name is Rashaverak," said the Overlord amiably. "I'm afraid I'm not being very sociable, but Rupert's library is a difficult place from which to escape."

Jean managed to suppress a nervous giggle. Their unexpected fellow guest was, she noticed, reading at the rate of a page every two seconds. She did not doubt that he was assimilating every word, and she wondered if he could manage to read a book with each eye. "And then, of course," she thought to herself, "he could go on to learn Braille so he could use his fingers. . . ." The resulting mental picture was too comic to be comfortable, so she tried to suppress it by entering into the conversation. After all, it was not every day that one had a chance of talking to one of the masters of Earth.

George let her chatter on, after he had made the introductions, hoping that she wouldn't say anything tactless. Like Jean, he had never seen an Overlord in the flesh. Though they mixed socially with government officials, scientists, and others who dealt with them in the course of business, he had never heard of one being present at an ordinary private party. One inference was that this party was not as private as it seemed. Rupert's possession of a piece of Overlord equipment also hinted at this, and George began to wonder, in capital letters, just What Was Going On. He would have to tackle Rupert about this when he could get him into a corner.

Since the chairs were too small for him, Rashaverak was sitting on the floor, apparently quite at ease, since he had ignored the cushions only a meter away. As a result, his head was a mere two meters from the ground, and George had a unique chance of studying extraterrestrial biology. Unfortunately, as he knew little about terrestrial biology either, he was not able to learn much that he did not already know. Only the peculiar, and by no means unpleasant, acid odor was new to him. He wondered how humans smelt to the Overlords, and hoped for the best.

There was nothing really anthropomorphic about Rashaverak. George could understand the way in which, if seen from a distance by ignorant, terrified savages, the Overlords could be mistaken for winged men, and so could have given rise to the conventional portrait of the Devil. From as close as this, however, some of the illusion vanished. The little horns (what function did they serve? wondered George) were as per specification, but the body was neither like that of a man nor that of any animal Earth had ever known. Coming from a totally alien evolutionary tree, the Overlords were neither mammals, insects, nor reptiles. It was not even certain that they were vertebrates: their hard, external armor might well be their only supporting framework.

Rashaverak's wings were folded so that George could not see them clearly, but his tail, looking like a piece of armored pipe, lay neatly curled under him. The famous barb was not so much an arrowhead as a large, flat diamond. Its purpose, it was now generally accepted, was to give stability in flight, like the tail feathers of a bird. From scanty facts and suppositions such as these, scientists had concluded that the Overlords came from a world of low gravity and very dense atmosphere.

Rupert's voice suddenly bellowed from a concealed speaker.

"Jean! George! Where the hell are you hiding? Come down and join the party. People are beginning to talk."

"Perhaps I'd better go, too," said Rashaverak, putting his book back on the shelf. He did that quite easily, without moving from the floor, and George noticed for the first time that he had two opposed thumbs, with five fingers between them. I'd hate to do arithmetic, George thought to himself, in a system based on fourteen.

Rashaverak getting to his feet was an impressive sight, and as the Overlord bent to avoid the ceiling it became obvious that, even if they were anxious to mix with human beings, the practical difficulties would be considerable.

Several more cargoes of guests had arrived in the last half hour, and the room was now quite crowded. Rashaverak's arrival made matters a good deal worse, because everyone in the adjacent rooms came running in to see him. Rupert was obviously very pleased with the sensation. Jean and George were much less gratified, as no one took any notice of them. Indeed, few people could see them, because they were standing behind the Overlord.

"Come over here, Rashy, and meet some of the folks,"

shouted Rupert. "Sit on this divan—then you can stop scraping the ceiling."

Rashaverak, his tail draped over his shoulder, moved across the room like an icebreaker worrying its way through a pack. As he sat down beside Rupert, the room seemed to become much larger again and George let out a sigh of relief.

"It gave me claustrophobia when he was standing. I wonder how Rupert got hold of him—this could be an interesting party."

"Fancy Rupert addressing him like that, in public too. But he didn't seem to mind. It's all very peculiar."

"I bet you he *did* mind. The trouble with Rupert is that he likes to show off, and he's got no tact. And that reminds me—some of those questions you asked!"

"Such as?"

"Well—'How long have you been here?' 'How do you get on with Supervisor Karellen?' 'Do you like it on Earth?' Really, darling! You just *don't* talk to Overlords that way!"

"I don't see why not. It's about time someone did."

Before the discussion could get acrimonious, they were accosted by the Shoenbergers and fission rapidly occurred. The girls went off in one direction to discuss Mrs. Boyce; the men went in another and did exactly the same thing, though from a different viewpoint. Benny Shoenberger, who was one of George's oldest friends, had a good deal of information on the subject.

"For heaven's sake don't tell anyone," he said. "Ruth doesn't know this, but *I* introduced her to Rupert."

"I think," George remarked enviously, "that she's much too good for Rupert. However, it can't possibly last. She'll soon get fed up with him." This thought seemed to cheer him considerably.

"Don't you believe it! Besides being a beauty, she's a really nice person. It's high time someone took charge of Rupert, and she's just the girl to do it."

Both Rupert and Maia were now sitting beside Rashaverak, receiving their guests in state. Rupert's parties seldom had any focal point, but usually consisted of half a dozen independent groups intent on their own affairs. This time, however, the whole gathering had found a center of attraction. George felt rather sorry for Maia. This should have been her day, but Rashaverak had partially eclipsed her.

"Look," said George, nibbling at a sandwich, "how the devil has Rupert got hold of an Overlord? I've never heard of such a thing—but he seems to take it for granted. He never even mentioned it when he invited us."

Benny chuckled.

"Just another of his little surprises. You'd better ask him about it. But this isn't the first time it's happened, after all. Karellen's been to parties at the White House and Buckingham Palace, and—"

"Heck, *that's* different! Rupert's a perfectly ordinary citizen."

"And maybe Rashaverak's a very minor Overlord. But you'd better ask them."

"I will," said George, "just as soon as I can get Rupert by himself."

"Then you'll have to wait a long time."

Benny was right, but as the party was now warming up it was easy to be patient. The slight paralysis which the appearance of Rashaverak had cast over the assembly had now vanished. There was still a small group around the Overlord, but elsewhere the usual fragmentation had taken place and everyone was behaving quite naturally.

Without bothering to turn his head, George could see a famous film producer, a minor poet, a mathematician, two actors, an atomic power engineer, a game warden, the editor of a weekly news magazine, a statistician from the World Bank, a violin virtuoso, a professor of archaeology, and an astrophysicist. There were no other representatives of George's own profession, television studio design—which was a good thing as he wanted to get away from shop. He loved his work: indeed, in this age, for the first time in human history, no one worked at tasks they did not like. But George was the kind of man who could lock the studio doors behind him at the end of the day.

He finally trapped Rupert in the kitchen, experimenting with drinks. It seemed a pity to bring him back to earth when he had such a faraway look in his eye, but George could be ruthless when necessary.

"Look here, Rupert," he began, perching himself on the nearest table. "I think you owe us all some explanations."

"Um," said Rupert thoughtfully, rolling his tongue round his mouth. "Just a teeny bit too much gin, I'm afraid."

"Don't hedge, and don't pretend you're not still sober, because I know perfectly well you are. Where does your Overlord friend come from, and what's he doing here?"

"Didn't I tell you?" said Rupert. "I thought I'd explained it to everybody. You couldn't have been around —of course, you were hiding up in the library." He chuckled in a manner which George found offensive. "It's the library, you know, that brought Rashy here."

"How extraordinary!"

"Why?"

George paused, realizing that this would require tact. Rupert was very proud of his peculiar collection.

"Er—well, when you consider what the Overlords know about science, I should hardly think they'd be interested in psychic phenomena and all that sort of nonsense."

"Nonsense or not," replied Rupert, "they're interested in human psychology, and I've got some books that can teach them a lot. Just before I moved here some Deputy Under-Overlord, or Over-Underlord, got in touch with me and asked if they could borrow about fifty of my rarest volumes. One of the keepers of the British Museum library had put him on to me, it seemed. Of course, you can guess what I said."

"I can't imagine."

"Well, I replied very politely that it had taken me twenty years to get my library together. They were welcome to study my books, *but* they'd darn well have to read them here. So Rashy came along and has been absorbing about twenty volumes a day. I'd love to know what he makes of them."

George thought this over, then shrugged his shoulders in disgust.

"Frankly," he said, "my opinion of the Overlords goes down. I thought they had better things to do with their time."

"You're an incorrigible materialist, aren't you? I don't think Jean will agree at all. But even from your oh-so-practical viewpoint, it still makes sense. Surely you'd study the superstitions of any primitive race you were having dealings with!"

"I suppose so," said George, not quite convinced. The table top was feeling hard, so he rose to his feet. Rupert had now mixed the drinks to his satisfaction and was heading back to his guests. Querulous voices could already be heard demanding his presence.

"Hey!" protested George, "just before you disappear there's one other question. How did you get hold of that two-way television gadget you tried to frighten us with?"

"Just a bit of bargaining. I pointed out how valuable it would be for a job like mine, and Rashy passed the suggestion on to the right quarters."

"Forgive me for being so obtuse, but what *is* your new job? I suppose, of course, it's something to do with animals."

"That's right. I'm a supervet. My practice covers about ten thousand square kilometers of jungle, and as my patients won't come to me I've got to look for them."

"Rather a full time job."

"Oh, of course it isn't practical to bother about the small fry. Just lions, elephants, rhinos, and so on. Every morning I set the controls for a height of a hundred meters, sit down in front of the screen and go cruising over the countryside. When I find anyone in trouble I climb into my flyer and hope my bedside manner will work. Sometimes it's a bit tricky. Lions and suchlike are easy—but trying to puncture a rhino from the air with an anesthetic dart is the devil of a job."

"*Rupert!*" yelled someone from the next room.

"Now look what you've done! You've made me forget my guests. There—you take that tray. Those are the ones with vermouth—I don't want to get them mixed up."

It was just before sunset that George found his way up to the roof. For a number of excellent reasons he had a slight headache and felt like escaping from the noise and confusion downstairs. Jean, who was a much better dancer than he was, still seemed to be enjoying herself hugely, and refused to leave. This annoyed George, who was beginning to feel alcoholically amorous, and he decided to have a quiet sulk beneath the stars.

One reached the roof by taking the escalator to the first floor and then climbing the spiral stairway round the intake of the air-conditioning plant. This led, through a hatchway, out onto the wide, flat roof. Rupert's flyer was parked at one end: the center area was a garden—already showing signs of running wild—and the rest was simply an observation platform with a few deck chairs placed on it. George flopped into one of these and regarded his surroundings with an imperial eye. He felt very much monarch of all he surveyed.

It was, to put it mildly, quite a view. Rupert's house had been built on the edge of a great basin, which sloped downwards towards the east into swamplands and lakes five kilometers away. Westward the land was flat and the jungle came almost to Rupert's back door. But beyond the jungle, at a distance that must have been at least fifty kilometers, a line of mountains ran like a great wall out of sight, to north and south. Their summits were streaked with snow, and the clouds above them were turning to fire as the sun descended, in the last few minutes of its daily journey. As he looked at those remote ramparts, George felt awed into a sudden sobriety.

The stars that sprang out in such indecent haste the moment the sun had set were completely strange to him. He looked for the Southern Cross, but without success. Though he knew very little of astronomy, and could recognize only a few constellations, the absence of familiar friends was disturbing. So were the noises drifting in from the jungle, uncomfortably close at hand. Enough of this fresh air, thought George. I'll go back to the party before a vampire bat, or something equally pleasant, comes flying up to investigate.

He was just starting to walk back when another guest emerged from the hatchway. It was now so dark that George could not see who it was, so he called out: "Hello, there. Have you had enough of it too?" His invisible companion laughed.

"Rupert's starting to show some of his movies. I've seen them all before."

"Have a cigarette," said George.

"Thanks."

By the flame of the lighter—George was fond of such antiques—he could now recognize his fellow guest, a strikingly handsome young Negro whose name George had been told but had immediately forgotten, like those of the twenty other complete strangers at the party. However, there seemed something familiar about him, and suddenly George guessed the truth.

"I don't think we've really met," he said, "but aren't you Rupert's new brother-in-law?"

"That's right. I'm Jan Rodricks. Everyone says that Maia and I look rather alike."

George wondered whether to commiserate with Jan for his newly acquired relative. He decided to let the poor fellow find out for himself; after all, it *was* just possible that Rupert would settle down this time.

"I'm George Greggson. This the first time you've been to one of Rupert's famous parties?"

"Yes. You certainly meet a lot of new people this way."

"And not only humans," added George. "This is the first chance I've had of meeting an Overlord socially."

The other hesitated for a moment before replying, and George wondered what sensitive spot he had struck. But the answer revealed nothing.

"I've never seen one before, either—except of course on TV."

There the conversation languished, and after a moment George realized that Jan wanted to be alone. It was getting cold, anyway, so he took his leave and rejoined the party.

The jungle was quiet now; as Jan leaned against the

curving wall of the air intake, the only sound he could
hear was the faint murmur of the house as it breathed
through its mechanical lungs. He felt very much alone,
which was the way he wanted to be. He also felt highly
frustrated—and that was something he had no desire to
be at all.

8

No UTOPIA can ever give satisfaction to everyone, all the
time. As their material conditions improve, men raise
their sights and become discontented with power and possessions that once would have seemed beyond their wildest dreams. And even when the external world has
granted all it can, there still remain the searchings of the
mind and the longings of the heart.

Jan Rodricks, though he seldom appreciated his luck,
would have been even more discontented in an earlier
age. A century before, his color would have been a tremendous, perhaps an overwhelming, handicap. Today, it
meant nothing. The inevitable reaction that had given
early twenty-first-century Negroes a slight sense of su-
periority had already passed away. The convenient word
"nigger" was no longer taboo in polite society, but was
used without embarrassment by everyone. It had no more
emotional content than such labels as republican or
methodist, conservative or liberal.

Jan's father had been a charming but somewhat feck-
less Scot, who had made a considerable name for himself as a professional magician. His death at the early
age of forty-five had been brought about by the excessive
consumption of his country's most famous product.
Though Jan had never seen his father drunk, he was not
sure that he had ever seen him sober.

Mrs. Rodricks, still very much alive, lectured in advanced probability theory at Edinburgh University. It was typical of the extreme mobility of Twenty-first-century Man that Mrs. Rodricks, who was coal black, had been born in Scotland, whereas her expatriate and blond husband had spent almost all his life in Haiti. Maia and Jan had never had a single home, but had oscillated between their parents' families like two small shuttlecocks. The treatment had been good fun, but had not helped to correct the instability they had both inherited from their father.

At twenty-seven, Jan still had several years of college life ahead of him before he needed to think seriously about his career. He had taken his bachelors' degrees without any difficulty, following a curriculum that would have seemed very strange a century before. His main subjects had been mathematics and physics, but as subsidiaries he had taken philosophy and music appreciation. Even by the high standards of the time, he was a first-rate amateur pianist.

In three years he would take his doctorate in engineering physics, with astronomy as a second subject. This would involve fairly hard work, but Jan rather welcomed that. He was studying at what was perhaps the most beautifully situated place of higher education in the world— the University of Cape Town, nestling at the foot of Table Mountain.

He had no material worries, yet he was discontented and saw no cure for his condition. To make matters worse, Maia's own happiness—though he did not grudge it in the least—had underlined the chief cause of his own trouble.

For Jan was still suffering from the romantic illusion— the cause of so much misery and so much poetry—that every man has only one real love in his life. At an unusually late age, he had lost his heart for the first time, to a lady more renowned for beauty than constancy. Rosita Tisen claimed, with perfect truth, to have the blood of Manchu emperors flowing in her veins. She still possessed many subjects, including most of the Faculty of Science at Cape. Jan had been taken prisoner by her delicate, flowerlike beauty, and the affair had proceeded far enough to make its termination all the more galling. He could not imagine what had gone wrong. . . .

He would get over it, of course. Other men had survived similar catastrophes without irreparable damage, had even reached the stage when they could say, "I'm sure I could never have been *really* serious about a woman like that!" But such detachment still lay far in the future, and at the moment Jan was very much at odds with life.

His other grievance was less easily remedied, for it concerned the impact of the Overlords upon his own ambitions. Jan was a romantic not only in heart but in mind. Like so many other young men since the conquest of the air had been assured, he had let his dreams and his imagination roam the unexplored seas of space.

A century before, Man had set foot upon the ladder that could lead him to the stars. At that very moment—could it have been coincidence?—the door to the planets had been slammed in his face. The Overlords had imposed few positive bans on any form of human activity (the conduct of war was perhaps the major exception) but research into space flight had virtually ceased. The challenge presented by the science of the Overlords was too great. For the moment, at least, Man had lost heart and had turned to other fields of activity. There was no point in developing rockets when the Overlords had infinitely superior means of propulsion, based on principles of which they had never given any hint.

A few hundred men had visited the Moon, for the purpose of establishing a lunar observatory. They had traveled as passengers in a small vessel loaned by the Overlords —and driven by rockets. It was obvious that little could be learned from a study of this primitive vehicle, even if its owners handed it over without reservation to inquisitive terrestrial scientists.

Man was, therefore, still a prisoner on his own planet. It was a much fairer, but a much smaller, planet than it had been a century before. When the Overlords had abolished war and hunger and disease, they had also abolished adventure.

The rising moon was beginning to paint the eastern sky with a pale, milky glow. Up there, Jan knew, was the main base of the Overlords, lying within the ramparts of Plato. Though the supply ships must have been coming and going for more than seventy years, it was only in Jan's lifetime that all concealment had been dropped and they had made their departure in clear sight of Earth. In the two hundred inch telescope, the shadows of the great ships could be clearly seen when the morning or evening sun cast them for miles across the lunar plains. Since everything that the Overlords did was of immense interest to mankind, a careful watch was kept of their comings and goings, and the pattern of their behavior (though not the reason for it) was beginning to emerge. One of those great shadows had vanished a few hours ago. That meant, Jan knew, that somewhere off the Moon an Overlord ship was lying in space, carrying out whatever routine was necessary before it began its journey to its distant, unknown home.

He had never seen one of those returning ships launch itself towards the stars. If conditions were good the sight was visible over half the world, but Jan had always been unlucky. One could never tell exactly when the take-off would be—and the Overlords did not advertise the fact. He decided he would wait another ten minutes, then rejoin the party.

What was that? Only a meteor sliding down through Eridanus. Jan relaxed, discovered his cigarette had gone out, and lit another.

He was halfway through it when, half a million kilometers away, the Stardrive went on. Up from the heart of the spreading moonglow a tiny spark began to climb towards the zenith. At first its movement was so slow that it could hardly be perceived, but second by second it was gaining speed. As it climbed it increased in brilliance, then suddenly faded from sight. A moment later it had reappeared, gaining speed and brightness. Waxing and waning with a peculiar rhythm, it ascended ever more swiftly into the sky, drawing a fluctuating line of light across the stars. Even if one did not know its real distance, the impression of speed was breath-taking; when one knew that the departing ship was somewhere beyond the moon, the mind reeled at the speeds and energies involved.

. It was an unimportant by-product of those energies, Jan knew, that he was seeing now. The ship itself was invisible, already far ahead of that ascending light. As a high-flying jet may leave a vapor trail behind it, so the outward bound vessel of the Overlords left its own peculiar wake. The generally accepted theory—and there seemed little doubt of its truth—was that the immense accelerations of the Stardrive caused a local distortion of space. What Jan was seeing, he knew, was nothing less than the light of distant stars, collected and focused into his eye whenever conditions were favorable along the track of the ship. It was a visible proof of relativity—the bending of light in the presence of a colossal gravitational field.

Now the end of that vast, pencil-thin lens seemed to be moving more slowly, but that was only due to perspective. In reality the ship was still gaining speed: its path was merely being foreshortened as it hurled itself outwards to the stars. There would be many telescopes following it, Jan knew, as Earth's scientists tried to uncover the secrets of the Drive. Dozens of papers had already been published on the subject; no doubt the Overlords had read them with the greatest interest.

The phantom light was beginning to wane. Now it was a fading streak, pointing to the heart of the constellation Carina, as Jan had known that it would. The home of the Overlords was somewhere out there, but it might circle any one of a thousand stars in that sector of space. There was no way of telling its distance from the solar system.

It was all over. Though the ship had scarcely begun its journey, there was nothing more that human eyes could see. But in Jan's mind the memory of that shining path still burned, a beacon that would never fade as long as he possessed ambition and desire.

The party was over. Almost all the guests had climbed back into the sky and were now scattering to the four corners of the globe. There were, however, a few exceptions.

One was Norman Dodsworth, the poet, who had got unpleasantly drunk but had been sensible enough to pass out before any violent action proved necessary. He had been deposited, not very gently, on the lawn, where it was hoped that a hyaena would give him a rude awakening. For all practical purposes he could, therefore, be regarded as absent.

The other remaining guests were George and Jean. This was not George's idea at all: he wanted to go home. He disapproved of the friendship between Rupert and Jean, though not for the usual reason. George prided himself on being a practical, levelheaded character, and regarded the interest which drew Jean and Rupert together as being not only childish in this age of science, but more than a little unhealthy. That anyone should still place the slightest credence in the supernormal seemed extraordinary to him, and finding Rashaverak here had shaken his faith in the Overlords.

It was now obvious that Rupert had been plotting some surprise, probably with Jean's connivance. George resigned himself gloomily to whatever nonsense was coming.

"I tried all sorts of things before I settled on *this*," said Rupert proudly. "The big problem is to reduce friction so that you get complete freedom of movement. The old-fashioned polished table and tumbler setup isn't bad, but it's been used for centuries now and I was sure that modern science could do better. And here's the result. Draw up your chairs—are you quite sure you don't want to join, Rashy?"

The Overlord seemed to hesitate for a fraction of a second. Then he shook his head. (Had they learned that habit on Earth? George wondered.)

"No, thank you," he replied. "I would prefer to observe. Some other time, perhaps."

"Very well—there's plenty of time to change your mind later."

Oh, is there? thought George, looking gloomily at his watch.

Rupert had shepherded his friends round a small but massive table, perfectly circular in shape. It had a flat plastic top which he lifted off to reveal a glittering sea of closely packed ball bearings. They were prevented from escaping by the table's slightly raised rim, and George found it quite impossible to imagine their purpose. The hundreds of reflected points of light formed a fascinating and hypnotic pattern, and he felt himself becoming slightly dizzy.

As they drew up their chairs, Rupert reached under the table and brought forth a disc some ten centimeters in diameter, which he placed on the surface of the ball bearings.

"There you are," he said, "You put your fingers on this, and it moves around with no resistance at all."

George eyed the device with profound distrust. He noted that the letters of the alphabet were placed at regular intervals—though in no particular order—round the circumference of the table. In addition there were the numbers 1 to 9, scattered at random among the letters, and two cards bearing the words "Yes" and "No." These were on opposite sides of the table.

"It looks like a lot of mumbo jumbo to me," he muttered. "I'm surprised that anyone takes it seriously in this age." He felt a little better after delivering this mild protest, which was aimed at Jean quite as much as Rupert. Rupert didn't pretend to have more than a detached scientific interest in these phenomena. He was open-minded, but not credulous. Jean, on the other hand—well, George was sometimes a little worried about her. She really seemed to think that there was something in this business of telepathy and second sight.

Not until he had made his remark did George realize that it also implied a criticism of Rashaverak. He glanced nervously round but the Overlord showed no reaction. Which, of course, proved absolutely nothing at all.

Everyone had now taken up their positions. Going in a clockwise direction round the table were Rupert, Maia,

Jan, Jean, George, and Benny Shoenberger. Ruth Shoenberger was sitting outside the circle with a notebook. She
apparently had some objection to taking part in the proceedings, which had caused Benny to make obscurely sar-
castic remarks about people who still took the Talmud
seriously. However, she seemed perfectly willing to act as
a recorder.

"Now listen," began Rupert, "for the benefit of skeptics
like George, let's get this quite straight. Whether or not
there's anything supernormal about this, *it works*. Personally, I think there's a purely mechanical explanation.
When we put our hands on the disc, even though we may
try to avoid influencing its movements, our subconscious
starts playing tricks. I've analyzed lots of these seances,
and I've never got answers that someone in the group
mightn't have known or guessed—though sometimes they
weren't aware of the fact. However, I'd like to carry out
the experiment in these rather—ah—peculiar circumstances."

The Peculiar Circumstance sat watching them silently,
but doubtless not with indifference. George wondered just
what Rashaverak thought of these antics. Were his reactions those of an anthropologist watching some primitive religious rite? The whole setup was really quite fantastic, and George felt as big a fool as he had ever done
in his life.

If the others felt equally foolish, they concealed their
emotions. Only Jean looked flushed and excited, though
that might have been the drinks.

"All set?" asked Rupert. "Very well." He paused im-
pressively; then, addressing no one in particular, he called
out: "Is there anybody there?"

George could feel the plate beneath his fingers tremble
slightly. That was not surprising, considering the pressure
being exerted upon it by the six people in the circle. It
slithered around in a small figure "8," then came to rest
back at the center.

"Is there anybody there?" repeated Rupert. In a more
conversational tone of voice he added, "It's often ten or
fifteen minutes before we get started. But sometimes—"

"Hush!" breathed Jean.

The plate was moving. It began to swing in a wide arc between the cards labelled "YES" and "NO." With some difficulty, George suppressed a giggle. Just what would it prove, he wondered, if the answer was "NO"? He remembered the old joke: "There's nobody here but us chickens, Massa. . . ."

But the answer was "YES." The plate came swiftly back to the center of the table. Somehow it now seemed alive, waiting for the next question. Despite himself, George began to be impressed.

"Who are you?" asked Rupert.

There was no hesitation now as the letters were spelled out. The plate darted across the table like a sentient thing, moving so swiftly that George sometimes found it hard to keep his fingers in contact. He could swear that he was not contributing to its motion. Glancing quickly round the table, he could see nothing suspicious in the faces of his friends. They seemed as intent, and as expectant, as he himself.

"IAMALL" spelled the plate, and returned to its point of equilibrium.

" 'I am all,' " repeated Rupert. "That's a typical reply. Evasive, yet stimulating. It probably means that there's nothing here except our combined minds." He paused for a moment, obviously deciding upon his next question. Then he addressed the air once more.

"Have you a message for anyone here?"

"NO" replied the plate promptly.

Rupert looked around the table.

"It's up to us; sometimes it volunteers information, but this time we'll have to ask definite questions. Anyone like to start?"

"Will it rain tomorrow?" said George jestingly.

At once the plate began to swing back and forth in the YES-NO line.

"That's a silly question," reproved Rupert. "It's bound to be raining *somewhere* and to be dry somewhere else. Don't ask questions that have ambiguous answers."

George felt appropriately squashed. He decided to let someone else have the next turn.

"What is my favorite color?" asked Maia.

"BLUE" came the prompt reply.

"That's quite correct."

"But is doesn't prove anything. At least three people here knew that," George pointed out.

"What's Ruth's favorite color?" asked Benny.

"RED."

"Is that right, Ruth?"

The recorder looked up from her notebook.

"Yes, it is. But Benny knows that, and he's in the circle."

"I didn't know," retorted Benny.

"You darn well ought to—I've told you enough times."

"Subconscious memory," murmured Rupert. "That often happens. But can we have some more *intelligent* questions, please? Now that this has started so well, I don't want it to peter out."

Curiously enough, the very triviality of the phenomenon was beginning to impress George. He was sure that there was no supernormal explanation; as Rupert had said, the plate was simply responding to their unconscious muscular movements. But this fact in itself was surprising and impressive: he would never have believed that such precise, swift replies could have been obtained. Once he tried to see if he could influence the board by making it spell out his own name. He got the "G," but that was all: the rest was nonsense. It was virtually impossible, he decided, for one person to take control without the remainder of the circle knowing it.

After half an hour, Ruth had taken down more than a dozen messages, some of them quite long ones. There were occasional spelling mistakes, and curiosities of grammar, but they were few. Whatever the explanation, George was not convinced that he was not contributing consciously to the results. Several times, as a word was being spelt out, he had anticipated the next letter and hence the meaning of the message. And on each occasion the plate had gone in a quite unexpected direction and spelt something totally different. Sometimes indeeed—since there was no pause to indicate the end of one word and the beginning of the next—the entire message was meaningless until it was complete and Ruth had read it back.

The whole experience gave George an uncanny impression of being in contact with some purposeful, independent mind. And yet there was no *conclusive* proof one way or the other. The replies were so trivial, so ambiguous. What, for example, could one make of:

BELIEVEINMANNATUREISWITHYOU.

Yet sometimes there were suggestions of profound, even disturbing truths:

REMEMBERMANISNOTALONENEARMANIS-
COUNTRYOFOTHERS.

But of course everyone knew that—though could one be sure that the message merely referred to the Overlords?

George was growing very sleepy. It was high time, he thought drowsily, that they headed for home. This was all very intriguing, but it wasn't getting them anywhere and you could have too much of a good thing. He glanced around the table. Benny looked as if he might be feeling the same way, Maia and Rupert both appeared slightly glazed, and Jean—well, she had been taking it too seriously all along. Her expression worried George; it was almost as if she were afraid to stop—yet afraid to go on.

That left only Jan. George wondered what he thought of his brother-in-law's eccentricities. The young engineer had asked no questions, shown no surprise at any of the answers. He seemed to be studying the movement of the plate as if it was just another scientific phenomenon.

Rupert roused himself from the lethargy into which he appeared to have fallen.

"Let's have one more question," he said, "then we'll call it a day. What about you, Jan? You've not asked anything."

Surprisingly, Jan never hesitated. It was as if he had made his choice a long time ago, and had been waiting for the opportunity. He glanced once at the impassive bulk of Rashaverak, then called out in a clear, steady voice:

"Which star is the Overlord's sun?"

Rupert checked a whistle of surprise. Maia and Benny showed no reaction at all. Jean had closed her eyes and seemed to be asleep. Rashaverak had leaned forward so that he could look down into the circle over Rupert's shoulder.

And the plate began to move.

When it came to rest again, there was a brief pause: then Ruth asked, in a puzzled voice:

"What does NGS 549672 mean?"

She got no reply, for at the same moment George called out anxiously:

"Give me a hand with Jean. I'm afraid she's fainted."

9

"THIS MAN BOYCE," said Karellen. "Tell me all about him."

The Supervisor did not use those actual words, of course, and the thoughts he really expressed were far more subtle. A human listener would have heard a short burst of rapidly modulated sound, not unlike a high-speed Morse sender in action. Though many samples of Overlord language had been recorded, they all defied analysis because of their extreme complexity. The speed of transmission made it certain that no interpreter, even if he had mastered the elements of the language, could ever keep up with the Overlords in their normal conversation.

The Supervisor for Earth stood with his back to Rashaverak, staring out across the multicolored gulf of the Grand Canyon. Ten kilometers away, yet scarcely veiled by distance, the terraced walls were catching the full force of the sun. Hundreds of meters down the shadowed slope at whose brim Karellen stood, a mule-train was slowly winding its way into the valley's depths.

It was strange, Karellen thought, that so many human beings still seized every opportunity for primitive behavior. They could reach the bottom of the canyon in a fraction of the time, and in far greater comfort, if they chose. Yet they preferred to be jolted along tracks which were probably as unsafe as they looked.

Karellen made an imperceptible gesture with his hand. The great panorama faded from view, leaving only a shadowy blankness of indeterminate depth. The realities of his office and of his position crowded in upon the Supervisor once more.

"Rupert Boyce is a somewhat curious character," Rashaverak answered. "Professionally, he's in charge of animal welfare over an important section of the main African reservation. He's quite efficient, and interested in his work. Because he has to keep watch over several thousand square kilometers, he has one of the fifteen panoramic viewers we've so far issued on loan—with the usual safeguards, of course. It is, incidentally, the only one with full projection facilities. He was able to make a good case for these, so we let him have them."

"What was his argument?"

"He wanted to appear to various wild animals so that they could get used to seeing him, and so wouldn't attack when he was physically present. The theory has worked out quite well with animals that rely on sight rather than smell—though he'll probably get killed eventually. And, of course, there was another reason why we let him have the apparatus."

"It made him more co-operative?"

"Precisely. I originally contacted him because he has one of the world's finest libraries of books on parapsychology and allied subjects. He politely but firmly refused to lend any of them, so there was nothing to do but to visit him. I've now read about half his library. It has been a considerable ordeal."

"That I can well believe," said Karellen dryly. "Have you discovered anything among all the rubbish?"

"Yes—eleven clear cases of partial breakthrough, and twenty-seven probables. The material is so selective, however, that one cannot use it for sampling purposes. And the evidence is confused with mysticism—perhaps the prime aberration of the human mind."

"And what is Boyce's attitude to all this?"

"He pretends to be open-minded and skeptical, but it's clear that he would never have spent so much time and effort in this field unless he had some subconscious faith. I challenged him on this and he admitted that I was probably right. He would like to find some convincing proof. That is why he is always carrying out these experiments, even though he pretends that they are only games."

"You are sure he doesn't suspect that your interest is more than academic?"

"Quite sure. In many ways Boyce is remarkably obtuse and simple-minded. That makes his attempts to do research in this, of all fields, rather pathetic. There is no need to take any special action regarding him."

"I see. And what about the girl who fainted?"

"This is the most exciting feature of the entire affair. Jean Morrel was, almost certainly, the channel through which the information came. But she is twenty-six—far too old to be a Prime Contact herself, judging by all our previous experience. It must, therefore, be someone closely linked to her. The conclusion is obvious. We cannot have many more years to wait. We must transfer her to Category Purple: she may be the most important human being alive."

"I will do that. And what of the young man who asked the question? Was it random curiosity, or did he have some other motive?"

"It was chance that brought him there—his sister has just married Rupert Boyce. He had never met any of the other guests before. I am sure the question was unpremeditated, being inspired by the unusual conditions—and probably by my presence. Given these factors, it is hardly surprising that he acted in the way he did. His great interest is astronautics: he is secretary of the space-travel group at Cape Town University, and obviously intends to make this field his life study."

"His career should be interesting. Meanwhile, what action do you think he will take, and what shall we do about him?"

"He will undoubtedly make some checks as soon as he can. But there is no way in which he can prove the accuracy of his information, and because of its peculiar origin he is hardly likely to publish it. Even if he does, will it affect matters in the slightest?"

"I will have both situations evaluated," Karellen replied. "Though it is part of our Directive not to reveal our base, there is no way in which the information could be used against us."

"I agree. Rodricks will have some information which is of doubtful truth, and of no practical value."

"So it would seem," said Karellen. "But let us not be too certain. Human beings are remarkably ingenious, and often very persistent. It is never safe to underrate them, and it will be interesting to follow Mr. Rodricks' career. I must think about this further."

Rupert Boyce never really got to the bottom of it. When his guests had departed, rather less boisterously than usual, he had thoughtfully rolled the table back into its corner. The mild alcoholic fog prevented any profound analysis of what had happened, and even the actual facts were already slightly blurred. He had a vague idea that something of great but elusive importance had happened, and wondered if he should discuss it with Rashaverak. On second thought, he decided it might be tactless. After all, his brother-in-law had caused the trouble, and Rupert felt vaguely annoyed with young Jan. But was it Jan's fault? Was it anybody's fault? Rather guiltily, Rupert remembered that it had been *his* experiment. He decided, fairly successfully, to forget the whole business.

Perhaps he might have done something if the last page of Ruth's notebook could have been found, but it had vanished in the confusion. Jan always feigned innocence —and, well, one could hardly accuse Rashaverak. And no one could ever remember exactly what had been spelled out, except that it didn't seem to make any sense. . . .

The person most immediately affected had been George Greggson. He could never forget his feeling of terror as Jean pitched into his arms. Her sudden helplessness transformed her in that moment from an amusing companion to an object of tenderness and affection. Women had fainted—not always without forethought—since time immemorial, and men had invariably responded in the desired way. Jean's collapse was completely spontaneous, but it could not have been better planned. In that instant, as he realized later, George came to one of the most important decisions of his life. Jean was definitely the girl who mattered, despite her queer ideas and queerer friends. He had no intention of totally abandoning Naomi or Joy or Elsa or—what *was* her name? Denise; but the time had come for something more permanent. He had no doubt that Jean would agree with him, for her feelings had been quite obvious from the start.

Behind his decision there was another factor of which he was unaware. Tonight's experience had wakened his contempt and scepticism for Jean's peculiar interests. He would never recognize the fact, but it was so—and it had removed the last barrier between them.

He looked at Jean as she lay, pale but composed, in the reclining chair of the flyer. There was darkness below, stars above. George had no idea, to within a thousand kilometers, where they might be—nor did he care. *That* was the business of the robot that was guiding them homewards and would land them in, so the control board announced, fifty-seven minutes from now.

Jean smiled back at him and gently dislodged her hand from his.

"Just let me restore the circulation," she pleaded, rubbing her fingers. "I wish you'd believe me when I tell you I'm perfectly all right now."

"Then what do you think happened? Surely you remember *something?*"

"No—it's just a complete blank. I heard Jan ask his

question—and then you were all making a fuss over me. I'm sure it was some kind of trance. After all—"

She paused, then decided not to tell George that this sort of thing had happened before. She knew how he felt about these matters, and had no desire to upset him further—and perhaps scare him away completely.

"After all—what?" asked George.

"Oh, nothing. I wonder what that Overlord thought about the whole business. We probably gave him more material than he bargained for."

Jean shivered slightly, and her eyes clouded.

"I'm afraid of the Overlords, George. Oh, I don't mean they're evil, or anything foolish like that. I'm sure they mean well and are doing what they think is best for us. I wonder just what their plans really are?"

George shifted uncomfortably.

"Men have been wondering *that* ever since they came to Earth," he said. "They'll tell us when we're ready for it—and, frankly, I'm not inquisitive. Besides, I've got more important things to bother about." He turned towards Jean and grasped her hands.

"What about going to Archives tomorrow and signing a contract for—let's say—five years?"

Jean looked at him steadfastly, and decided that, on the whole, she liked what she saw.

"Make it ten," she said.

Jan bided his time. There was no hurry, and he wanted to think. It was almost as if he feared to make any checks, lest the fantastic hope that had come into his mind be too swiftly destroyed. While he was still uncertain, he could at least dream.

Moreover, to take any further action he would have to see the Observatory librarian. She knew him and his interests too well, and would certainly be intrigued by his request. Probably it would make no difference, but Jan was determined to leave nothing to chance. There would be a better opportunity in a week. He was being supercautious, he knew, but that added a schoolboy zest to the enterprise. Jan also feared ridicule quite as much as anything that the Overlords might conceivably do to thwart him. If he was embarking on a wild goose chase, no one else would ever know.

He had a perfectly good reason for going to London: the arrangements had been made weeks ago. Though he was too young and too unqualified to be a delegate, he was one of the three students who had managed to attach themselves to the official party going to the meeting of the International Astronomical Union. The vacancies had been there, and it seemed a pity to waste the opportunity, as he had not visited London since his childhood. He knew that very few of the dozens of papers to be delivered to the I.A.U. would be of the slightest interest to him, even if he could understand them. Like a delegate to any scientific congress, he would attend the lectures that looked promising, and spend the rest of the time talking with fellow enthusiasts, or simply sight-seeing.

London had changed enormously in the last fifty years. It now contained scarcely two million people, and a hundred times as many machines. It was no longer a great port, for with every country producing almost all its needs, the entire pattern of world trade had been altered. There were some goods that certain countries still made best, but they went directly by air to their destinations. The trade routes that had once converged on the great harbors, and later on the great airports, had finally dispersed into an intricate web-work covering the whole world, with no major nodal points.

Yet some things had not altered. The city was still a center of administration, of art, of learning. In these matters, none of the continental capitals could rival it— not even Paris, despite many claims to the contrary. A Londoner from a century before could still have found his way around, at least at the city's center, with no difficulty. There were new bridges over the Thames, but in the old places. The great, grimy railway stations had gone—banished to the suburbs. But the Houses of Parliament were unchanged: Nelson's solitary eye still stared down Whitehall: the dome of St. Paul's still stood above

Ludgate Hill, though now there were taller buildings to challenge its pre-eminence.

And the guard still marched in front of Buckingham Palace.

All these things, thought Jan, could wait. It was vacation time, and he was lodged, with his two fellow students, in one of the University hostels. Bloomsbury also had not changed its character in the last century: it was still an island of hotels and boarding houses, though they no longer jostled each other so closely, or formed such endless, identical rows of soot-coated brick.

It was not until the second day of the Congress that Jan got his opportunity. The main papers were being read in the great assembly chamber of the Science Center, not far from the Concert Hall that had done so much to make London the musical metropolis of the world. Jan wanted to hear the first of the day's lectures, which, it was rumored, would completely demolish the current theory of the formation of the planets.

Perhaps it did, but Jan was little the wiser when he left after the interval. He hurried down to the directory, and looked up the rooms he wanted.

Some humorous civil servant had put the Royal Astronomical Society on the top floor of the great building, a gesture which the Council members fully appreciated as it gave them a magnificent view across the Thames and over the entire northern part of the city. There seemed to be nobody around, but Jan—clutching his membership card like a passport in case he was challenged—had no difficulty in locating the library.

It took him almost an hour to find what he wanted, and to learn how to handle the great star catalogues with their millions of entries. He was trembling slightly as he neared the end of his quest, and felt glad that there was no one around to see his nervousness.

He put the catalogue back among its fellows, and for a long time sat quite still, staring sightlessly at the wall of volumes before him. Then he slowly walked out into the still corridors, past the secretary's office (there was somebody there now, busily unpacking parcels of books) and down the stairs. He avoided the elevator, for he wanted to be free and unconfined. There was another lecture he had intended to hear, but that was no longer important now.

His thoughts were still in turmoil as he crossed to the embankment wall and let his eye follow the Thames on its unhurried way to the sea. It was hard for anyone with his training in orthodox science to accept the evidence that had now come into his hands. He could never be certain of its truth, yet the probability was overwhelming. As he paced slowly beside the river wall, he marshalled the facts one by one.

Fact one: no one at Rupert's party could possibly have known that he was going to ask that question. He had not known it himself: it had been a spontaneous reaction to the circumstances. Therefore, no one could have prepared any answer, or had it already lying in their minds.

Fact two: "NGS 549672" probably meant nothing to anyone except an astronomer. Though the great National Geographic Survey had been completed half a century before, its existence was known only to a few thousand specialists. And taking any number from it at random, no one could have said where that particular star lay in the heavens.

But—and this was Fact Three, which he had only this moment discovered—the small and insignificant star known as NGS 549672 was in precisely the right place. It lay in the heart of the constellation Carina, at the end of that shining trail Jan himself had seen, so few nights ago, leading from the solar system out across the depths of space.

It was an impossible coincidence. NGS 549672 *must* be the home of the Overlords. Yet to accept the fact violated all Jan's cherished ideas of scientific method. Very well—let them be violated. He must accept the fact that, somehow, Rupert's fantastic experiment had tapped a hitherto unknown source of knowledge.

Rashaverak? That seemed the most probable explanation. The Overlord had not been in the circle, but that was a minor point. However, Jan was not concerned with the mechanism of paraphysics: he was only interested in using the results.

Very little was known about NGS 549672: there had been nothing to distinguish it from a million other stars. But the catalogue gave its magnitude, its co-ordinates, and its spectral type. Jan would have to do a little research, and make a few simple calculations: then he would know, at least approximately, how far the world of the Overlords was from Earth.

A slow smile spread over Jan's face as he turned away from the Thames, back towards the gleaming white façade of the Science Center. Knowledge was power—and he was the only man on Earth who knew the origin of the Overlords. How he would use that knowledge he could not guess. It would lie safely in his mind, awaiting the moment of destiny.

10

THE HUMAN RACE continued to bask in the long, cloudless summer afternoon of peace and prosperity. Would there ever be a winter again? It was unthinkable. The age of reason, prematurely welcomed by the leaders of the French Revolution two and a half centuries before, had now really arrived. This time, there was no mistake.

There were drawbacks, of course, though they were willingly accepted. One had to be very old indeed to realize that the papers which the telecaster printed in every home were really rather dull. Gone were the crises that had once produced banner headlines. There were no mysterious murders to baffle the police and to arouse in a million breasts the moral indignation that was often suppressed envy. Such murders as did occur were never mysterious: it was only necessary to turn a dial—and the crime could be seen re-enacted. That instruments capable of such feats existed had at first caused considerable panic among quite law-abiding people. This was something that the Overlords, who had mastered most but not all the quirks of human psychology, had not anticipated. It had to be made perfectly clear that no Peeping Tom would be able to spy on his fellows, and that the very few instruments in human hands would be under strict control. Rupert Boyce's projector, for instance, could not operate beyond the borders of the reservation, so he and Maia were the only persons inside its range.

Even the few serious crimes that did occur received no particular attention in the news. For well-bred people do not, after all, care to read about the social *gaffes* of others.

The average working week was now twenty hours— but those twenty hours were no sinecure. There was little work left of a routine, mechanical nature. Men's minds were too valuable to waste on tasks that a few thousand transistors, some photoelectric cells, and a cubic meter of printed circuits could perform. There were factories that ran for weeks without being visited by a single human being. Men were needed for trouble-shooting, for making decisions, for planning new enterprises. The robots did the rest.

The existence of so much leisure would have created tremendous problems a century before. Education had overcome most of these, for a well-stocked mind is safe from boredom. The general standard of culture was at a level which would once have seemed fantastic. There was no evidence that the intelligence of the human race had improved, but for the first time everyone was given the fullest opportunity of using what brain he had.

Most people had two homes, in widely separated parts of the world. Now that the polar regions had been opened up, a considerable fraction of the human race oscillated from Arctic to Antarctic at six-monthly intervals, seeking the long, nightless polar summer. Others had gone into the deserts, up the mountains, or even into the sea. There was nowhere on the planet where science and technology could not provide one with a comfortable home, if one wanted it badly enough.

Some of the more eccentric dwelling places provided the few items of excitement in the news. In the most perfectly ordered society, there will always be accidents. Perhaps it was a good sign that people felt it worthwhile to risk, and occasionally break, their necks for the sake of a cozy villa tucked under the summit of Everest, or looking out through the spray of Victoria Falls. As a result, someone was always being rescued from somewhere. It had become a kind of game—almost a planetary sport.

People could indulge in such whims, because they had both the time and the money. The abolition of armed forces had at once almost doubled the world's effective wealth, and increased production had done the rest. As a result, it was difficult to compare the standard of living of twenty-first-century man with that of any of his predecessors. Everything was so cheap that the necessities of life were free, provided as a public service by the community, as roads, water, street lighting, and drainage had once been. A man could travel anywhere he pleased, eat whatever food he fancied—without handing over any money. He had earned the right to do this by being a productive member of the community.

There were, of course, some drones, but the number of people sufficiently strong-willed to indulge in a life of complete idleness is much smaller than is generally supposed. Supporting such parasites was considerably less of a burden than providing for the armies of ticket collectors, shop assistants, bank clerks, stock-brokers, and so forth, whose main function, when one took the global point of view, was to transfer items from one ledger to another.

Nearly a quarter of the human race's total activity, it had been calculated, was now expended on sports of various kinds, ranging from such sedentary occupations as chess to lethal pursuits like ski-gliding across mountain valleys. One unexpected result of this was the extinction of the professional sportsman. There were too many brilliant amateurs, and the changed economic conditions had made the old system obsolete.

Next to sport, entertainment, in all its branches, was the greatest single industry. For more than a hundred years there had been people who had believed that Hollywood was the center of the world. They could now make a better case for this claim that ever before, but it was safe to say that most of 2050's productions would have seemed incomprehensibly highbrow to 1950. There had been some progress: the box office was no longer lord of all it surveyed.

Yet among all the distractions and diversions of a planet which now seemed well on the way to becoming one vast playground, there were some who still found time to repeat an ancient and never-answered question:

"Where do we go from here?"

11

JAN LEANED against the elephant and rested his hands on the skin, rough as the bark of a tree. He looked up at the great tusks and the curving trunk, caught by the skill of the taxidermist in the moment of challenge or salutation. What still weirder creatures, he wondered, from what unknown worlds, would one day be looking at this exile from Earth?

"How many animals have you sent the Overlords?" he asked Rupert.

"At least fifty, though of course this is the biggest one. He's magnificent, isn't he? Most of the others have been quite small—butterflies, snakes, monkeys, and so on. Though I did get a hippo last year."

Jan gave a wry smile.

"It's a morbid thought, but I suppose they've got a fine

stuffed group of *Homo sapiens* in their collection by this time. I wonder who was honored?"

"You're probably right," said Rupert, rather indifferently. "It would be easy to arrange through the hospitals."

"What would happen," continued Jan thoughtfully, "if someone volunteered to go as a *live* specimen? Assuming that an eventual return was guaranteed, of course."

Rupert laughed, though not unsympathetically.

"Is that an offer? Shall I put it to Rashaverak?"

For a moment Jan considered the idea more than half seriously. Then he shook his head.

"Er—no. I was only thinking out loud. They'd certainly turn me down. By the way, do you ever see Rashaverak these days?"

"He called me up about six weeks ago. He'd just found a book I'd been hunting. Rather nice of him."

Jan walked slowly around the stuffed monster, admiring the skill that had frozen it forever at this instant of greatest vigor.

"Did you ever discover what he was looking for?" he asked. "I mean, it seems so hard to reconcile the Overlord's science with an interest in the occult."

Rupert looked at Jan a little suspiciously, wondering if his brother-in-law was poking fun at his hobby.

"His explanation seemed adequate. As an anthropologist, he was interested in every aspect of our culture. Remember, they have plenty of time. They can go into more detail than a human research worker ever could. Reading my entire library probably put only a slight strain on Rashy's resources."

That might be the answer, but Jan was not convinced. Sometimes he had thought of confiding his secret to Rupert, but his natural caution had held him back. When he met his Overlord friend again, Rupert would probably give something away—the temptation would be far too great.

"Incidentally," said Rupert, changing the subject abruptly, "if you think *this* is a big job, you should see the commission Sullivan's got. He's promised to deliver the two biggest creatures of all—a sperm whale and a giant squid. They'll be shown locked in mortal combat. What a tableau *that* will make!"

For a moment Jan did not answer. The idea that had exploded in his mind was too outrageous, too fantastic to be taken seriously. Yet, because of its very daring, it might succeed. . . .

"What's the matter?" said Rupert anxiously. "The heat getting you down?"

Jan shook himself back to present reality.

"I'm all right," he said. "I was just wondering how the Overlords would collect a little packet like that."

"Oh," said Rupert, "one of those cargo ships of theirs will come down, open a hatch, and hoist it in."

"That," said Jan, "is exactly what I thought."

It might have been the cabin of a spaceship, but it was not. The walls were covered with meters and instruments: there were no windows—merely a large screen in front of the pilot. The vessel could carry six passengers, but at the moment Jan was the only one.

He was watching the screen intently, absorbing each glimpse of this strange and unknown region as it passed before his eyes. Unknown—yes, as unknown as anything he might meet beyond the stars, if his mad plan succeeded. He was going into a realm of nightmare creatures, preying upon each other in a darkness undisturbed since the world began. It was a realm above which men had sailed for thousands of years: it lay no more than a kilometer below the keels of their ships—yet until the last hundred years they had known less about it than the visible face of the moon.

The pilot was dropping down from the ocean heights towards the still unexplored vastness of the South Pacific Basin. He was following, Jan knew, the invisible grid of sound waves created by beacons along the ocean floor. They were still sailing as far above that floor as clouds above the surface of the Earth. . . .

There was very little to see: the submarine's scanners were searching the waters in vain. The disturbance created by their jets had probably scared away the smaller fish: if any creature came to investigate, it would be something so large that it did not know the meaning of fear.

The tiny cabin vibrated with power—the power which could hold at bay the immense weight of the waters above their heads, and could create this little bubble of light and air within which men could live. If that power failed, thought Jan, they would become prisoners in a metal tomb, buried deep in the silt of the ocean bed.

"Time to get a fix," said the pilot. He threw a set of switches, and the submarine came to rest in a gentle surge of deceleration as the jets ceased their thrust. The vessel was motionless, floating in equilibrium as a balloon floats in the atmosphere.

It took only a moment to check their position on the sonar grid. When he had finished with his instrument readings, the pilot remarked: "Before we start the motors again, let's see if we can hear anything."

The loudspeaker flooded the quiet little room with a low, continuous murmur of sound. There was no outstanding noise that Jan could distingush from the rest. It was a steady background, into which all individual sounds had been blended. He was listening, Jan knew, to the myriad creatures of the sea talking together. It was as if he stood in the center of a forest that teemed with life—except that there he would have recognized some of the individual voices. Here, not one thread in the tapestry of sound could be disentangled and identified. It was so alien, so remote from anything he had ever known that it set Jan's scalp crawling. And yet this was part of his own world. . . .

The shriek cut across the vibrating background like a flash of lightning against a dark storm cloud. It faded swiftly away into a banshee wail, an ululation that dwindled and died, yet was repeated a moment later from a more distant source. Then a chorus of screams broke out, a pandemonium that caused the pilot to reach swiftly for the volume control.

"What in the name of God was *that?*" gasped Jan.

"Weird, isn't it? It's a school of whales, about ten kilometers away. I knew they were in the neighborhood and thought you'd like to hear them."

Jan shuddered.

"And I always thought the sea was silent! Why do they make such a din?"

"Talking to one another, I suppose. Sullivan could tell you—they say he can even identify some individual whales, though I find that hard to believe. Hello, we've got company!"

A fish with incredibly exaggerated jaws was visible in the viewing screen. It appeared to be quite large, but as Jan did not know the scale of the picture it was hard to judge. Hanging from a point just below its gills was a long tendril, ending in an unidentifiable, bell-shaped organ.

"We're seeing it on infrared," said the pilot. "Let's look at the normal picture."

The fish vanished completely. Only the pendant remained, glowing with its own vivid phosphorescence. Then, just for an instant, the shape of the creature flickered into visibility as a line of lights flashed on along its body.

"It's an angler: that's the bait it uses to lure other fish. Fantastic, isn't it? What I don't understand is—why doesn't his bait attract fish big enough to eat *him*? But we can't wait here all day. Watch him run when I switch on the jets."

The cabin vibrated once again as the vessel eased itself forward. The great luminous fish suddenly flashed on all its lights in a frantic signal of alarm, and departed like a meteor into the darkness of the abyss.

It was after another twenty minutes of slow descent that the invisible fingers of the scanner beams caught the first glimpse of the ocean bed. Far beneath, a range of low hills was passing, their outlines curiously soft and rounded. Whatever irregularities they might once have possessed had long ago been obliterated by the ceaseless rain from the watery heights above. Even here in mid Pacific, far from the great estuaries that slowly swept the continents out to sea, that rain never ceased. It came from the storm-scarred flanks of the Andes, from the bodies of a billion living creatures, from the dust of meteors that had wandered through space for ages and had come at last to rest. Here in the eternal night, it was laying the foundations of the lands to be.

The hills drifted behind. They were the frontier posts, as Jan could see from the charts, of a wide plain which lay at too great a depth for the scanners to reach.

The submarine continued on its gentle downward glide. Now another picture was beginning to form on the screen: because of the angle of view, it was some time before Jan could interpret what he saw. Then he realized that they were approaching a submerged mountain, jutting up from the hidden plain.

The picture was clearer now: at this short range the definition of the scanners improved and the view was almost as distinct as if the image was being formed by light waves. Jan could see fine detail, could watch the strange fish that pursued each other among the rocks. Once a venomous-looking creature with gaping jaws swam slowly across a half-concealed cleft. So swiftly that the eye could not follow the movement, a long tentacle flashed out and dragged the struggling fish down to its doom.

"Nearly there," said the pilot. "You'll be able to see the lab in a minute."

They were traveling slowly above a spur of rock jutting out from the base of the mountain. The plain beneath was now coming into view: Jan guessed that they were not more than a few hundred meters above the sea bed. Then he saw, a kilometer or so ahead, a cluster of spheres standing on tripod legs, and joined together by connecting tubes. It looked exactly like the tanks of some chemical plant, and indeed was designed on the same basic principles. The only difference was that here the pressures which had to be resisted were *outside*, not within.

"What's that?" gasped Jan suddenly. He pointed a shaky finger towards the nearest sphere. The curious pattern of lines on its surface had resolved itself into a network of giant tentacles. As the submarine came closer, he could see that they ended in a great, pulpy bag, from which peered a pair of enormous eyes.

"That," said the pilot indifferently, "is probably Lucifer. Someone's been feeding him again." He threw a switch and leaned over the control desk.

"S.2 calling Lab. I'm connecting up. Will you shoo away your pet?"

The reply came promptly.

"Lab to S.2. O.K.—go ahead and make contact. Lucey will get out of the way."

The curving metal walls began to fill the screen. Jan caught a last glimpse of a giant, sucker-studded arm whipping away at their approach. Then there was a dull clang, and a series of scratching noises as the clamps sought for their locking points on the submarine's smooth, oval hull. In a few minutes the vessel was pressed tightly against the wall of the base, the two entrance ports had locked together, and were moving forward through the hull of the submarine at the end of a giant hollow screw. Then came the "pressure equalized" signal, the hatches unsealed, and the way into Deep Sea Lab One was open.

Jan found Professor Sullivan in a small, untidy room that seemed to combine the attributes of office, workshop and laboratory. He was peeping through a microscope into what looked like a small bomb. Presumably it was a pressure-capsule containing some specimen of deep-sea life, still swimming happily around under its normal tons-to-the-square-centimeter conditions.

"Well," said Sullivan, dragging himself away from the eyepiece. "How's Rupert? And what can we do for you?"

"Rupert's fine," replied Jan. "He sends his best wishes, and says he'd love to visit you if it weren't for his claustrophobia."

"Then he'd certainly feel a little unhappy down here, with five kilometers of water on top of him. Doesn't it worry you, by the way?"

Jan shrugged his shoulders.

"No more than being in a stratoliner. If anything went wrong, the result would be the same in either case."

"That's the sensible approach, but it's surprising how few people see it that way." Sullivan toyed with the controls of his microscope, then shot Jan an inquisitive glance.

"I'll be very glad to show you around," he said, "but I must confess I was a little surprised when Rupert passed on your request. I couldn't understand why one of you spacehounds should be interested in our work. Aren't you going in the wrong direction?" He gave a chuckle of amusement. "Personally, I've never seen why you were in such a hurry to get out there. It will be centuries before we've got everything in the oceans nicely charted and pigeonholed."

Jan took a deep breath. He was glad that Sullivan had broached the subject himself, for it made his task that much easier. Despite the ichthyologist's jest, they had a great deal in common. It should not be too hard to build a bridge, to enlist Sullivan's sympathy and aid. He was a man of imagination, or he would never have invaded this underwater world. But Jan would have to be cautious, for the request he was going to make was, to say the least of it, somewhat unconventional.

There was one fact that gave him confidence. Even if Sullivan refused to co-operate, he would certainly keep Jan's secret. And here in this quiet little office on the bed of the Pacific, there seemed no danger that the Overlords —whatever strange powers they possessed—would be able to listen to their conversation.

"Professor Sullivan," he began, "if you were interested in the ocean, but the Overlords refused to let you go near it, how would you feel?"

"Exceedingly annoyed, no doubt."

"I'm sure you would. And suppose, one day, you had a chance of achieving your goal, without them knowing, what would you do? Would you take the opportunity?"

Sullivan never hesitated.

"Of course. And argue later."

Right into my hands! thought Jan. He can't retreat now —unless he's afraid of the Overlords. And I doubt if Sullivan is afraid of anything. He leaned forward across the cluttered table and prepared to present his case.

Professor Sullivan was no fool. Before Jan could speak, his lips twisted into a sardonic smile.

"So *that's* the game, is it?" he said slowly. "Very, very interesting! Now you go right ahead and tell me why I should help you."

12

AN EARLIER AGE would have regarded Professor Sullivan as an expensive luxury. His operations cost as much as a small war: indeed, he could be likened to a general conducting a perpetual campaign against an enemy who never relaxed. Professor Sullivan's enemy was the sea, and it fought him with weapons of cold and darkness and, above all, pressure. In his turn, he countered his adversary with intelligence and engineering skill. He had won many victories, but the sea was patient: it could wait. One day, Sullivan knew, he would make a mistake. At least he had the consolation of knowing that he could never drown. It would be far too quick for that.

He had refused to commit himself one way or the other when Jan made his request, but he knew what his answer was going to be. Here was the opportunity for a most interesting experiment. It was a pity that he would never know the result; still, that happened often enough in scientific research, and he had initiated other programs that would take decades to complete.

Professor Sullivan was a brave and an intelligent man, but looking back on his career he was conscious of the fact that it had not brought him the sort of fame that sends a scientist's name safely down the centuries. Here was a chance, totally unexpected and all the more attractive for that, of really establishing himself in the history books. It was not an ambition he would ever have admitted to anybody—and, to do him justice, he would still have helped Jan even if his part in the plot remained forever secret.

As for Jan, he was now having second thoughts. The momentum of his original discovery had carried him thus far almost without effort. He had made his investigations, but had taken no active steps to turn his dream into reality. In a few days, however, he must make his choice. If Professor Sullivan agreed to co-operate, there was no way in which he could retreat. He must face the future he had chosen, with all its implications.

What finally decided him was the thought that, if he neglected this incredible opportunity, he would never forgive himself. All the rest of his life would be spent in vain regrets—and nothing could be worse than that.

Sullivan's answer reached him a few hours later, and he knew that the die was cast. Slowly, because there was still plenty of time, he began to put his affairs in order.

"Dear Maia (the letter began), *this is going to be —to put it mildly—rather a surprise for you. When you get this letter, I shall no longer be on Earth. By that I don't mean that I shall have gone to the Moon, as many others have done. No: I shall be on my way to the home of the Overlords. I shall be the first man ever to leave the Solar System.*

"I am giving this letter to the friend who is helping me: he will hold it until he knows that my plan has succeeded—in its first phase, at least—and that it is too late for the Overlords to interfere. I shall be so far away, and traveling at such a speed, that I doubt if any recall message can overtake me. Even if it could, it seems most unlikely that the ship would be able to put back to Earth. And I very much doubt if I'm all that important anyway.

"First, let me explain what led to this. You know that I've always been interested in spaceflight, and have always felt frustrated because we've never been allowed to go to the other planets, or to learn anything about the civilization of the Overlords. If

they had never intervened, we might have reached Mars and Venus by now. I admit that it is equally probable that we would have destroyed ourselves with cobalt bombs and the other global weapons the twentieth century was developing. Yet sometimes I wish we could have had a chance of standing on our own feet.

"Probably the Overlords have their reasons for keeping us in the nursery, and probably they are excellent reasons. But even if I knew what they were, I doubt if it would make much difference to my own feelings—or my actions.

"Everything really began at that party of Rupert's. (He doesn't know about this, by the way, though he put me on the right track.) You remember that silly seance he arranged and how it ended when that girl—I forget her name—fainted? I'd asked what star the Overlords came from, and the reply was 'NGS 549672.' I'd not expected any answer, and had treated the whole business as a joke until then. But when I realized that this was a number in a star catalogue, I decided to look into it. I found that the star was in the constellation Carina —and one of the few facts that we do know about the Overlords is that they come from that direction.

"Now I don't pretend to understand how that information reached us, or where it originated. Did someone read Rashaverak's mind? Even if they had, it's hardly likely that he would have known the reference number of his sun in one of our catalogues. It's a complete mystery, and I leave it to people like Rupert to solve—if they can! I'm just content to take the information, and to act on it.

"We know a lot now, through our observations of their departure, about the speed of the Overlord ships. They leave the Solar System under such tremendous accelerations that they approach the velocity of light in less than an hour. That means that the Overlords must possess some kind of propulsive system that acts equally on every atom of their ships,

so that anything aboard won't be crushed instantly. I wonder why they employ such colossal accelerations, when they've got all space to play with and could take their time picking up speed? My theory is that they can somehow tap the energy fields round the stars, and so have to do their starting and stopping while they're fairly close to a sun. But that's all by the way. . . .

"The important fact was that I knew how far they had to travel, and therefore how long the journey took. NGS 549672 is forty light years from Earth. The Overlord ships reach more than 99 percent of the speed of light, so the trip must last forty years of our time. Our time: that's the crux of the matter.

"Now as you may have heard, strange things happen as one approaches the speed of light. Time itself begins to flow at a different rate—to pass more slowly, so that what would be months on Earth would be no more than days on the ships of the Overlords. The effect is quite fundamental: it was discovered by the great Einstein more than a hundred years ago.

"I have made calculations based on what we know about the Stardrive, and using the firmly established results of the Relativity theory. From the viewpoint of the passengers on one of the Overlord ships, the journey to NGS 549672 will last not more than two months—even though by Earth's reckoning forty years will have passed. I know this seems a paradox, and if it's any consolation it's puzzled the world's best brains ever since Einstein announced it.

"Perhaps this example will show you the sort of thing that can happen, and will give you a clearer picture of the situation. If the Overlords send me straight back to Earth, I shall arrive home having aged only four months. But on Earth itself, eighty years will have passed. So you understand, Maia, that whatever happens, this is good-by. . . .

"I have few ties binding me here, as you know well enough, so I can leave with a clear conscience. I've not told Mother yet: she would get hysterical, and I couldn't face that. It's better this way. Though I've tried to make allowances, ever since Father died —oh, there's no point now in going into all that again!

"I've terminated my studies and told the authorities that, for family reasons, I'm moving to Europe. Everything has been settled and there should be nothing for you to worry about.

"By this time, you may imagine that I'm crazy, since it seems impossible for anyone to get into one of the Overlord ships. But I've found a way. It doesn't happen very often, and after this it may never happen again, for I'm sure Karellen never makes the same mistake twice. Do you know the legend of the Wooden Horse, that got the Greek soldiers into Troy? But there's a story from the Old Testament that's an even closer parallel. . . ."

"You'll certainly be much more comfortable than Jonah," said Sullivan. "There is no evidence that he was provided with electric light or sanitation. But you'll need a lot of provisions, and I see you're taking oxygen. Can you take enough for a two months' voyage in such a small space?"

He stubbed his finger on the careful sketches which Jan had laid on the table. The microscope acted as a paper weight at one end, the skull of some improbable fish held down the other.

"I hope the oxygen isn't necessary," said Jan. "We know that they can breathe our atmosphere, but they don't seem to like it very much and I might not be able to manage theirs at all. As for the supply situation, using narcosamine solves that. It's perfectly safe. When we're under way, I'll take a shot that will knock me out for six weeks, plus or minus a few days. I'll be nearly there by then. Actually, it wasn't the food and oxygen that was worrying me, so much as the boredom."

Professor Sullivan nodded thoughtfully.

"Yes, narcosamine is safe enough, and can be calibrated fairly accurately. But mind you've got plenty of food handy—you'll be ravening when you wake up, and as weak as a kitten. Suppose you starved to death because you hadn't the strength to use a can opener?"

"I'd thought of that," said Jan, a little hurt. "I'll work up through sugar and chocolate in the usual way."

"Good: I'm glad to see that you've been into the problem thoroughly, and aren't treating it like some stunt you can back out of if you don't like the way it's going. It's your life you're playing with, but I'd hate to feel I was helping you to commit suicide."

He picked up the skull and lifted it absentmindedly in his hands. Jan grabbed the plan to prevent it rolling up.

"Luckily," continued Professor Sullivan, "the equipment you need is all fairly standard, and our shop can put it together in a few weeks. And if you decide to change your mind—"

"I won't," said Jan.

"—I've considered all the risks I'm taking, and there seems to be no flaw in the plan. At the end of six weeks I'll emerge like any other stowaway and give myself up. By then—in my time, remember— the journey will be nearly over. We will be about to land on the world of the Overlords.

"Of course, what happens then is up to them. Probably I'll be sent home on the next ship—but at least I can expect to see something. I've got a four millimeter camera and thousands of meters of film: it won't be my fault if I can't use it. Even at the worst, I'll have proved that man can't be kept in quarantine forever. I'll have created a precedent that will compel Karellen to take some action.

"That, my dear Maia, is all I have to say. I know you won't miss me greatly: let's be honest and admit that we never had very strong ties, and now that you've married Rupert you'll be quite happy in your own private universe. At least, I hope so.

"*Good-by, then, and good luck. I shall look forward to meeting your grandchildren—make sure
that they know about me, won't you?*

Your affectionate brother
Jan."

13

WHEN JAN FIRST SAW IT, he found it hard to realize that
he was not watching the fuselage of a small airliner being
assembled. The metal skeleton was twenty meters long,
perfectly streamlined, and surrounded by light scaffolding over which the workmen were clambering with their
power tools.

"Yes," said Sullivan in reply to Jan's question. "We
use standard aeronautical techniques, and most of these
men are from the aircraft industry. It's hard to believe
that a thing this size could be alive, isn't it? Or could
throw itself clear out of the water, as I've seen them do."

It was all very fascinating, but Jan had other things
on his mind. His eyes were searching the giant skeleton
to find a suitable hiding-place for his little cell—the "air-
conditioned coffin," as Sullivan had christened it. On
one point he was immediately reassured. As far as space
was concerned, there would be room for a dozen stow-
aways.

"The framework looks nearly complete," said Jan.
"When will you be putting on the skin? I suppose you've
already caught your whale, or you wouldn't know how
large to make the skeleton."

Sullivan seemed highly amused by this remark.

"We haven't the slightest intention of catching a whale.
Anyway, they don't have skins in the usual sense of the
word. It would hardly be practicable to fold a blanket of

blubber twenty centimeters thick around that framework. No, the whole thing will be faked up with plastics and then accurately painted. By the time we've finished, no one will be able to tell the difference."

In that case, thought Jan, the sensible thing for the Overlords to have done would be to take photographs and make the full-sized model themselves, back on their home planet. But perhaps their supply ships returned empty, and a little thing like a twenty meter sperm whale would hardly be noticed. When one possessed such power and such resources, one could not be bothered with minor economies. . . .

Professor Sullivan stood by one of the great statues that had been such a challenge to archaeology since Easter Island was discovered. King, god, or whatever it might be, its eyeless gaze seemed to be following his as he looked upon his handiwork. He was proud of what he had done: it seemed a pity that it would soon be banished forever from human sight.

The tableau might have been the work of some mad artist in a drugged delirium. Yet it was a painstaking copy from life: Nature herself was the artist here. The scene was one that, until the perfection of underwater television, few men had ever glimpsed—and even then only for seconds on those rare occasions when the giant antagonists thrashed their way to the surface. These battles were fought in the endless night of the ocean depths, where the sperm whales hunted for their food. It was food that objected strongly to being eaten alive. . . .

The long, saw-toothed lower jaw of the whale was gaping wide, preparing to fasten upon its prey. The creature's head was almost concealed beneath the writhing network of white, pulpy arms with which the giant squid was fighting desperately for life. Livid sucker-marks, twenty centimeters or more in diameter, had mottled the whale's skin where those arms had fastened. One tentacle was already a truncated stump, and there could be no doubt as to the ultimate outcome of the battle. When the two greatest beasts on earth engaged in combat, the whale was always the winner. For all the vast strength of its forest of tentacles, the squid's only hope lay in escaping before that patiently grinding jaw had sawn it to pieces. Its great expressionless eyes, half a meter across, stared at its destroyer—though, in all probability, neither creature could see the other in the darkness of the abyss.

The entire exhibit was more than thirty meters long, and had now been surrounded by a cage of aluminum girders to which the lifting tackle had been connected. Everything was ready, awaiting the Overlords' pleasure. Sullivan hoped that they would act quickly: the suspense was beginning to be uncomfortable.

Someone had come out of the office into the bright sunlight, obviously looking for him. Sullivan recognized his chief clerk, and walked over to meet him.

"Hello, Bill—what's the fuss?"

The other was holding a message form and looked rather pleased.

"Some good news, Professor. We've been honored! The Supervisor himself wants to come and look at our tableau before it's shipped off. Just think of the publicity we'll get! It will help a lot when we apply for our new grant. I'd been hoping for something like this."

Professor Sullivan swallowed hard. He never objected to publicity, but this time he was afraid he might get altogether too much.

Karellen stood by the head of the whale and looked up at the great, blunt snout and the ivory-studded jaw. Sullivan, concealing his unease, wondered what the Supervisor was thinking. His behavior had not hinted at any suspicion, and the visit could be easily explained as a normal one. But Sullivan would be very glad when it was over.

"We've no creatures as large as this on our planet," said Karellen. "That is one reason why we asked you to make this group. My—er—compatriots will find it fascinating."

"With your low gravity," answered Sullivan, "I should have thought you would have had some very large animals. After all, look how much bigger you are than us!"

"Yes—but we have no oceans. And where size is concerned, the land can never compete with the sea."

That was perfectly true, thought Sullivan. And as far as he knew, this was a hitherto unrevealed fact about the world of the Overlords. Jan, confound him, would be very interested.

At the moment that young man was sitting in a hut a kilometer away, anxiously watching the inspection through field glasses. He kept telling himself that there was nothing to fear. No inspection of the whale, however close, could reveal its secret. But there was always the chance that Karellen suspected something—and was playing with them.

It was a suspicion that was growing in Sullivan's mind as the Supervisor peered into the cavernous throat.

"In your Bible," said Karellen, "there is a remarkable story of a Hebrew prophet, one Jonah, who was swallowed by a whale and thus carried safely to land after he had been cast from a ship. Do you think there could be any basis of fact in such a legend?"

"I believe," Sullivan replied cautiously, "that there is one fairly well-authenticated case of a whaleman being swallowed and then regurgitated with no ill effects. Of course, if he had been inside the whale for more than a few seconds he would have suffocated. And he must have been very lucky to miss the teeth. It's an almost incredible story, but not *quite* impossible."

"Very interesting," said Karellen. He stood for another moment staring at the great jaw, then moved on to examine the squid. Sullivan hoped he did not hear his sigh of relief.

"If I'd known what I was going to go through," said Professor Sullivan, "I'd have thrown you out of the office as soon as you tried to infect me with your insanity."

"I'm sorry about that," Jan replied. "But we've got away with it."

"I hope so. Good luck, anyway. If you want to change your mind, you've still got at least six hours."

"I won't need them. Only Karellen can stop me now.

Thanks for all that you've done. If I ever get back, and write a book about the Overlords, I'll dedicate it to you."

"Much good that will do me," said Sullivan gruffly. "I'll have been dead for years." To his surprise and mild consternation, for he was not a sentimental man, he discovered that this farewell was beginning to affect him. He had grown to like Jan during the weeks they had plotted together. Moreover, he had begun to fear he might be an accessory to a complicated suicide.

He steadied the ladder as Jan climbed into the great jaw, carefully avoiding the lines of teeth. By the light of the electric torch, he saw Jan turn and wave before he was lost in the cavernous hollow. There was the sound of the airlock hatch being opened and closed, and, thereafter, silence.

In the moonlight, that had transformed the frozen battle into a scene from a nightmare, Professor Sullivan walked slowly back to his office. He wondered what he had done, and where it would lead. But this, of course, he would never know. Jan might walk this spot again, having given no more than a few months of his life in traveling to the home of the Overlords and returning to Earth. Yet if he did so, it would be on the other side of Time's impassable barrier, for it would be eighty years in the future.

The lights went on in the tiny metal cylinder as soon as Jan had closed the inner door of the lock. He allowed himself no time for second thoughts, but began immediately upon the routine check he had already worked out. All the stores and provisions had been loaded days ago, but a final recheck would put him in the right frame of mind, by assuring him that nothing had been left undone.

An hour later, he was satisfied. He lay back on the sponge rubber couch and recapitulated his plans. The only sound was the faint whirr of the electric calender clock, which would warn him when the voyage was coming to its end.

He knew that he could expect to feel nothing here in

his cell, for whatever tremendous forces drove the ships of the Overlords must be perfectly compensated. Sullivan had checked that, pointing out that his tableau would collapse if subjected to more than a few gravities. His—clients—had assured him that there was no danger on this score.

There would, however, be a considerable change of atmospheric pressure. This was unimportant, since the hollow models could "breathe" through several orifices. Before he left his cell, Jan would have to equalize pressure, and he had assumed that the atmosphere inside the Overlord ship was unbreathable. A simple facemask and oxygen set would take care of that: there was no need for anything elaborate. If he could breathe without mechanical aid, so much the better.

There was no point in waiting any longer: it would only be a strain on the nerves. He took out the little syringe, already loaded with the carefully prepared solution. Narcosamine had been discovered during research into animal hibernation: it was not true to say—as was popularly believed—that it produced suspended animation. All it caused was a great slowing down of the vital processes, though metabolism still continued at a reduced level. It was as if one had banked up the fires of life, so that they smoldered underground. But when, after weeks or months, the effect of the drug wore off, they would burst out again and the sleeper would revive. Narcosamine was perfectly safe. Nature had used it for a million years to protect many of her children from the foodless winter.

So Jan slept. He never felt the tug of the hoisting cables as the huge metal framework was lifted into the hold of the Overlord freighter. He never heard the hatches close, not to open again for three hundred million million kilometers. He never heard, far-off and faint through the mighty walls, the protesting scream of Earth's atmosphere, as the ship climbed swiftly back to its natural element.

And he never felt the Stardrive go on.

14

THE CONFERENCE ROOM was always crowded for these weekly meetings, but today it was so closely packed that the reporters had difficulty in writing. For the hundredth time, they grumbled to each other at Karellen's conservatism and lack of consideration. Anywhere else in the world they could have brought TV cameras, tape recorders, and all the other tools of their highly mechanized trade. But here, they had to rely on such archaic devices as paper and pencil—and even, incredible to relate, *shorthand*.

There had, of course, been several attempts to smuggle in recorders. They had been successfully smuggled out again, but a single glance at their smoking interiors had shown the futility of the experiment. Everyone understood, then, why they had always been warned, in their own interest, to leave watches and other metallic objects outside the conference room.

To make things more unfair, Karellen himself recorded the whole proceedings. Reporters guilty of carelessness, or downright misrepresentation—though this was very rare —had been summoned to short and unpleasant sessions with Karellen's underlings, and had been required to listen attentively to playbacks of what the Supervisor had *really* said. The lesson was not one that ever had to be repeated.

It was strange how these rumors got around. No prior announcement was made, yet there was always a full house whenever Karellen had an important statement to make—which happened, on the average, two or three times a year.

Silence descended on the murmuring crowd as the

great doorway split open and Karellen came forward onto the dais. The light here was dim—no doubt approximating that of the Overlords' far distant sun—so that the Supervisor for Earth had discarded the dark glasses he normally wore when in the open.

He replied to the ragged chorus of greetings with a formal "Good morning, everybody," then turned to the tall, distinguished figure at the front of the crowd. Mr. Golde, *doyen* of the Press Club, might have been the original inspirer of the butler's announcement: "Two reporters, m'lud, and a gentleman from the *Times.*" He dressed and behaved like a diplomat of the old school: no one would ever hesitate to confide in him, and no one had ever regretted it subsequently.

"Quite a crowd today, Mr. Golde. There must be a shortage of news."

The gentleman from the *Times* smiled and cleared his throat.

"I hope you can rectify that, Mr. Supervisor."

He watched intently as Karellen considered his reply. It seemed so unfair that the Overlords' faces, rigid as masks, betrayed no trace of emotion. The great, wide eyes, their pupils sharply contracted even in this indifferent light, stared fathomlessly back into the frankly curious human ones. The twin breathing orifices on either cheek—if those fluted, basalt curves could be called cheeks—emitted the faintest of whistles as Karellen's hypothetical lungs labored in the thin air of Earth. Golde could just see the curtain of tiny white hairs fluttering to and fro, keeping accurately out of phase, as they responded to Karellen's rapid, double-action breathing cycle. Dust filters, they were generally believed to be, and elaborate theories concerning the atmosphere of the Overlords' home had been constructed on this slender foundation.

"Yes, I have some news for you. As you are doubtless aware, one of my supply ships recently left Earth to return to its base. We have just discovered that there was a stowaway on board."

A hundred pencils braked to a halt: a hundred pairs of eyes fixed themselves upon Karellen.

"A *stowaway,* did you say, Mr. Supervisor?" asked Golde. "May we ask who he was—and how he got aboard?"

"His name is Jan Rodricks: he is an engineering student from the University of Cape Town. Further details you can no doubt discover for yourselves through your own very efficient channels."

Karellen smiled. The Supervisor's smile was a curious affair. Most of the effect really resided in the eyes: the inflexible, lipless mouth scarcely moved at all. Was this, Golde wondered, another of the many human customs that Karellen had copied with such skill? For the total effect was, undoubtedly, that of a smile, and the mind readily accepted it as such.

"As for *how* he left," continued the Supervisor, "that is of secondary importance. I can assure you, or any other potential astronauts, that there is no possibility of repeating the exploit."

"What will happen to this young man?" persisted Golde. "Will he be sent back to Earth?"

"That is outside my jurisdiction, but I expect he will come back on the next ship. He would find conditions too —alien—for comfort where he has gone. And this leads me to the main purpose of our meeting today."

Karellen paused, and the silence grew even deeper.

"There has been some complaint, among the younger and more romantic elements of your population, because outer space has been closed to you. We had a purpose in doing this: we do not impose bans for the pleasure of it. But have you ever stopped to consider—if you will excuse a slightly unflattering analogy—what a man from your Stone Age would have felt, if he suddenly found himself in a modern city?"

"Surely," protested the *Herald Tribune,* "there is a fundamental difference. We are accustomed to Science. On your world there are doubtless many things which we might not understand—but they wouldn't seem magic to us."

"Are you quite sure of that?" said Karellen, so softly that it was hard to hear his words. "Only a hundred years lies between the age of electricity and the age of steam, but what would a Victorian engineer have made of a television set or an electronic computer? And how long would he have lived if he started to investigate their workings? The gulf between two technologies can easily become so great that it is—lethal."

("Hello," whispered Reuters to the B.B.C. "We're in luck. He's going to make a major policy statement. I know the symptoms.")

"And there are other reasons why we have restricted the human race to Earth. Watch."

The lights dimmed and vanished. As they faded, a milky opalescence formed in the center of the room. It congealed into a whirlpool of stars—a spiral nebula seen from a point far beyond its outermost sun.

"No human eyes have ever seen this sight before," said Karellen's voice from the darkness. "You are looking at your own Universe, the island galaxy of which your sun is a member, from a distance of a million light-years."

There was a long silence. Then Karellen continued, and now his voice held something that was not quite pity and not precisely scorn.

"Your race had shown a notable incapacity for dealing with the problems of its own rather small planet. When we arrived, you were on the point of destroying yourselves with the powers that science had rashly given you. Without our intervention, the Earth today would be a radioactive wilderness.

"Now you have a world at peace, and a united race. Soon you will be sufficiently civilized to run your planet without our assistance. Perhaps you could eventually handle the problems of an entire solar system—say fifty moons and planets. But do you really imagine that you could ever cope with *this?*"

The nebula expanded. Now the individual stars were rushing past, appearing and vanishing as swiftly as sparks from a forge. And each of those transient sparks was a sun, with who knew how many circling worlds. . . .

"In this galaxy of ours," murmured Karellen, "there

are eighty seven thousand million suns. Even that figure
gives only a faint idea of the immensity of space. In challenging it, you would be like ants attempting to label and
classify all the grains of sand in all the deserts of the
world.

"Your race, in its present stage of evolution, cannot
face that stupendous challenge. One of my duties has
been to protect you from the powers and forces that lie
among the stars—forces beyond anything that you can
ever imagine."

The image of the galaxy's swirling fire-mists faded:
light returned to the sudden silence of the great chamber.

Karellen turned to go: the audience was over. At the
door he paused and looked back upon the hushed crowd.

"It is a bitter thought, but you must face it. The planets
you may one day possess. But the stars are not for Man."

"The stars are not for Man." Yes, it would annoy them
to have the celestial portals slammed in their faces. But
they must learn to face the truth—or as much of the
truth as could mercifully be given to them.

From the lonely heights of the stratosphere, Karellen
looked down upon the world and the people that had
been given into his reluctant keeping. He thought of all
that lay ahead, and what this world would be only a
dozen years from now.

They would never know how lucky they had been. For
a lifetime, mankind had achieved as much happiness as
any race can ever know. It had been the Golden Age.
But gold was also the color of sunset, of autumn: and only
Karellen's ears could catch the first wailings of the winter storms.

And only Karellen knew with what inexorable swiftness the Golden Age was rushing to its close.

III

The Last Generation

15

"LOOK AT THIS!" exploded George Greggson, hurling the paper across at Jean. It came to rest, despite her efforts to intercept it, spread listlessly across the breakfast table. Jean patiently scraped away the jam and read the offending passage, doing her best to register disapproval. She was not very good at this, because all too often she agreed with the critics. Usually she kept these heretical opinions to herself, and not merely for the sake of peace and quiet. George was perfectly prepared to accept praise from her (or anyone else) but if she ventured any criticism of his work she would receive a crushing lecture on her artistic ignorance.

She read the review twice, then gave up. It appeared quite favorable, and she said so.

"He seemed to like the performance. What are you grumbling about?"

"This," snarled George, stubbing his finger at the middle of the column. "Just read it again."

" 'Particularly restful on the eyes were the delicate pastel greens of the background to the ballet sequence.' Well?"

"They *weren't* greens! I spent a lot of time getting that exact shade of blue! And what happens? Either some blasted engineer in the control room upsets the color balance, or that idiot of a reviewer's got a cockeyed set. Hey, what color did it look on *our* receiver?"

"Er—I can't remember," confessed Jean. "The Poppet started squealing about then and I had to go and find what was wrong with her."

"Oh," said George, relapsing into a gently simmering quiescence. Jean knew that another eruption could be expected at any moment. When it came, however, it was fairly mild.

"I've invented a new definition for TV," he muttered gloomily. "I've decided it's a device for *hindering* communication between artist and audience."

"What do you want to do about it?" retorted Jean. "Go back to the live theater?"

"And why not?" asked George. "That's exactly what I *have* been thinking about. You know that letter I received from the New Athens people? They've written to me again. This time I'm going to answer."

"Indeed?" said Jean, faintly alarmed. "I think they're a lot of cranks."

"Well, there's only one way to find out. I intend to go and see them in the next two weeks. I must say that the literature they put out looks perfectly sane. And they've got some very good men there."

"If you expect me to start cooking over a wood fire, or learning to dress in skins, you'll have—"

"Oh, don't be silly! Those stories are just nonsense. The colony's got everything that's really needed for civilized life. They don't believe in unnecessary frills, that's all. Anyway, it's a couple of years since I visited the Pacific. It will make a nice trip for us both."

"I agree with you there," said Jean. "But I don't intend Junior and the Poppet to grow up into a couple of Polynesian savages."

"They won't," said George. "I can promise you that."

He was right, though not in the way he had intended.

"As you noticed when you flew in," said the little man on the other side of the veranda, "the colony consists of two islands, linked by a causeway. This is Athens, the other we've christened Sparta. It's rather wild and rocky, and is a wonderful place for sport or exercise." His eye flickered momentarily over his visitor's waistline, and George squirmed slightly in the cane chair. "Sparta is an extinct volcano, by the way. At least the geologists *say* it's extinct, ha-ha!

"But back to Athens. The idea of the colony, as you've gathered, is to build up an independent, stable cultural group with its own artistic traditions. I should point out that a vast amount of research took place before we started this enterprise. It's really a piece of applied social engineering, based on some exceedingly complex mathematics which I wouldn't pretend to understand. All I know is that the mathematical sociologists have computed how large the colony should be, how many types of people it should contain—and, above all, what constitution it should have for long-term stability.

"We're ruled by a council of eight directors, representing production, power, social engineering, art, economics, science, sport, and philosophy. There's no permanent chairman or president. The chair's held by each of the directors in rotation for a year at a time.

"Our present population is just over fifty thousand, which is a little short of the desired optimum. That's why we keep our eyes open for recruits. And, of course, there is a certain wastage: we're not yet quite self-supporting in some of the more specialized talents.

"Here on this island we're trying to save something of humanity's independence, its artistic traditions. We've no hostility towards the Overlords: we simply want to be left alone to go our own way. When they destroyed the old nations and the way of life man had known since the beginning of history, they swept away many good things with the bad. The world's now placid, featureless, and culturally dead: nothing really new has been created since the Overlords came. The reason's obvious. There's nothing left to struggle for, and there are too many distractions and entertainments. Do you realize that *every day* something like five hundred hours of radio and TV pour out over the various channels? If you went without sleep and did nothing else, you could follow less than a twentieth of the entertainment that's available at the turn of a switch! No wonder that people are becoming passive sponges—absorbing but never creating. Did you know that the *average* viewing time per person is now three hours a day? Soon people won't be living their own lives any more. It will be a full-time job keeping up with the various family serials on TV!

"Here in Athens, entertainment takes its proper place. Moreover, it's live, not canned. In a community this size it is possible to have almost complete audience participation, with all that that means to the performers and artists. Incidentally we've got a very fine symphony orchestra—probably among the world's half-dozen best.

"But I don't want you to take my word for all this. What usually happens is that prospective citizens stay here a few days, getting the feel of the place. If they decide they'd like to join us, then we let them take the battery of psychological tests which are really our main line of defense. About a third of the applicants are rejected, usually for reasons which don't reflect on them and which wouldn't matter outside. Those who pass go home long enough to settle their affairs, and then rejoin us. Sometimes, they change their minds at this stage, but that's very unusual and almost invariably through personal reasons outside their control. Our tests are practically a hundred percent reliable now: the people they pass are the people who really want to come."

"Suppose anyone changed their mind *later?*" asked Jean anxiously.

"Then they could leave. There'd be no difficulty. It's happened once or twice."

There was a long silence. Jean looked at George, who was rubbing thoughtfully at the side whiskers currently popular in artistic circles. As long as they weren't burning their boats behind them, she was not unduly worried. The colony looked an interesting place, and certainly wasn't as cranky as she'd feared. And the children would love it. That, in the final analysis, was all that mattered.

They moved in six weeks later. The single-storied house was small, but quite adequate for a family which had no intention of being greater than four. All the basic labor-saving devices were in evidence: at least, Jean admitted, there was no danger of reverting to the dark ages of domestic drudgery. It was slightly disturbing, however, to discover that there was a kitchen. In a community of this size, one would normally expect to dial Food Central, wait five minutes, and then get whatever meal had been selected. Individuality was all very well, but this, Jean feared, might be taking things a little *too* far. She wondered darkly if she would be expected to make the family's clothes as well as to prepare its meals. But there was no spinning wheel between the automatic dishwasher and the radar range, so it wasn't quite as bad as that. . . .

Of course, the rest of the house still looked very bare and raw. They were its first occupants, and it would be some time before all this aseptic newness had been converted into a warm, human home. The children, doubtless, would catalyze the process rather effectively. There was already (though Jean did not know it yet) an unfortunate victim of Jeffrey's expiring in the bath, as a result of that young man's ignorance of the fundamental difference between fresh and salt water.

Jean moved to the still-uncurtained window and looked across the colony. It was a beautiful place, there was no doubt of that. The house stood on the western slope of the low hill that dominated, because of the absence of any other competition, the island of Athens. Two kilometers to the north she could see the causeway—a thin knife-edge dividing the water—that led to Sparta. That rocky island, with its brooding volcanic cone, was such a contrast to this peaceful spot that it sometimes frightened her. She wondered how the scientists could be so certain that it would never reawaken and overwhelm them all.

A wavering figure coming up the slope, keeping care-

fully to the palm trees' shade in defiance of the rule of
the road, attracted her eye. George was returning from
his first conference. It was time to stop daydreaming and
get busy about the house.

A metallic crash announced the arrival of George's bicycle. Jean wondered how long it was going to take them
both to learn to ride. This was yet another unexpected
aspect of life on the island. Private cars were not per-
mitted, and indeed were unnecessary since the greatest
distance one could travel in a straight line was less than
fifteen kilometers. There were various community-owned
service vehicles—trucks, ambulances, and fire engines,
all restricted, except in cases of real emergency, to fifty
kilometers an hour. As a result the inhabitants of Athens
had plenty of exercise, uncongested streets—and no traffic accidents.

George gave his wife a perfunctory peck and collapsed
with a sigh of relief into the nearest chair.

"Phew!" he said, mopping his brow. "Everyone raced
past me on the way up the hill, so I suppose people *do*
get used to it. I think I've lost ten kilograms already."

"What sort of day did you have?" asked Jean dutifully.
She hoped George would not be too exhausted to help
with the unpacking.

"Very stimulating. Of course I can't remember half the
people I met, but they all seemed very pleasant. And the
theater is just as good as I'd hoped. We're starting work
next week on Shaw's *Back to Methuselah*. I'll be in complete charge of sets and stage design. It'll make a change,
not having a dozen people to tell me what I can't do. Yes,
I think we're going to like it here."

"Despite the bicycles?"

George summoned up enough energy to grin.

"Yes," he said. "In a couple of weeks, I won't even notice this little hill of ours."

He didn't really believe it—but it was perfectly true.
It was another month, however, before Jean ceased to
pine for the car, and discovered all the things one could
do with one's own kitchen.

New Athens was not a natural and spontaneous growth like the city whose name it bore. Everything about the colony was deliberately planned, as the result of many years of study by a group of very remarkable men. It had begun as an open conspiracy against the Overlords, an implicit challenge to their policy if not to their power. At first the colony's sponsors had been more than half certain that Karellen would neatly frustrate them, but the Supervisor had done nothing—absolutely nothing. This was not quite as reassuring as might have been expected. Karellen had plenty of time: he might be preparing a delayed counterstroke. Or he might be so certain of the project's failure that he felt no need to take any action against it.

That the colony would fail had been the prediction of most people. Yet even in the past, long before any real knowledge of social dynamics had existed, there had been many communities devoted to special religious or philosophical ends. It was true that their mortality rate had been high, but some had survived. And the foundations of New Athens were as secure as modern science could make them.

There were many reasons for choosing an island site. Not the least important were psychological. In an age of universal air transport, the ocean meant nothing as a physical barrier, but it still gave a sense of isolation. Moreover, a limited land area made it impossible for too many people to live in the colony. The maximum population was fixed at a hundred thousand: more than that, and the advantages inherent in a small, compact community would be lost. One of the aims of the founders was that any member of New Athens should know all the other citizens who shared his interests—and as many as one or two percent of the remainder as well.

The man who had been the driving force behind New Athens was a Jew. And, like Moses, he had never lived to enter his promised land, for the colony had been founded three years after his death.

He had been born in Israel, the last independent nation ever to come into existence—and, therefore, the shortest lived. The end of national sovereignty had been felt here perhaps more bitterly than anywhere else, for it is hard to lose a dream which one has just achieved after centuries of striving.

Ben Salomon was no fanatic, but the memories of his childhood must have determined, to no small extent, the philosophy he was to put into practice. He could just remember what the world had been before the advent of the Overlords, and had no wish to return to it. Like not a few other intelligent and well-meaning men, he could appreciate all that Karellen had done for the human race, while still being unhappy about the Supervisor's ultimate plans. Was it possible, he sometimes said to himself, that despite all their enormous intelligence the Overlords did not really understand mankind, and were making a terrible mistake from the best of motives? Suppose, in their altruistic passion for justice and order, they had determined to reform the world, but had not realized that they were destroying the soul of man?

The decline had barely started, yet the first symptoms of decay were not hard to discover. Salomon was no artist, but he had an acute appreciation of art and knew that his age could not match the achievements of previous centuries in any single field. Perhaps matters would right themselves in due course, when the shock of encountering the Overlord civilization had worn off. But it might not, and a prudent man would consider taking out an insurance policy.

New Athens was that policy. Its establishment had taken twenty years and some billions of Pounds Decimal —a relatively trivial fraction, therefore, of the world's total wealth. Nothing had happened for the first fifteen years; everything had happened in the last five.

Salomon's task would have been impossible had he not been able to convince a handful of the world's most famous artists that his plan was sound. They had sympathized because it appealed to their egos, not because it was important for the race. But, once convinced, the world had listened to them and given both moral and material support. Behind this spectacular façade of temperamental talent, the real architects of the colony had laid their plans.

A society consists of human beings whose behavior as individuals is unpredictable. But if one takes enough of the basic units, then certain laws begin to appear—as was discovered long ago by life insurance companies. No one can tell what individuals will die in a given time—yet the total number of deaths can be predicted with considerable accuracy.

There are other, subtler laws, first glimpsed in the early twentieth century by mathematicians such as Weiner and Rashavesky. They had argued that such events as economic depressions, the results of armament races, the stability of social groups, political elections, and so on, could be analyzed by the correct mathematical techniques. The great difficulty was the enormous number of variables, many of them hard to define in numerical terms. One could not draw a set of curves and state definitely: "When this line is reached, it will mean war." And one could never wholly allow for such utterly unpredictable events as the assassination of a key figure or the effects of some new scientific discovery—still less such natural catastrophes as earthquakes or floods, which might have a profound effect on large numbers of people and the social groups in which they lived.

Yet one could do much, thanks to the knowledge patiently accumulated during the past hundred years. The task would have been impossible without the aid of the giant computing machines that could perform the work of a thousand human calculators in a matter of seconds. Such aids had been used to the utmost when the colony was planned.

Even so, the founders of New Athens could only provide the soil and the climate in which the plant they wished to cherish might—or might not—come to flower. As Salomon himself had remarked: "We can be sure of talent: we can only pray for genius." But it was a reasonable hope that in such a concentrated society some interesting reactions would take place. Few artists thrive in solitude, and nothing is more stimulating than the conflict of minds with similar interests.

So far, the conflict had produced worthwhile results in sculpture, music, literary criticism, and film-making. It was still too early to see if the group working on historical research would fulfill the hopes of its instigators, who were frankly aiming at restoring mankind's pride in its own achievements. Painting still languished, which supported the view of those who considered that static, two-dimensional forms of art had no further possibilities.

It was noticeable—though a satisfactory explanation for this had not yet been produced—that Time played an essential part in the colony's most successful artistic achievements. Even its sculpture was seldom immobile. Andrew Carson's intriguing volumes and curves changed slowly as one watched, according to complex patterns that the mind could appreciate, even if it could not fully comprehend them. Indeed, Carson claimed, with some truth, to have taken the "mobiles" of a century before to their ultimate conclusion, and thus to have wedded sculpture and ballet.

Much of the colony's musical experimenting was, quite consciously, concerned with what might be called "time span." What was the briefest note that the mind could grasp—or the longest that it could tolerate without boredom? Could the result be varied by conditioning or by the use of appropriate orchestration? Such problems were discussed endlessly, and the arguments were not purely academic. They had resulted in some extremely interesting compositions.

But it was in the art of the cartoon film, with its limitless possibilities, that New Athens had made its most successful experiments. The hundred years since the time of Disney had still left much undone in this most flexible of all mediums. On the purely realistic side, results could be produced indistinguishable from actual photography—much to the contempt of those who were developing the cartoon along abstract lines.

The group of artists and scientists that had so far done least was the one that had attracted the greatest interest—and the greatest alarm. This was the team working on "total identification." The history of the cinema gave the clue to their actions. First, sound, then color, then stereoscopy, then Cinerama, had made the old "moving pictures" more and more like reality itself. Where was the end of the story? Surely, the final stage would be reached when the audience forgot it was an audience, and became part of the action. To achieve this would involve stimulation of all the senses, and perhaps hypnosis as well, but many believed it to be practical. When the goal was attained, there would be an enormous enrichment of human experience. A man could become—for a while, at least—any other person, and could take part in any conceivable adventure, real or imaginary. He could even be a plant or an animal, if it proved possible to capture and record the sense impressions of other living creatures. And when the "program" was over, he would have acquired a memory as vivid as any experience in his actual life—indeed, indistinguishable from reality itself.

The prospect was dazzling. Many also found it terrifying, and hoped that the enterprise would fail. But they knew in their hearts that once science had declared a thing possible, there was no escape from its eventual realization. . . .

This, then, was New Athens and some of its dreams. It hoped to become what the old Athens might have been had it possessed machines instead of slaves, science instead of superstition. But it was much too early yet to tell if the experiment would succeed.

16

JEFFREY GREGGSON was one islander who, as yet, had no interest in esthetics or science, the two main preoccupations of his elders. But he heartily approved of the colony, for purely personal reasons. The sea, never more than a few kilometers away in any direction, fascinated him. Most of his short life had been spent far inland, and he was not yet accustomed to the novelty of being surrounded by water. He was a good swimmer, and would often cycle off with other young friends, carrying his fins and mask, to go exploring the shallower water of the lagoon. At first Jean was not very happy about this, but after she had made a few dives herself, she lost her fear of the sea and its strange creatures and let Jeffrey enjoy himself as he pleased—on condition that he never swam alone.

The other member of the Greggson household who approved of the change was Fey, the beautiful golden retriever who nominally belonged to George but could seldom be detached from Jeffrey. The two were inseparable, both by day and—if Jean had not put her foot down—by night. Only when Jeffrey went off on his bicycle did Fey remain at home, lying listlessly in front of the door and staring down the road with moist, mournful eyes, her muzzle resting on her paws. This was rather mortifying to George, who had paid a stiff price for Fey and her pedigree. It looked as if he would have to wait for the next generation—due in three months—before he could have a dog of his own. Jean had other views on the subject. She liked Fey, but felt that one hound per house was quite sufficient.

Only Jennifer Anne had not yet decided whether she

liked the colony. That, however, was hardly surprising, for she had so far seen nothing of the world beyond the plastic panels of her cot, and had, as yet, very little suspicion that such a place existed.

George Greggson did not often think about the past: he was too busy with plans for the future, too much occupied by his work and his children. It was seldom indeed that his mind went back across the years to that evening in Africa, and he never talked about it with Jean. By mutual consent, the subject was avoided, and since that day they had never visited the Boyces again, despite repeated invitations. They called Rupert with fresh excuses several times a year, and lately he had ceased to bother them. His marriage to Maia, rather to everyone's surprise, still seemed to be flourishing.

One result of that evening was that Jean had lost all desire to dabble with mysteries at the borders of known science. The naïve and uncritical wonder that had drawn her to Rupert and his experiments had completely vanished. Perhaps she had been convinced and wanted no more proof: George preferred not to ask her. Possibly the cares of maternity had banished such interests from her mind.

There was no point, George knew, in worrying about a mystery that could never be solved, yet sometimes in the stillness of the night he would wake and wonder. He remembered his meeting with Jan Rodricks on the roof of Rupert's house, and the few words that were all he had spoken with the only human being successfully to defy the Overlords' ban. Nothing in the realm of the supernatural, thought George, could be more eerie than the plain scientific fact that though almost ten years had passed since he had spoken to Jan, that now-far-distant voyager would have aged by only a few days.

The universe was vast, but that fact terrified him less than its mystery. George was not a person who thought deeply on such matters, yet sometimes it seemed to him that men were like children amusing themselves in some secluded playground, protected from the fierce realities of the outer world. Jan Rodricks had resented that protection and had escaped from it—into no one knew what. But in this matter, George found himself on the side of the Overlords. He had no wish to face whatever lurked in the unknown darkness, just beyond the little circle of light cast by the lamp of Science.

"How is it," said George plaintively, "that Jeff's always off somewhere when I happen to be home? Where's he gone today?"

Jean looked up from her knitting—an archaic occupation which had recently been revived with much success. Such fashions came and went on the island with some rapidity. The main result of this particular craze was that the men had now all been presented with multicolored sweaters, far too hot to wear in the daytime but quite useful after sundown.

"He's gone off to Sparta with some friends," Jean replied. "He promised to be back for dinner."

"I really came home to do some work," said George thoughtfully. "But it's a nice day, and I think I'll go out there and have a swim myself. What kind of fish would you like me to bring back?"

George had never caught anything, and the fish in the lagoon were much too wily to be trapped. Jean was just going to point this out when the stillness of the afternoon was shattered by a sound that still had power, even in this peaceful age, to chill the blood and set the scalp crawling with apprehension.

It was the wail of a siren, rising and falling, spreading its message of danger in concentric circles out to sea.

For almost a hundred years the stresses had been slowly increasing, here in the burning darkness deep beneath the ocean's floor. Though the submarine canyon had been formed geological ages ago, the tortured rocks had never reconciled themselves to their new positions. Countless times the strata had creaked and shifted, as the unimaginable weight of water disturbed their precarious equilibrium. They were ready to move again.

Jeff was exploring the rock pools along the narrow Spartan beach—an occupation he found endlessly absorbing. One never knew what exotic creatures one might find, sheltered here from the waves that marched forever across the Pacific to spend themselves against the reef. It was a fairyland for any child, and at the moment he possessed it all himself, for his friends had gone up into the hills.

The day was quiet and peaceful. There was not a breath of wind, and even the perpetual muttering beyond the reef had sunk to a sullen undertone. A blazing sun hung halfway down the sky, but Jeff's mahogany-brown body was now quite immune to its onslaughts.

The beach here was a narrow belt of sand, sloping steeply towards the lagoon. Looking down into the glass-clear water, Jeff could see the submerged rocks which were as familiar to him as any formations on the land. About ten meters down, the weed-covered ribs of an ancient schooner curved up towards the world it had left almost two centuries ago. Jeff and his friends had often explored the wreck, but their hopes of hidden treasure had been disappointed. All that they had ever retrieved was a barnacle-encrusted compass.

Very firmly, something took hold of the beach and gave it a single, sudden jerk. The tremor passed so swiftly that Jeff wondered if he had imagined it. Perhaps it was a momentary giddiness, for all around him remained utterly unchanged. The waters of the lagoon were unruffled, the sky empty of cloud or menace. And then a very strange thing began to happen.

Swifter than any tide could ebb, the water was receding from the shore. Jeff watched, deeply puzzled and not in the least afraid, as the wet sands were uncovered and lay sparkling in the sun. He followed the retreating ocean, determined to make the most of whatever miracle had opened up the underwater world for his inspection. Now the level had sunk so far that the broken mast of the old wreck was climbing into the air, its weeds hanging limply from it as they lost their liquid support. Jeff hastened forward, eager to see what wonders would be uncovered next.

It was then that he noticed the sound from the reef. He had never heard anything like it before, and he stopped to think the matter over, his bare feet slowly sinking into the moist sand. A great fish was thrashing in its death agonies a few meters away, but Jeff scarcely noticed it. He stood, alert and listening, while the noise from the reef grew steadily around him.

It was a sucking, gurgling sound, as of a river racing through a narrow channel. It was the voice of the reluctantly retreating sea, angry at losing, even for a moment, the lands it rightfully possessed. Through the graceful branches of the coral, through the hidden submarine caves, millions of tons of water were draining out of the lagoon into the vastness of the Pacific.

Very soon, and very swiftly, they would return.

One of the salvage parties, hours later, found Jeff on a great block of coral that had been hurled twenty meters above the normal water level. He did not seem particularly frightened, though he was upset over the loss of his bicycle. He was also very hungry, as the partial destruction of the causeway had cut him off from home. When rescued he was contemplating swimming back to Athens, and unless the currents had changed drastically, would doubtless have managed the crossing without much trouble.

Jean and George had witnessed the whole sequence of events when the *tsunami* hit the island. Though the damage to the low-lying areas of Athens had been severe, there had been no loss of life. The seismographs had been able to give only fifteen minutes warning, but that had been long enough to get everyone above the danger line. Now the colony was licking its wounds and collecting together a mass of legends that would grow steadily more hair-raising through the years to come.

Jean burst into tears when her son was restored to her, for she had quite convinced herself that he had been swept out to sea. She had watched with horrified eyes as the black, foam-capped wall of water had moved roaring in from the horizon to smother the base of Sparta in spume and spray. It seemed incredible that Jeff could have reached safety in time.

It was scarcely surprising that he could not give a very rational account of what had happened. When he had eaten and was safely in bed, Jean and George gathered by his side.

"Go to sleep, darling, and forget all about it," said Jean. "You're all right now."

"But it was fun, Mummy," protested Jeff. "I wasn't *really* frightened."

"That's fine," said George. "You're a brave lad, and it's a good thing you were sensible and ran in time. I've heard about these tidal waves before. A lot of people get drowned because they go out on the uncovered beach to see what's happened."

"That's what I did," confessed Jeff. "I wonder who it was helped me?"

"What do you mean? There wasn't anyone with you. The other boys were up the hill."

Jeff looked puzzled.

"But someone told me to run."

Jean and George glanced at each other in mild alarm.

"You mean—you imagined you heard something?"

"Oh, don't bother him now," said Jean anxiously, and with a little too much haste. But George was stubborn.

"I want to get to the bottom of this. Tell me just what happened, Jeff."

"Well, I was right down the beach, by that old wreck, when the voice spoke."

"What did it say?"

"I can't quite remember, but it was something like 'Jeffrey, get up the hill as quickly as you can. You'll be drowned if you stay here.' I'm sure it called me Jeffrey, not Jeff. So it couldn't have been anyone I knew."

"Was it a man's voice? And where did it come from?"

"It was ever so close beside me. And it sounded like a man. . . ." Jeff hesitated for a moment, and George prompted him.

"Go on—just imagine that you're back on the beach, and tell us exactly what happened."

"Well, it wasn't quite like anyone I've ever heard talking before. I think he was a very *big* man."

"Is that all the voice said?"

"Yes—until I started to climb the hill. Then another funny thing happened. You know the path up the cliff?"

"Yes."

"I was running up that, because it was the quickest way. I knew what was happening now, for I'd seen the big wave coming in. It was making an awful noise, too. And then I found there was a great big rock in the way. It wasn't there before, and I couldn't get past it."

"The quake must have brought it down," said George.

"Shush! Go on, Jeff."

"I didn't know what to do, and I could hear the wave coming closer. Then the voice said 'Close your eyes, Jeffrey, and put your hand in front of your face.' It seemed a funny thing to do, but I tried it. And then there was a great flash—I could feel it all over—and when I opened my eyes the rock was gone."

"Gone?"

"That's right—it just wasn't there. So I started running again, and that's when I nearly burnt my feet, because the path was awful hot. The water hissed when it went over it, but it couldn't catch me then—I was too far up the cliff. And that's all. I came down again when there weren't any more waves. Then I found that my bike had gone, and the road home had been knocked down."

"Don't worry about the bicycle, dear," said Jean, squeezing her son thankfully. "We'll get you another one. The only thing that matters is that you're safe. We won't worry about *how* it happened."

That wasn't true, of course, for the conference began immediately they had left the nursery. It decided nothing, but it had two sequels. The next day, without telling George, Jean took her small son to the colony's child psychologist. He listened carefully while Jeff repeated his story, not in the least overawed by his novel surround-

ings. Then, while his unsuspecting patient rejected seria-
tim the toys in the next room, the doctor reassured Jean.

"There's nothing on his card to suggest any mental ab-
normality. You must remember that he's been through
a terrifying experience, and he's come out of it remarkably well. He's a highly imaginative child, and probably
believes his own story. So just accept it, and don't worry
unless there are any later symptoms. Then let me know
at once."

That evening, Jean passed the verdict on to her husband. He did not seem as relieved as she had hoped, and
she put it down to worry over the damage to his beloved theater. He just grunted "That's fine," and settled
down with the current issue of *Stage and Studio*. It
looked as if he had lost interest in the whole affair, and
Jean felt vaguely annoyed with him.

But three weeks later, on the first day that the causeway was reopened, George and his bicycle set off briskly
toward Sparta. The beach was still littered with masses
of shattered coral, and in one place the reef itself seemed
to have been breached. George wondered how long it
would take the myriads of patient polyps to repair the
damage.

There was only one path up the face of the cliff, and
when he had recovered his breath George began the
climb. A few dried fragments of weed, trapped among
the rocks, marked the limit of the ascending waters.

For a long time George Greggson stood on that lonely track, staring at the patch of fused rock beneath his
feet. He tried to tell himself that it was some freak of the
long-dead volcano, but soon abandoned this attempt at
self-deception. His mind went back to that night, years
ago, when he and Jean had joined that silly experiment
of Rupert Boyce's. No one had ever really understood
what had happened then, and George knew that in some
unfathomable way these two strange events were linked
together. First it had been Jean, now her son. He did not
know whether to be glad or fearful, and in his heart
he uttered a silent prayer:

"Thank you, Karellen, for whatever your people did for Jeff. But I wish I knew *why* they did it."

He went slowly down to the beach, and the great white gulls wheeled around him, annoyed because he had brought no food to throw them as they circled in the sky.

17

KARELLEN'S REQUEST, though it might have been expected at any time since the foundation of the colony, was something of a bombshell. It represented, as everyone was fully aware, a crisis in the affairs of Athens, and nobody could decide whether good or bad would come of it.

Until now, the colony had gone its way without any form of interference from the Overlords. They had left it completely alone, as indeed they ignored most human activities that were not subversive or did not offend their codes of behavior. Whether the colony's aims could be called subversive was uncertain. They were nonpolitical, but they represented a bid for intellectual and artistic independence. And from that, who knew what might come? The Overlords might well be able to foresee the future of Athens more clearly than its founders—and they might not like it.

Of course, if Karellen wished to send an observer, inspector, or whatever one cared to call him, there was nothing that could be done about it. Twenty years ago the Overlords had announced that they had discontinued all use of their surveillance devices, so that humanity need no longer consider itself spied upon. However, the fact that such devices still existed meant that nothing could be hidden from the Overlords if they really wanted to see it.

There were some on the island who welcomed this visit as a chance of settling one of the minor problems of Overlord psychology—their attitude towards art. Did they regard it as a childish aberration of the human race? Did they have any forms of art themselves? In that case, was the purpose of this visit purely esthetic, or did Karellen have less innocent motives?

All these matters were debated endlessly while the preparations were under way. Nothing was known of the visiting Overlord, but it was assumed that he could absorb culture in unlimited amounts. The experiment would at least be attempted, and the reactions of the victim observed with interest by a battery of very shrewd minds.

The current chairman of the council was the philosopher, Charles Yan Sen, an ironic but fundamentally cheerful man not yet in his sixties and therefore still in the prime of life. Plato would have approved of him as an example of the philosopher-statesman, though Sen did not altogether approve of Plato, whom he suspected of grossly misrepresenting Socrates. He was one of the islanders who was determined to make the most of this visit, if only to show the Overlords that men still had plenty of initiative and were not yet, as he put it, "fully domesticated."

Nothing in Athens was done without a committee, that ultimate hallmark of the democratic method. Indeed, someone had once defined the colony as a system of interlocking committees. But the system worked, thanks to the patient studies of the social psychologists who had been the real founders of Athens. Because the community was not too large, everyone in it could take some part in its running and could be a citizen in the truest sense of the word.

It was almost inevitable that George, as a leading member of the artistic hierarchy, should be one of the reception committee. But he made doubly sure by pulling a few strings. If the Overlords wanted to study the colony, George wanted equally to study them. Jean was not very happy about this. Ever since that evening at the Boyces', she had felt a vague hostility towards the Overlords, though she could never give any reason for it. She just wished to have as little to do with them as possible, and to her one of the island's main attractions had been its hoped-for independence. Now she feared that this independence might be threatened.

The Overlord arrived without ceremony in an ordinary man-made flyer, to the disappointment of those who had hoped for something more spectacular. He might have been Karellen himself, for no one had ever been able to distinguish one Overlord from another with any degree of confidence. They all seemed duplicates from a single, master mold. Perhaps, by some unknown biological process, they were.

After the first day, the islanders ceased to pay much attention when the official car murmured past on its sightseeing tours. The visitor's correct name, Thanthalteresco, proved too intractable for general use, and he was soon christened "the Inspector." It was an accurate enough name, for his curiosity and appetite for statistics were insatiable.

Charles Yan Sen was quite exhausted when, long after midnight, he had seen the Inspector back to the flyer which was serving as his base. There, no doubt, he would continue to work throughout the night while his human hosts indulged in the frailty of sleep.

Mrs. Sen greeted her husband anxiously on his return. They were a devoted couple, despite his playful habit of calling her Xantippe when they were entertaining guests. She had long ago threatened to make the appropriate retort by brewing him a cup of hemlock, but fortunately this herbal beverage was less common in the new Athens than the old.

"Was it a success?" she asked as her husband settled down to a belated meal.

"I think so—but you can never tell what goes on inside those remarkable minds. He was certainly interested—even complimentary. I apologized, by the way, for not inviting him here. He said he quite understood, and had no wish to bang his head on our ceiling."

"What did you show him today?"

"The bread-and-butter side of the colony, which he didn't seem to find as boring as I always do. He asked every question you could imagine about production, how we balanced our budget, our mineral resources, the birth rate, how we got our food, and so on. Luckily I had Secretary Harrison with me, and *he'd* come prepared with every Annual Report since the colony began. You should have heard them swapping statistics. The Inspector's borrowed the lot, and I'm prepared to bet that when we see him tomorrow he'll be able to quote any figure back at us. I find that kind of mental performance frightfully depressing."

He yawned and began to peck halfheartedly at his food.

"Tomorrow should be more interesting. We're going to do the schools and the Academy. That's when *I'm* going to ask some questions for a change. I'd like to know how the Overlords bring up their kids—assuming, of course, that they have any."

That was not a question that Charles Sen was ever to have answered, but on other points the Inspector was remarkably talkative. He would evade awkward queries in a manner that was a pleasure to behold, and then, quite unexpectedly, would become positively confiding.

Their first real intimacy occurred while they were driving away from the school that was one of the colony's chief prides. "It's a great responsibility," Dr. Sen had remarked, "training these young minds for the future. Fortunately, human beings are extraordinarily resilient: it takes a pretty bad upbringing to do permanent damage. Even if our aims are mistaken, our little victims will probably get over it. And as you've seen, they appear to be perfectly happy." He paused for a moment, then glanced mischievously up at the towering figure of his passenger. The Inspector was completely clothed in some reflecting silvery cloth so that not an inch of his body was exposed to the fierce sunlight. Behind the dark glasses,

Dr. Sen was aware of the great eyes watching him emotionlessly—or with emotions which he could never understand. "Our problem in bringing up these children must, I imagine, be very similar to yours when confronted with the human race. Would you agree?"

"In some ways," admitted the Overlord gravely. "In others perhaps a better analogy can be found in the history of your colonial powers. The Roman and British Empires, for that reason, have always been of considerable interest to us. The case of India is particularly instructive. The main difference between us and the British in India was that they had no real motives for going there—no conscious objectives, that is, except such trivial and temporary ones as trade or hostility to other European powers. They found themselves possessors of an empire before they knew what to do with it, and were never really happy until they had got rid of it again."

"And will you," asked Dr. Sen, quite unable to resist the opportunity, "get rid of your empire when the time arises?"

"Without the slightest hesitation," replied the Inspector.

Dr. Sen did not press the point. The forthrightness of the reply was not altogether flattering: moreover, they had now arrived at the Academy, where the assembled pedagogues were waiting to sharpen their wits on a real, live Overlord.

"As our distinguished colleague will have told you," said Professor Chance, Dean of the University of New Athens, "our main purpose is to keep the minds of our people *alert*, and to enable them to realize all their potentialities. Beyond this island"—his gesture indicated, and rejected, the rest of the globe—"I fear that the human race has lost its *initiative*. It has peace, it has plenty—but it has no *horizons*."

"Yet here, of course . . . ?" interjected the Overlord blandly.

Professor Chance, who lacked a sense of humor and

was vaguely aware of the fact, glanced suspiciously at his visitor.

"Here," he continued, "we do not suffer from the ancient obsession that leisure is wicked. But we do not consider that it is enough to be passive receptors of entertainment.

"Everybody on this island has one ambition, which may be summed up very simply. It is to do *something,* however small it may be, better than anyone else. Of course, it's an ideal we don't all achieve. But in this modern world the great thing is to *have* an ideal. Achieving it is considerably less important."

The Inspector did not seem inclined to comment. He had discarded his protective clothing, but still wore dark glasses even in the subdued light of the Common Room. The Dean wondered if they were physiologically necessary, or whether they were merely camouflage. Certainly they made quite impossible the already difficult task of reading the Overlord's thoughts. He did not, however, seem to object to the somewhat challenging statements that had been thrown at him, or the criticisms of his race's policy with regard to Earth which they implied.

The Dean was about to press the attack when Professor Sperling, head of the Science Department, decided to make it a three-cornered fight.

"As you doubtless know, Sir, one of the great problems of our culture has been the dichotomy between art and science. I'd very much like to know your views on the matter. Do you subscribe to the view that all artists are abnormal? That their work—or at any rate the impulse behind it—is the result of some deep-seated psychological dissatisfaction?"

Professor Chance cleared his throat purposefully, but the Inspector forestalled him.

"I've been told that all men are artists to a certain extent, so that everyone is capable of creating something, if only on a rudimentary level. At your schools yesterday, for example, I noticed the emphasis placed on self-expression in drawing, painting, and modeling. The impulse seemed quite universal, even among those clearly destined to be specialists in science. So if all artists are abnormal, and all men are artists, we have an interesting syllogism. . . ."

Everyone waited for him to complete it. But when it suited their purpose, the Overlords could be impeccably tactful.

The Inspector came through the symphony concert with flying colors, which was a good deal more than could be said for many human members of the audience. The only concession to popular taste had been Stravinsky's "Symphony of Psalms": the rest of the program was aggressively modernistic. Whatever one's views on its merits, the performance was superb, for the colony's boast that it possessed some of the finest musicians in the world was no idle one. There had been much wrangling among the various rival composers for the honor of being included in the program, though a few cynics wondered if it would be an honor at all. For all that anyone knew to the contrary, the Overlords might be tone deaf.

It was observed, however, that after the concert Thanthalteresco sought out the three composers who had been present and complimented them all on what he called their "great ingenuity." This caused them to retire with pleased but vaguely baffled expressions.

It was not until the third day that George Greggson had a chance of meeting the Inspector. The theater had arranged a kind of mixed grill rather than a single dish— two one-act plays, a sketch by a world-famous impersonator, and a ballet sequence. Once again all these items were superbly executed and one critic's prediction —"Now at least we'll discover if the Overlords can yawn"—was falsified. Indeed, the Inspector laughed several times, and in the correct places.

And yet—no one could be sure. He might himself be putting on a superb act, following the performance by logic alone and with his own strange emotions completely untouched, as an anthropologist might take part in some primitive rite. The fact that he uttered the appropriate sounds, and made the expected responses, really proved nothing at all.

Though George had been determined to have a talk with the Inspector, he failed utterly. After the performance they exchanged a few words of introduction, then the visitor was swept away. It was completely impossible to isolate him from his entourage, and George went home in a state of extreme frustration. He was by no means certain what he wished to say, even if he had had the chance, but somehow, he felt sure, he could have turned the conversation round to Jeff. And now the opportunity had gone.

His bad temper lasted two days. The Inspector's flyer had departed, amid many protestations of mutual regard, before the sequel emerged. No one had thought of questioning Jeff, and the boy must have been thinking it over for a long time before he approached George.

"Daddy," he said, just prior to bedtime. "You know the Overlord who came to see us?"

"Yes," replied George grimly.

"Well, he came to our school, and I heard him talk to some of the teachers. I didn't really understand what he said—but I think I recognized his voice. That's who told me to run when the big wave came."

"You are quite sure?"

Jeff hesitated for a moment.

"Not *quite*—but if it wasn't him, it was another Overlord. I wondered if I ought to thank him. But he's gone now, hasn't he?"

"Yes," said George, "I'm afraid he has. Still, perhaps we'll have another chance. Now go to bed like a good boy and don't worry about it any more."

When Jeff was safely out of the way, and Jenny had been attended to, Jean came back and sat on the rug beside George's chair, leaning against his legs. It was a habit that struck him as annoyingly sentimental, but not worth creating a fuss about. He merely made his knees as knobbly as possible.

"What do you think about it now?" asked Jean in a tired, flat voice. "Do you believe it really happened?"

"It happened," George replied, "but perhaps we're foolish to worry. After all, most parents would be grateful—and of course, I *am* grateful. The explanation may be perfectly simple. We know that the Overlords have got interested in the colony, so they've undoubtedly been observing it with their instruments—despite that promise they made. Suppose one was just prowling round with that viewing gadget of theirs, and saw the wave coming. It would be natural enough to warn anyone who was in danger."

"But he knew Jeff's name, don't forget that. No, we're being watched. There's something peculiar about us, something that attracts their attention. I've felt it ever since Rupert's party. It's funny how that changed both our lives."

George looked down at her with sympathy, but nothing more. It was strange how much one could alter in so short a time. He was fond of her: she had borne his children and was part of his life. But of the love which a not clearly remembered person named George Greggson had once known towards a fading dream called Jean Morrel, how much remained? His love was divided now between Jeff and Jennifer on the one hand—and Carolle on the other. He did not believe that Jean knew about Carolle, and he intended to tell her before anyone else did. But somehow he had never got round to it.

"Very well—Jeff is being watched—protected, in fact. Don't you think that should make us proud? Perhaps the Overlords have planned a great future for him. I wonder what it can be?"

He was talking to reassure Jean, he knew. He was not greatly disturbed himself, only intrigued and baffled. And quite suddenly another thought struck him, something that should have occurred to him before. His eyes turned automatically towards the nursery.

"I wonder if it's only Jeff they're after," he said.

In due course the Inspector presented his report. The Islanders would have given much to see it. All the statistics and records went into the insatiable memories of the great computers which were some, but not all, of the unseen powers behind Karellen. Even before these impersonal electric minds had arrived at their conclusions, however, the Inspector had given his own recommendations. Expressed in the thoughts and language of the human race, they would have run as follows:

"We need take no action regarding the colony. It is an interesting experiment, but cannot in any way affect the future. Its artistic endeavors are no concern of ours, and there is no evidence that any scientific research is progressing along dangerous channels.

"As planned, I was able to see the school records of subject Zero, without arousing curiosity. The relevant statistics are attached, and it will be seen that there are still no signs of any unusual development. Yet, as we know, breakthrough seldom gives much prior warning.

"I also met the subject's father, and gathered the impression that he wished to speak to me. Fortunately I was able to avoid this. There is no doubt that he suspects something, though of course he can never guess the truth nor affect the outcome in any way.

"I grow more and more sorry for these people."

George Greggson would have agreed with the Inspector's verdict that there was nothing unusual about Jeff. There was just that one baffling incident, as startling as a single clap of thunder on a long, calm day. And after that—nothing.

Jeff had all the energy and inquisitiveness of any other seven year old. He was intelligent—when he bothered to be—but was in no danger of becoming a genius. Sometimes, Jean thought a little wearily, he filled to perfection the classic recipe for a small boy: "a noise surrounded by dirt." Not that it was very easy to be certain about the dirt, which had to accumulate for a considerable time before it showed against Jeff's normal sunburn.

By turns he could be affectionate or morose, reserved or ebullient. He showed no preference for one parent rather than the other, and the arrival of his little sister had not produced any signs of jealousy. His medical card was spotless; he had never had a day's illness in his life.

But in these times, and in such a climate, there was nothing unusual about this.

Unlike some boys, Jeff did not grow quickly bored by his father's company and desert him whenever possible for associates of his own age. It was obvious that he shared George's artistic talents, and almost as soon as he was able to walk had become a regular backstage visitor to the colony's theater. Indeed, the theater had adopted him as an unofficial mascot and he was now highly skilled at presenting bouquets to visiting celebritics of stage and screen.

Yes, Jeff was a perfectly ordinary boy. So George reassured himself as they went for walks or rides together over the Island's rather restricted terrain. They would talk as sons and fathers had done since the beginning of time—except that in this age there was so much more to talk about. Though Jeff never left the Island, he could see all that he wished of the surrounding world through the ubiquitous cycs of the television screen. He felt, like all the colonists, a slight disdain for the rest of mankind. They were the clite, the vanguard of progress. They would take mankind to the heights that the Overlords had reached—and perhaps beyond. Not tomorrow, certainly, but one day. . . .

They never guessed that that day would be all too soon.

18

THE DREAMS BEGAN six weeks later.

In the darkness of the subtropical night, George Greggson swam slowly upwards towards consciousness. He did not know what had awakened him, and for a moment he lay in a puzzled stupor. Then he realized that he was alone. Jean had got up and gone silently into the nursery. She was talking quietly to Jeff, too quietly for him to hear what she was saying.

George heaved himself out of bed and went to join her. The Poppet had made such nocturnal excursions common enough, but then there had been no question of his remaining asleep through the uproar. This was something quite different and he wondered what had disturbed Jean.

The only light in the nursery came from the fluoropaint patterns on the walls. By their dim glow, George could see Jean sitting beside Jeff's bed. She turned as he came in, and whispered, "Don't disturb the Poppet."

"What's the matter?"

"I knew that Jeff wanted me, and that woke me up."

The very matter-of-fact simplicity of that statement gave George a feeling of sick apprehension. *I knew that Jeff wanted me.* How did you know? he wondered. But all he asked was:

"Has he been having nightmares?"

"I'm not sure," said Jean, "he seems all right now. But he was frightened when I came in."

"I *wasn't* frightened, Mummy," came a small, indignant voice. "But it was such a strange place."

"What was?" asked George. "Tell me all about it."

"There were mountains," said Jeff dreamily. "They were ever so high and there was no snow on them, like on all the mountains I've ever seen. Some of them were burning."

"You mean—volcanoes?"

"Not really. They were burning all over, with funny blue flames. And while I was watching, the sun came up."

"Go on—why have you stopped?"

Jeff turned puzzled eyes towards his father.

"That's the other thing I don't understand, Daddy. It came up so quickly, and it was much too big. And—it wasn't the right color. It was such a pretty blue."

There was a long, heart-freezing silence. Then George said quietly, "Is that all?"

"Yes. I began to feel kind of lonely, and that's when Mummy came and woke me up."

George tousled his son's untidy hair with one hand, while tightening his dressing gown around him with the other. He felt suddenly very cold and very small. But there was no hint of this in his voice when he spoke to Jeff.

"It's just a silly dream: you've eaten too much for supper. Forget all about it and go back to sleep, there's a good boy."

"I will, Daddy," Jeff replied. He paused for a moment, then added thoughtfully, "I think I'll try and go there again."

"A blue sun?" said Karellen, not many hours later. "That must have made identification fairly easy."

"Yes," Rashaverak answered. "It is undoubtedly Alphanidon Two. The Sulphur Mountains confirm the fact. And it's interesting to notice the distortion of the time scale. The planet rotates fairly slowly, so he must have observed many hours in a few minutes."

"That's all you can discover?"

"Yes, without questioning the child directly."

"We dare not do that. Events must take their natural course without our interference. When his parents approach us—then, perhaps, we can question him."

"They may never come to us. And when they do, it may be too late."

"That, I am afraid, cannot be helped. We should never forget this fact—that in these matters our curiosity is of no importance. It is no more important, even, than the happiness of mankind."

His hand reached out to break the connection.

"Continue the surveillance, of course, and report all results to me. But do not interfere in any way."

Yet when he was awake, Jeff still seemed just the same. That at least, thought George, was something for which they could be thankful. But the dread was growing in his heart.

To Jeff, it was only a game; it had not yet begun to frighten him. A dream was merely a dream, no matter how strange it might be. He was no longer lonely in the worlds that sleep opened up to him. Only on that first night had his mind called out to Jean across whatever unknown gulfs had sundered them. Now he went alone and fearless into the universe that was opening up before him.

In the mornings they would question him, and he would tell what he could remember. Sometimes his words stumbled and failed as he tried to describe scenes which were clearly not only beyond all his experience, but beyond the imagination of man. They would prompt him with new words, show him pictures and colors to refresh his memory, then build up what pattern they could from his replies. Often they could make nothing of the result, though it seemed that in Jeff's own mind his dream worlds were perfectly plain and sharp. He was simply unable to communicate them to his parents. Yet some were clear enough. . . .

Space—no planet, no surrounding landscape, no world underfoot. Only the stars in the velvet night, and hanging against them a great red sun that was beating like a heart. Huge and tenuous at one moment, it would slowly shrink, brightening at the same time as if new fuel was being fed to its internal fires. It would climb the spectrum and hover at the edge of yellow, and then the cycle would reverse itself, the star would expand and cool, becoming once more a ragged, flame-red cloud. . . .

("Typical pulsating variable," said Rashaverak eagerly. "Seen, too, under tremendous time-acceleration. I can't identify it precisely, but the nearest star that fits the description is Rhamsandron 9. Or it may be Pharanidon 12."

"Whichever it is," replied Karellen, "he's getting further away from home."

"Much further," said Rashaverak. . . .)

It might have been Earth. A white sun hung in a blue sky flecked with clouds, which were racing before a storm. A hill sloped gently down to an ocean torn into spray by the ravening wind. Yet nothing moved: the scene was frozen as if glimpsed in a flash of lightning. And far, far away on the horizon was something that was not of Earth—a line of misty columns, tapering slightly as they soared out of the sea and lost themselves among the clouds. They were spaced with perfect precision along the rim of the planet—too huge to be artificial, yet too regular to be natural.

("Sideneus 4 and the Pillars of the Dawn," said Rashaverak, and there was awe in his voice. "He has reached the center of the Universe."

"And he has barely begun his journey," answered Karellen.)

The planet was absolutely flat. Its enormous gravity had long ago crushed into one uniform level the mountains of its fiery youth—mountains whose mightiest peaks had never exceeded a few meters in height. Yet there was life here, for the surface was covered with a myriad geometrical patterns that crawled and moved and changed their color. It was a world of two dimensions, inhabited by beings who could be no more than a fraction of a centimeter in thickness.

And in its sky was such a sun as no opium eater could have imagined in his wildest dreams. Too hot to be white, it was a searing ghost at the frontiers of the ultraviolet, burning its planets with radiations which would be instantly lethal to all earthly forms of life. For millions of kilometers around extended great veils of gas and dust, fluorescing in countless colors as the blasts of ultraviolet tore through them. It was a star against which Earth's pale sun would have been as feeble as a glowworm at noon.

("Hexanerax 2, and nowhere else in the known universe," said Rashaverak. "Only a handful of our ships have ever reached it—and they have never risked any landings, for who would have thought that life could exist on such planets?"

"It seems," said Karellen, "that you scientists have not

been as thorough as you had believed. If those—*patterns* —are intelligent, the problem of communication will be interesting. I wonder if they have any knowledge of the third dimension?")

It was a world that could never know the meaning of night and day, of years or seasons. Six colored suns shared its sky, so that there came only a change of light, never darkness. Through the clash and tug of conflicting gravitational fields, the planet traveled along the loops and curves of its inconceivably complex orbit, never retracing the same path. Every moment was unique: the configuration which the six suns now held in the heavens would not repeat itself this side of eternity.

And even here there was life. Though the planet might be scorched by the central fires in one age, and frozen in the outer reaches in another, it was yet the home of intelligence. The great, many-faceted crystals stood grouped in intricate geometrical patterns, motionless in the eras of cold, growing slowly along the veins of mineral when the world was warm again. No matter if it took a thousand years for them to complete a thought. The universe was still young, and time stretched endlessly before them. . . .

("I have searched all our records," said Rashaverak. "We have no knowledge of such a world, or such a combination of suns. If it existed inside our universe, the astronomers would have detected it, even if it lay beyond the range of our ships."

"Then he has left the galaxy."

"Yes. Surely it cannot be much longer now."

"Who knows? He is only dreaming. When he awakes, he is still the same. It is merely the first phase. We will know soon enough when the change begins.")

"We have met before, Mr. Greggson," said the Overlord gravely. "My name is Rashaverak. No doubt you remember."

"Yes," said George. "That party of Rupert Boyce's. I am not likely to forget. And I thought we should meet again."

"Tell me—why have you asked for this interview?"

"I think you already know."

"Perhaps: but it will help us both if you tell me in your own words. It may surprise you a good deal, but I also am trying to understand, and in some ways my ignorance is as great as yours."

George stared at the Overlord in astonishment. This was a thought that had never occurred to him. He had subconsciously assumed that the Overlords possessed all knowledge and all power—that they understood, and were probably responsible for, the things that had been happening to Jeff.

"I gather," George continued, "that you have seen the reports I gave to the island psychologist, so you know about the dreams."

"Yes: we know about them."

"I never believed that they were simply the imaginings of a child. They were so incredible that—I know this sounds ridiculous—they *had* to be based on some reality."

He looked anxiously at Rashaverak, not knowing whether to hope for confirmation or denial. The Overlord said nothing, but merely regarded him with his great, calm eyes. They were sitting almost face to face, for the room —which had obviously been designed for such interviews—was on two levels, the Overlord's massive chair being a good meter lower than George's. It was a friendly gesture, reassuring to the men who asked for these meetings and who were seldom in an easy frame of mind.

"We were worried, but not really alarmed at first. Jeff seemed perfectly normal when he woke up, and his dreams didn't appear to bother him. And then one night"—he hesitated and glanced defensively at the Overlord. "I've never believed in the supernatural: I'm no scientist, but I think there's a rational explanation for everything."

"There is," said Rashaverak. "I know what you saw: I was watching."

"I always suspected it. But Karellen had promised that you'd never spy on us with your instruments. Why have you broken that promise?"

"I have not broken it. The Supervisor said that the human race would no longer be under surveillance. That is a promise we have kept. I was watching your children, not you."

It was several seconds before George understood the implications of Rashaverak's words. Then the color drained slowly from his face.

"You mean? . . ." he gasped. His voice trailed away and he had to begin again. "Then what in God's name *are* my children?"

"That," said Rashaverak solemnly, "is what we are trying to discover."

Jennifer Anne Greggson, lately known as the Poppet, lay on her back with her eyes tightly closed. She had not opened them for a long time; she would never open them again, for sight was now as superfluous to her as to the many-sensed creatures of the lightless ocean depths. She was aware of the world that surrounded her: indeed, she was aware of much more than that.

One reflex remained from her brief babyhood, by some unaccountable trick of development. The rattle which had once delighted her sounded incessantly now, beating a complex, everchanging rhythm in her cot. It was that strange syncopation which had roused Jean from her sleep and sent her flying into the nursery. But it was not the sound alone that had started her screaming for George.

It was the sight of that commonplace, brightly colored rattle beating steadily in airy isolation half a meter away from any support, while Jennifer Anne, her chubby fingers clasped tightly together, lay with a smile of calm contentment on her face.

She had started later, but she was progressing swiftly. Soon she would pass her brother, for she had so much less to unlearn.

"You were wise," said Rashaverak, "not to touch her toy. I do not believe you could have moved it. But if you had succeeded, she might have been annoyed. And then, I do not know what would have happened."

"Do you mean," said George dully, "that you can do nothing?"

"I will not deceive you. We can study and observe, as we are doing already. But we cannot interfere, because we cannot understand."

"Then what are we to do? And why has this thing happened to *us?*"

"It had to happen to someone. There is nothing exceptional about you, any more than there is about the first neutron that starts the chain reaction in an atomic bomb. It simply happens to be the first. Any other neutron would have served—just as Jeffrey might have been any boy in the world. We call it Total Breakthrough. There is no need for any secrecy now, and I am very glad. We have been waiting for this to happen, ever since we came to Earth. There was no way to tell when and where it would start—until, by pure chance, we met at Rupert Boyce's party. Then I knew that, almost certainly, your wife's children would be the first."

"But—we weren't married then. We hadn't even—"

"Yes, I know. But Miss Morrel's mind was the channel that, if only for a moment, let through knowledge which no one alive at that time could possess. It could only come from another mind, intimately linked to hers. The fact that it was a mind not yet born was of no consequence, for Time is very much stranger than you think."

"I begin to understand. Jeff knows these things—he can see other worlds and can tell where you come from. And somehow Jean caught his thoughts, even before he was born."

"There is far more to it than that—but I do not imagine you will ever get much closer to the truth. All through history there have been people with inexplicable powers which seemed to transcend space and time. They never understood them: almost without exception, their attempted explanations were rubbish. I should know—I have read enough of them!

"But there is one analogy which is—well, suggestive and helpful. It occurs over and over again in your literature. Imagine that every man's mind is an island, surrounded by ocean. Each seems isolated, yet in reality all are linked by the bedrock from which they spring. If the ocean were to vanish, that would be the end of the islands. They would all be part of one continent, but their individuality would have gone.

"Telepathy, as you have called it, is something like this. In suitable circumstances minds can merge and share each other's contents, and carry back memories of the experience when they are isolated once more. In its highest form, this power is not subject to the usual limitations of time and space. That is why Jean could tap the knowledge of her unborn son."

There was a long silence while George wrestled with these astounding thoughts. The pattern was beginning to take shape. It was an unbelievable pattern, but it had its own inherent logic. And it explained—if the word could be used for anything so incomprehensible—all that had happened since that evening at Rupert Boyce's home. It also accounted, he realized now, for Jean's own curiosity about the supernormal.

"What has started this thing?" asked George. "And where is it going to lead?"

"That is something we cannot answer. But there are many races in the universe, and some of them discovered these powers long before your species—or mine—appeared on the scene. They have been waiting for you to join them, and now the time has come."

"Then where do *you* come into the picture?"

"Probably, like most men, you have always regarded us as your masters. That is not true. We have never been more than guardians, doing a duty imposed upon us from —above. That duty is hard to define: perhaps you can best think of us as midwives attending a difficult birth. We are helping to bring something new and wonderful into being."

Rashaverak hesitated: for a moment it almost seemed as if he was at a loss for words.

"Yes, we are the midwives. But we ourselves are barren."

In that instant, George knew he was in the presence of a tragedy transcending his own. It was incredible—and yet somehow just. Despite all their powers and their brilliance, the Overlords were trapped in some evolutionary cul-de-sac. Here was a great and noble race, in almost every way superior to mankind; yet it had no future, and it was aware of it. In the face of this, George's own problems seemed suddenly trivial.

"Now I know," he said, "why you have been watching Jeffrey. He was the guinea pig in this experiment."

"Exactly—though the experiment was beyond our control. We did not start it—we were merely trying to observe. We did not interfere except when we had to."

Yes, thought George—the tidal wave. It would never do to let a valuable specimen be destroyed. Then he felt ashamed of himself: such bitterness was unworthy.

"I've only one more question," he said. "What shall we do about our children?"

"Enjoy them while you may," answered Rashaverak gently. "They will not be yours for long."

It was advice that might have been given to any parent in any age: but now it contained a threat and a terror it had never held before.

19

THERE CAME THE TIME when the world of Jeffrey's dreams was no longer sharply divided from his everyday existence. He no longer went to school, and for Jean and George also the routine of life was completely broken, as it was soon to break down throughout the world.

They avoided all their friends, as if already conscious that soon no one would have sympathy to spare for them.

Sometimes, in the quietness of the night when there were few people about, they would go for long walks together. They were closer now than they had been since the first days of their marriage, united again in the face of the still unknown tragedy that soon would overwhelm them.

At first it had given them a feeling of guilt to leave the sleeping children alone in the house, but now they realized that Jeff and Jenny could look after themselves in ways beyond the knowledge of their parents. And, of course, the Overlords would be watching too. That thought was reassuring: they felt that they were not alone with their problem, but that wise and sympathetic eyes shared their vigil.

Jennifer slept: there was no other word to describe the state she had entered. To all outward appearances, she was still a baby, but round her now was a sense of latent power so terrifying that Jean could no longer bear to enter the nursery.

There was no need to do so. The entity that had been Jennifer Anne Greggson was not yet fully developed, but even in its sleeping chrysalis state it already had enough control of its evironment to take care of all its needs. Jean had only once attempted to feed it, without success. It chose to take nourishment in its own time, and in its own manner.

For food vanished from the freezer in a slow, steady stream: yet Jennifer Anne never moved from her cot.

The rattling had ceased, and the discarded toy lay on the nursery floor where no one dared to touch it, lest Jennifer Anne might need it again. Sometimes she caused the furniture to stir itself into peculiar patterns, and it seemed to George that the fluoropaint on the wall was glowing more brilliantly than it had ever done before.

She gave no trouble; she was beyond their assistance, and beyond their love. It could not last much longer, and in the time that was left they clung desperately to Jeff.

He was changing too, but he still knew them. The boy whose growth they had watched from the formless mists of babyhood was losing his personality, dissolving hour by hour before their very eyes. Yet sometimes he still spoke to them as he had always done, and talked of his toys and friends as if unconscious of what lay ahead. But much of the time he did not see them, or show any awareness of their presence. He no longer slept, as they were forced to do, despite their overwhelming need to waste as few as possible of these last remaining hours.

Unlike Jenny, he seemed to possess no abnormal powers over physical objects—perhaps because, being already partly grown, he had less need for them. His strangeness was entirely in his mental life, of which the dreams were now only a small part. He would stay quite still for hours on end, his eyes tightly closed, as if listening to sounds which no one else could hear. Into his mind was flooding knowledge—from somewhere or somewhen—which soon would overwhelm and destroy the half-formed creature who had been Jeffrey Angus Greggson.

And Fey would sit watching, looking up at him with tragic, puzzled eyes, wondering where her master had gone and when he would return to her.

Jeff and Jenny had been the first in all the world, but soon they were no longer alone. Like an epidemic spreading swiftly from land to land, the metamorphosis infected the entire human race. It touched practically no one above the age of ten, and practically no one below that age escaped.

It was the end of civilization, the end of all that men had striven for since the beginning of time. In the space of a few days, humanity had lost its future, for the heart of any race is destroyed, and its will to survive is utterly broken, when its children are taken from it.

There was no panic, as there would have been a century before. The world was numbed, the great cities stilled and silent. Only the vital industries continued to function. It was as though the planet was in mourning, lamenting all that now could never be.

And then, as he had done once before in a now forgotten age, Karellen spoke for the last time to mankind.

20

"My work here is nearly ended," said Karellen's voice from a million radios. "At last, after a hundred years, I can tell you what it was.

"There are many things we have had to hide from you, as we hid ourselves for half our stay on Earth. Some of you, I know, thought that concealment unnecessary. You are accustomed to our presence: you can no longer imagine how your ancestors would have reacted to us. But at least you can understand the purpose of our concealment, and know that we had a reason for what we did.

"The supreme secret we kept from you was our purpose in coming to earth—that purpose about which you have speculated so endlessly. We could not tell you until now, for the secret was not ours to reveal.

"A century ago we came to your world and saved you from self-destruction. I do not believe that anyone would deny that fact—but what that self-destruction was, you never guessed.

"Because we banned nuclear weapons and all the other deadly toys you were accumulating in your armories, the danger of physical annihilation was removed. You thought that was the only danger. We wanted you to believe that, but it was never true. The greatest danger that confronted you was of a different character altogether—and it did not concern your race alone.

"Many worlds have come to the crossroads of nuclear power, have avoided disaster, have gone on to build peaceful and happy civilizations—and have then been utterly destroyed by forces of which they knew nothing. In the twentieth century, you first began to tamper seriously with those forces. That was why it became necessary to act.

"All through that century, the human race was drawing slowly nearer to the abyss—never even suspecting its existence. Across that abyss, there is only one bridge. Few races, unaided, have ever found it. Some have turned back while there was still time, avoiding both the danger and the achievement. Their worlds have become Elysian islands of effortless content, playing no further part in the story of the universe. That would never have been your fate—or your fortune. Your race was too vital for that. It would have plunged into ruin and taken others with it, for you would never have found the bridge.

"I am afraid that almost all I have to say now must be by means of such analogies. You have no words, no conceptions, for many of the things I wish to tell you—and our own knowledge of them is also sadly imperfect.

"To understand, you must go back into the past and recover much that your ancestors would have found familiar, but which you have forgotten—which, in fact, we deliberately helped you to forget. For all our sojourn here has been based on a vast deception, a concealment of truths which you were not ready to face.

"In the centuries before our coming, your scientists uncovered the secrets of the physical world and led you from the energy of steam to the energy of the atom. You had put superstition behind you: Science was the only real religion of mankind. It was the gift of the western minority to the remainder of mankind, and it had destroyed all other faiths. Those that still existed when we came were already dying. Science, it was felt, could explain everything: there were no forces which did not come within its scope, no events for which it could not ultimately account. The origin of the universe might be forever unknown, but all that had happened since obeyed the laws of physics.

"Yet your mystics, though they were lost in their own delusions, had seen part of the truth. There are powers of the mind, and powers beyond the mind, which your science could never have brought within its framework without shattering it entirely. All down the ages there have been countless reports of strange phenomena—poltergeists, telepathy, precognition—which you had named but never explained. At first science ignored them, even denied their existence, despite the testimony of five thousand years. But they exist, and, if it is to be complete, any theory of the universe must account for them.

"During the first half of the twentieth century, a few of your scientists began to investigate these matters. They did not know it, but they were tampering with the lock of Pandora's box. The forces they might have unleashed transcended any perils that the atom could have brought. For the physicists could only have ruined the earth: the paraphysicists could have spread havoc to the stars.

"That could not be allowed. I cannot explain the full nature of the threat you represented. It would not have been a threat to us, and therefore we do not comprehend it. Let us say that you might have become a telepathic cancer, a malignant mentality which in its inevitable dissolution would have poisoned other and greater minds.

"And so we came—we were *sent*—to Earth. We interrupted your development on every cultural level, but in particular we checked all serious work on paranormal phenomena. I am well aware of the fact that we have also inhibited, by the contrast between our civilizations, all other forms of creative achievement as well. But that was a secondary effect, and it is of no importance.

"Now I must tell you something which you may find very surprising, perhaps almost incredible. All these potentialities, all these latent powers—we do not possess them, nor do we understand them. Our intellects are far more powerful than yours, but there is something in your minds that has always eluded us. Ever since we came to Earth we have been studying you; we have learned a great deal, and will learn more, yet I doubt if we shall discover all the truth.

"Our races have much in common—that is why we were chosen for this task. But in other respects, we represent the ends of two different evolutions. Our minds have reached the end of their development. So, in their present form, have yours. Yet you can make the jump to the next stage, and therein lies the difference between us. Our potentialities are exhausted, but yours are still untapped. They are linked, in ways we do not understand, with the powers I have mentioned—the powers that are now awakening on your world.

"We held the clock back, we made you mark time while those powers developed, until they could come flooding out into the channels that were being prepared for them. What we did to improve your planet, to raise your standards of living, to bring justice and peace—those things we should have done in any event, once we were forced to intervene in your affairs. But all that vast transformation diverted you from the truth, and therefore helped to serve our purpose.

"We are your guardians—no more. Often you must have wondered what position my race held in the hierarchy of the universe. As we are above you, so there is something above us, using us for its own purposes. We have never discovered what it is, though we have been its tool for ages and dare not disobey it. Again and again we have received our orders, have gone to some world in the early flower of its civilization, and have guided it along the road that we can never follow—the road that you are traveling now.

"Again and again we had studied the process we have been sent to foster, hoping that we might learn to escape from our own limitations. But we have glimpsed only the vague outlines of the truth. You called us the Overlords, not knowing the irony of that title. Let us say that above us is the *Overmind*, using us as the potter uses his wheel.

"And your race is the clay that is being shaped on that wheel.

"We believe—it is only a theory—that the Overmind is trying to grow, to extend its powers and its awareness of the universe. By now it must be the sum of many races, and long ago it left the tyranny of matter behind. It is conscious of intelligence, everywhere. When it knew that you were almost ready, it sent us here to do its bidding, to prepare you for the transformation that is now at hand.

"All the earlier changes your race has known took countless ages. But this is a transformation of the mind, not of the body. By the standards of evolution, it will be cataclysmic—instantaneous. It has already begun. You must face the fact that yours is the last generation of *Homo sapiens*.

"As to the nature of that change, we can tell you very little. We do not know how it is produced—what trigger impulse the Overmind employs when it judges that the time is ripe. All we have discovered is that it starts with a single individual—always a child—and then spreads explosively, like the formation of crystals round the first nucleus in a saturated solution. Adults will not be affected, for their minds are already set in an unalterable mould.

"In a few years, it will all be over, and the human race will have divided in twain. There is no way back, and no future for the world you know. All the hopes and dreams of your race are ended now. You have given birth to your successors, and it is your tragedy that you will never understand them—will never even be able to communicate with their minds. Indeed, they will not possess minds as you know them. They will be a single entity, as you yourselves are the sums of your myriad cells. You will not think them human, and you will be right.

"I have told you these things so that you will know what faces you. In a few hours, the crisis will be upon us. My task and my duty is to protect those I have been sent here to guard. Despite their wakening powers, they could be destroyed by the multitudes around them— yes, even by their parents, when they realized the truth. I must take them away and isolate them, for their protection, and for yours. Tomorrow my ships will begin the evacuation. I shall not blame you if you try to interfere, but it will be useless. Greater powers than mine are wakening now; I am only one of their instruments.

"And then—what am I to do with you, the survivors, when your purpose has been fulfilled? It would be simplest, and perhaps most merciful, to destroy you—as you yourselves would destroy a mortally wounded pet you loved. But this I cannot do. Your future will be your own to choose in the years that are left to you. It is my hope that humanity will go to its rest in peace, knowing that it has not lived in vain.

"For what you will have brought into the world may be utterly alien, it may share none of your desires or hopes, it may look upon your greatest achievements as childish toys—yet it is something wonderful, and you will have created it.

"When our race is forgotten, part of yours will still exist. Do not, therefore, condemn us for what we were compelled to do. And remember this—we shall always envy you."

21

JEAN HAD WEPT BEFORE, but she was not weeping now. The island lay golden in the heartless, unfeeling sunlight as the ship came slowly into sight above the twin peaks of Sparta. On that rocky island, not long ago, her son had escaped death by a miracle she now understood all too well. Sometimes she wondered if it might not have been better had the Overlords stood aside and left him to his fate. Death was something she could face as she had faced it before: it was in the natural order of things. But this was stranger than death—and more final. Until this day, men had died, yet the race had continued.

There was no sound or movement from the children. They stood in scattered groups along the sand, showing no more interest in one another than in the homes they were leaving forever. Many carried babies who were too small to walk—or who did not wish to assert the powers that made walking unnecessary. For surely, thought George, if they could move inanimate matter, they could move their own bodies. Why, indeed, were the Overlord ships collecting them at all?

It was of no importance. They were leaving, and this was the way they chose to go. And then George realized what it was that had been teasing his memory. Somewhere long ago, he had seen a century-old newsreel of such an exodus. It must have been at the beginning of the First World War—or the Second. There had been long lines of trains, crowded with children, pulling slowly out of the threatened cities, leaving behind the parents that so many of them would never see again. Few were crying: some were puzzled, clutching nervously at their small belongings, but most seemed to be looking forward with eagerness to some great adventure.

And yet—the analogy was false. History never repeated itself. These who were leaving now were no longer children, whatever they might be. And this time, there would be no reunion.

The ship had grounded along the water's edge, sinking deeply into the soft sand. In perfect unison, the line of great curving panels slid upwards and the gangways extended themselves towards the beach like metal tongues. The scattered, unutterably lonely figures began to converge, to gather into a crowd that moved precisely as a human crowd might do.

Lonely? Why had he thought that, wondered George. For *that* was the one thing they could never be again. Only individuals can be lonely—only human beings. When the barriers were down at last, loneliness would vanish as personality faded. The countless raindrops would have merged into the ocean.

He felt Jean's hand increase its pressure on his in a sudden spasm of emotion.

"Look," she whispered. "I can see Jeff. By that second door."

It was a long way away, and very hard to be certain.

There was a mist before his eyes which made it hard to see. But it was Jeff—he was sure of that: George could recognize his son now, as he stood with one foot already on the metal gangway.

And Jeff turned and looked back. His face was only a white blur: at this distance, there was no way of telling if it bore any hint of recognition, any remembrance for all that he was leaving behind. Nor would George ever know if Jeff had turned towards them by pure chance—or if he knew, in those last moments while he was still their son, that they stood watching him as he passed into the land that they could never enter.

The great doors began to close. And in that moment Fey lifted up her muzzle and gave a low, desolate moan. She turned her beautiful, limpid eyes towards George, and he knew that she had lost her master. He had no rival now.

For those who were left there were many roads but only one destination. There were some who said: "The world is still beautiful; one day we must leave it, but why should we hasten our departure?"

But others, who had set more store by the future than the present, and who had lost all that made life worth living, did not wish to stay. They took their leave alone, or with their friends, according to their nature.

It was thus with Athens. The island had been born in fire; in fire it chose to die. Those who wished to leave did so, but most remained, to meet the end among the broken fragments of their dreams.

No one was supposed to know when the time would be. Yet Jean awoke in the stillness of the night, and lay for a moment staring at the ghostly glimmer from the ceiling. Then she reached out to grasp George's hand. He was a sound sleeper, but this time he woke at once. They did not speak, for the words that were wanted did not exist.

Jean was no longer frightened, or even sad. She had come through to the calm waters and was beyond emotion now. But there was one thing still to be done, and she knew that there was barely time to do it.

Still without a word, George followed her through the silent house. They went across the patch of moonlight that had entered through the studio roof, moving as quietly as the shadows it cast, until they came to the deserted nursery.

Nothing had been changed. The fluoro-patterns that George had painted so carefully still glowed on the walls. And the rattle that had once belonged to Jennifer Anne still lay where she had dropped it, when her mind turned into the unknowable remoteness it inhabited now.

She has left her toys behind, thought George, but ours go hence with us. He thought of the royal children of the Pharaohs, whose dolls and beads had been buried with them five thousand years ago. So it would be again. No one else, he told himself, will ever love our treasures: we will take them with us, and will not part with them.

Slowly Jean turned towards him, and rested her head upon his shoulder. He clasped his arms about her waist, and the love he had once known came back to him, faint yet clear, like an echo from a distant range of hills. It was too late now to say all that was due to her, and the regrets he felt were less for his deceits than for his past indifference.

Then Jean said quietly: "Good-by, my darling," and tightened her arms about him. There was no time for George to answer, but even at that final moment he felt a brief astonishment as he wondered how she knew that the moment had arrived.

Far down in the rock, the segments of uranium began to rush together, seeking the union they could never achieve.

And the island rose to meet the dawn.

22

THE SHIP OF THE OVERLORDS came sliding in along its glowing meteor-trail through the heart of Carina. It had begun its mad deceleration among the outer planets, but even while passing Mars it had still possessed an appreciable fraction of the velocity of light. Slowly the immense fields surrounding the sun were absorbing its momentum, while for a million kilometers behind, the stray energies of the stardrive were painting the heavens with fire.

Jan Rodricks was coming home, six months older, to the world he had left eighty years before.

This time he was no longer a stowaway, hidden in a secret chamber. He stood behind the three pilots (why, he wondered, did they need so many?) watching the patterns come and go on the great screen that dominated the control room. The colors and shapes it showed were meaningless to him: he assumed that they were conveying information which in a vessel designed by men would have been displayed on banks of meters. But sometimes the screen showed the surrounding star fields, and soon, he hoped, it would be showing Earth.

He was glad to be home, despite the effort he had devoted to escaping from it. In these few months, he had grown up. He had seen so much, traveled so far, and now was weary for his own familiar world. He understood, now, why the Overlords had sealed Earth from the stars. Humanity still had very far to go before it could play any part in the civilization he had glimpsed.

It might be—though this he refused to accept—that mankind could never be more than an inferior species, preserved in an out-of-the-way zoo with the Overlords as keepers. Perhaps that was what Vindarten had meant when he gave Jan that ambiguous warning, just before his departure. "Much may have happened," the Overlord had said, "in the time that has passed on your planet. You may not know your world when you see it again."

Perhaps not, thought Jan: eighty years was a long time, and though he was young and adaptable, he might find it hard to understand all the changes that had come to pass. But of one thing he was certain—men would want to hear his story, and to know what he had glimpsed of the civilization of the Overlords.

They had treated him well, as he had assumed they would. Of the outward journey he had known nothing: when the injection had worn off and he had emerged, the ship was already entering the Overlord system. He had climbed out of his fantastic hiding place, and found to his relief that the oxygen set was not needed. The air was thick and heavy, but he could breathe without difficulty. He had found himself in the ship's enormous red-lit hold, among countless other packing cases and all the impedimenta one would expect on a liner of space or of sea. It had taken him almost an hour to find his way to the control room and to introduce himself to the crew.

Their lack of surprise had puzzled him: he knew that the Overlords showed few emotions, but he had expected *some* reaction. Instead, they simply continued with their work, watching the great screen and playing the countless keys on their control panels. It was then that he knew that they were landing, for from time to time the image of a planet—larger at each appearance—would flash upon the screen. Yet there was never the slightest sense of motion or acceleration—only a perfectly constant gravity which he judged to be about a fifth of Earth's. The immense forces that drove the ship must have been compensated with exquisite precision.

And then, in unison, the three Overlords had risen from their seats, and he knew that the voyage was over. They did not speak to their passenger or to each other, and when one of them beckoned to him to follow, Jan realized something that he should have thought of before. There might well be no one here, at this end of Karellen's enormously long supply line, who understood a word of English.

They watched him gravely as the great doors opened before his eager eyes. This was the supreme moment of his life: now he was to be the first human being ever to look upon a world lit by another sun. The ruby light of NGS 549672 came flooding into the ship, and there before him lay the planet of the Overlords.

What had he expected? He was not sure. Vast buildings, cities whose towers were lost among the clouds, machines beyond imagination—these would not have surprised him. Yet what he saw was an almost featureless plain, reaching out to an unnaturally close horizon, and broken only by three more of the Overlords' ships, a few kilometers away.

For a moment Jan felt a surge of disappointment. Then he shrugged his shoulders, realizing that, after all, one would expect to find a spaceport in some such remote and uninhabited region as this.

It was cold, though not uncomfortably so. The light from the great red sun low down on the horizon was quite ample for human eyes, but Jan wondered how long it would be before he yearned for greens and blues. Then he saw that enormous, wafer-thin crescent reaching up the sky like a great bow placed beside the sun. He stared at it for a long time before he realized that his journey was not yet altogether ended. *That* was the world of the Overlords. This must be its satellite, merely the base from which their vessels operated.

They had taken him across in a ship no larger than a terrestrial airliner. Feeling a pygmy, he had climbed up into one of the great seats to try and see something of the approaching planet through the observation windows.

The journey was so swift that he had time to make out few details on the expanding globe beneath. Even so near to home, it seemed, the Overlords used some version of the stardrive, for in a matter of minutes they were falling down through a deep, cloud-flecked atmosphere. When the doors opened, they stepped out into a vaulted chamber with a roof that must have swung swiftly shut behind them, for there was no sign of any entrance overhead.

It was two days before Jan left this building. He was an unexpected consignment, and they had nowhere to put him. To make matters worse, not one of the Overlords could understand English. Communication was practically impossible, and Jan realized bitterly that getting in touch with an alien race was not as easy as it was so often depicted in fiction. Sign language proved singularly unsuccessful, for it depended too much on a body of gestures, expressions and attitudes which the Overlords and mankind did not possess in common.

It would be more than frustrating, thought Jan, if the only Overlords who spoke his language were all back on Earth. He could only wait and hope for the best. Surely some scientist, some expert on alien races, would come and take charge of him! Or was he so unimportant that no one could be bothered?

There was no way he could get out of the building, because the great doors had no visible controls. When an Overlord walked up to them, they simply opened. Jan had tried the same trick, had waved objects high in the air to interrupt any controlling light-beam, had tried everything he could imagine—with no result at all. He realized that a man from the Stone Age, lost in a modern city or building, might be equally helpless. Once he had tried to walk out when one of the Overlords left, but had been gently shooed back. As he was very anxious not to annoy his hosts, he did not persist.

Vindarten arrived before Jan had begun to get desperate. The Overlord spoke very bad English, much too rapidly, but improved with amazing speed. In a few days they were able to talk together with little trouble on any subject that did not demand a specialized vocabulary.

Once Vindarten had taken charge of him, Jan had no more worries. He also had no opportunity of doing the things he wished, for almost all his time was spent meeting Overlord scientists anxious to carry out obscure tests with complicated instruments. Jan was very wary of

these machines, and after one session with some kind
of hypnotic device had a splitting headache for several
hours. He was perfectly willing to co-operate, but was
not sure if his investigators realized his limitations, both
mental and physical. It was certainly a long time before
he could convince them that he had to sleep at regular
intervals.

Between these investigations, he caught momentary
glimpses of the city, and realized how difficult—and dangerous—it would be for him to travel around in it.
Streets were practically nonexistent, and there seemed to
be no surface transport. This was the home of creatures
who could fly, and who had no fear of gravity. It was
nothing to come without warning upon a vertiginous
drop of several hundred meters, or to find that the only
entrance into a room was an opening high up in the wall.
In a hundred ways, Jan began to realize that the psychology of a race with wings must be fundamentally different from that of earthbound creatures.

It was strange to see the Overlords flying like great
birds among the towers of their city, their pinions moving with slow, powerful beats. And there was a scientific problem here. This was a large planet—larger than
Earth. Yet its gravity was low, and Jan wondered why it
had so dense an atmosphere. He questioned Vindarten on
this, and discovered, as he had half expected, that this
was not the original planet of the Overlords. They had
evolved on a much smaller world and then conquered
this one, changing not only its atmosphere but even its
gravity.

The architecture of the Overlords was bleakly func-
tional: Jan saw no ornaments, nothing that did not
serve a purpose, even though that purpose was often
beyond his understanding. If a man from medieval times
could have seen this red-lit city, and the beings moving
through it, he would certainly have believed himself in
Hell. Even Jan, for all his curiosity and scientific detachment, sometimes found himself on the verge of unreason-
ing terror. The absence of a single familiar reference

point can be utterly unnerving even to the coolest and clearest minds.

And there was so much he did not understand, and which Vindarten could or would not attempt to explain. What were those flashing lights and changing shapes, the things that flickered through the air so swiftly that he could never be certain of their existence? They could have been something tremendous and awe-inspiring—or as spectacular yet trivial as the neon signs of old-time Broadway.

Jan also sensed that the world of the Overlords was full of sounds that he could not hear. Occasionally he caught complex rhythmical patterns racing up and down through the audible spectrum, to vanish at the upper or lower edge of hearing. Vindarten did not seem to understand what Jan meant by music, so he was never able to solve this problem to his satisfaction.

The city was not very large: it was certainly far smaller than London or New York had been at their heyday. According to Vindarten, there were several thousand such cities scattered over the planet, each one designed for some specific purpose. On Earth, the closest parallel to this place would have been a university town—except that the degree of specialization had gone much further. This entire city was devoted, Jan soon discovered, to the study of alien cultures.

In one of their first trips outside the bare cell in which Jan lived, Vindarten had taken him to the museum. It had given Jan a much needed psychological boost to find himself in a place whose purpose he could fully understand. Apart from the scale upon which it was built, this museum might well have been on Earth. They had taken a long time to reach it, falling steadily on a great platform that moved like a piston in a vertical cylinder of unknown length. There were no visible controls, and the sense of acceleration at the beginning and ending of the descent was quite noticeable. Presumably the Overlords did not waste their compensating field devices for domestic uses. Jan wondered if the whole interior of this world was riddled with excavations: and why had they limited the size of the city, going underground instead of outwards? That was just another of the enigmas he never solved.

One could have spent a lifetime exploring these colossal chambers. Here was the loot of planets, the achievements of more civilizations than Jan could guess. But there was no time to see much. Vindarten placed him carefully on a strip of flooring that at first sight seemed an ornamental pattern. Then Jan remembered that there were no ornaments here—and at the same time, something invisible grasped him gently and hurried him forward. He was moving past the great display cases, past vistas of unimaginable worlds, at a speed of twenty or thirty kilometers an hour.

The Overlords had solved the problem of museum fatigue. There was no need for anyone to walk.

They must have travelled several kilometers before Jan's guide grasped him again, and with a surge of his great wings lifted him away from whatever force was propelling them. Before them stretched a huge, half-empty hall, flooded with a familiar light that Jan had not seen since leaving Earth. It was faint, so that it would not pain the sensitive eyes of the Overlords, but it was, unmistakably, sunlight. Jan would never have believed that anything so simple or so commonplace could have evoked such yearning in his heart.

So this was the exhibit for Earth. They walked for a few meters past a beautiful model of Paris, past art treasures from a dozen centuries grouped incongruously together, past modern calculating machines and paleolithic axes, past television receivers and Hero of Alexandra's steam turbine. A great doorway opened ahead of them, and they were in the office of the Curator for Earth.

Was he seeing a human being for the first time? Jan wondered. Had he ever been to Earth, or was it just another of the many planets in his charge, of whose exact location he was not precisely sure? Certainly he neither spoke nor understood English, and Vindarten had to act as interpreter.

Jan had spent several hours here, talking into a recording device while the Overlords presented various terrestrial objects to him. Many of these, he discovered to his shame, he could not identify. His ignorance of his own race and its achievements was enormous: he wondered if the Overlords, for all their superb mental gifts, could really grasp the complete pattern of human culture.

Vindarten took him out of the museum by a different route. Once again they floated effortlessly through great vaulted corridors, but this time they were moving past the creations of nature, not of conscious mind. Sullivan, thought Jan, would have given his life to be here, to see what wonders evolution had wrought on a hundred worlds. But Sullivan, he remembered, was probably already dead. . . .

Then, without any warning, they were on a gallery high above a large circular chamber, perhaps a hundred meters across. As usual, there was no protective parapet, and for a moment Jan hesitated to go near the edge. But Vindarten was standing on the very brink, looking calmly downwards, so Jan moved cautiously forward to join him.

The floor was only twenty meters below—far, far too close. Afterwards, Jan was sure that his guide had not intended to surprise him, and was completely taken aback by his reaction. For he had given one tremendous yell and jumped backwards from the gallery's edge, in an involuntary effort to hide what lay below. It was not until the muffled echoes of his shout had died away in the thick atmosphere that he steeled himself to go forward again.

It was lifeless, of course—not, as he had thought in that first moment of panic, consciously staring up at him. It filled almost all that great circular space, and the ruby light gleamed and shifted in its crystal depths.

It was a single giant eye.

"Why did you make that noise?" asked Vindarten.

"I was frightened," Jan confessed sheepishly.

"But why? Surely you did not imagine that there could be any danger here?"

Jan wondered if he could explain what a reflex action was, but decided not to attempt it.

"Anything completely unexpected is frightening. Until a novel situation is analyzed, it is safest to assume the worst."

His heart was still pounding violently as he stared down once more at that monstrous eye. Of course, it might have been a model, enormously enlarged as were microbes and insects in terrestrial museums. Yet even as he asked the question, Jan knew, with a sickening certainty, that it was no larger than life.

Vindarten could tell him little: this was not his field of knowledge, and he was not particularly curious. From the Overlord's description, Jan built up a picture of a cyclopean beast living among the asteroidal rubble of some distant sun, its growth uninhibited by gravity, depending for food and life upon the range and resolving power of its single eye.

There seemed no limit to what Nature could do if she was pressed, and Jan felt an irrational pleasure at discovering something which the Overlords would not attempt. They had brought a full-sized whale from Earth—but they had drawn the line at *this*.

* * *

And there was the time when he had gone up, endlessly up, until the walls of the elevator had faded through opalescence into a crystal transparency. He was standing, it seemed, unsupported among the uppermost peaks of the city, with nothing to protect him from the abyss. But he felt no more vertigo than one does in an airplane, for there was no sense of contact with the distant ground.

He was above the clouds, sharing the sky with a few pinnacles of metal or stone. A rose-red sea, the cloud-layer rolled sluggishly beneath him. There were two pale and tiny moons in the sky, not far from the somber sun. Near the center of that bloated red disc was a small, dark shadow, perfectly circular. It might have been a sunspot, or another moon in transit.

Jan slowly moved his gaze along the horizon. The cloud-cover extended clear to the edge of this enormous world, but in one direction, at an unguessable distance, there was a mottled patch that might have marked the towers of another city. He stared at it for a long while, then continued his careful survey.

When he had turned half-circle he saw the mountain. It was not on the horizon, but *beyond* it—a single serrated peak, climbing up over the edge of the world, its lower slopes hidden as the bulk of an iceberg is concealed below the water line. He tried to guess its size, and failed completely. Even on a world with gravity as low as this, it seemed hard to believe that such mountains could exist. Did the Overlords, he wondered, sport themselves upon its slopes and sweep like eagles around those immense buttresses?

And then, slowly, the mountain began to change. When he saw it first, it was a dull and almost sinister red, with a few faint markings near its crown that he could not clearly distinguish. He was trying to focus on them when he realized that they were moving. . . .

At first he could not believe his eyes. Then he forced himself to remember that all his preconceived ideas were worthless here: he must not let his mind reject any message his senses brought into the hidden chamber of the brain. He must not try to understand—only to observe. Understanding would come later, or not at all.

The mountain—he still thought of it as such, for there was no other word that could serve—seemed to be alive. He remembered that monstrous eye in its buried vault—but no, that was inconceivable. It was not organic life that he was watching: it was not even, he suspected, matter as he knew it.

The somber red was brightening to an angrier hue. Streaks of vivid yellow appeared, so that for a moment Jan felt he was looking at a volcano pouring streams of lava down on to the land beneath. But these streams, as he could tell by occasional flecks and mottlings, were moving *upwards*.

Now something else was rising out of the ruby clouds around the mountain's base. It was a huge ring, perfectly horizontal and perfectly circular—and it was the color of all that Jan had left so far behind, for the skies of Earth had held no lovelier blue. Nowhere else on the world of the Overlords had he seen such hues, and his throat contracted with the longing and the loneliness they evoked.

The ring was expanding as it climbed. It was higher than the mountain now, and its nearer arc was sweeping swiftly towards him. Surely, thought Jan, it must be a vortex of some kind—a smoke ring already many kilometers across. But it showed none of the rotation he expected, and it seemed to grow no less solid as its size increased.

Its shadow rushed past long before the ring itself had swept majestically overhead, still rising into space. He watched until it had dwindled to a thin thread of blue, hard for the eye to focus upon in the surrounding redness of the sky. When it vanished at last, it must already have been many thousands of kilometers across. And it was still growing.

He looked back at the mountain. It was golden now, and devoid of all markings. Perhaps it was imagination —he could believe anything by this time—but it seemed taller and narrower, and appeared to be spinning like the funnel of a cyclone. Not until then, still numbed and with his powers of reason almost in abeyance, did he remember his camera. He raised it to eye level, and sighted towards that impossible, mind-shaking enigma.

Vindarten moved swiftly into his line of vision. With implacable firmness, the great hands covered the lens turret and forced him to lower the camera. Jan did not attempt to resist: it would have been useless, of course, but he felt a sudden deathly fear of that thing out there at the edge of the world, and wanted no further part of it.

There was nothing else in all his travels that they

would not let him photograph, and Vindarten gave no explanations. Instead, he spent much time getting Jan to describe in minute detail what he had witnessed.

It was then that Jan realized that Vindarten's eyes had seen something totally different: and it was then that he guessed, for the first time, that the Overlords had masters, too.

Now he was coming home, and all the wonder, the fear and the mystery were far behind. It was the same ship, he believed, though surely not the same crew. However long their lives, it was hard to believe that the Overlords would willingly cut themselves off from their home for all the decades consumed on an interstellar voyage.

The Relativity time-dilation effect worked both ways, of course. The Overlords would age only four months on the round trip, but when they returned their friends would be eighty years older.

Had he wished, Jan could doubtless have stayed here for the remainder of his life. But Vindarten had warned him that there would be no other ship going to Earth for several years, and had advised him to take this opportunity. Perhaps the Overlords realized that even in this relatively short time, his mind had nearly reached the end of its resources. Or he might merely have become a nuisance, and they could spare no more time for him.

It was of no importance now, for Earth was there ahead. He had seen it thus a hundred times before, but always through the remote, mechanical eye of the television camera. Now at last he himself was out here in space, as the final act of his dream unfolded itself, and Earth spun beneath on its eternal orbit.

The great blue-green crescent was in its first quarter: more than half the visible disc was still in darkness. There was little cloud—a few bands scattered along the line of the trade winds. The arctic cap glittered brilliantly, but was far outshone by the dazzling reflection of the sun in the north Pacific.

One might have thought it was a world of water:

this hemisphere was almost devoid of land. The only continent visible was Australia, a darker mist in the atmospheric haze along the limb of the planet.

The ship was driving into Earth's great cone of shadow: the gleaming crescent dwindled, shrank to a burning bow of fire, and winked out of existence. Below was darkness and night. The world was sleeping.

It was then that Jan realized what was wrong. There was land down there—but where were the gleaming necklaces of light, where were the glittering corruscations that had been the cities of man? In all that shadowy hemisphere, there was no single spark to drive back the night. Gone without a trace were the millions of kilowatts that once had been splashed carelessly towards the stars. He might have been looking down on Earth as it had been before the coming of man.

This was not the homecoming he had expected. There was nothing he could do but watch, while the fear of the unknown grew within him. Something had happened—something unimaginable. And yet the ship was descending purposefully in a long curve that was taking it again over the sunlit hemisphere.

He saw nothing of the actual landing, for the picture of Earth suddenly winked out and was replaced by that meaningless pattern of lines and lights. When vision was restored, they were on the ground. There were great buildings in the distance, machines moving about, and a group of Overlords watching them.

Somewhere there was the muffled roar of air as the ship equalized pressure, then the sound of great doors opening. He did not wait: the silent giants watched him with tolerance or indifference as he ran from the control room.

He was home, seeing once more by the sparkling light of his own familiar sun, breathing the air that had first washed through his lungs. The gangway was already down, but he had to wait for a moment until the glare outside no longer blinded him.

Karellen was standing, a little apart from his companions, beside a great transport vehicle loaded with crates.

Jan did not stop to wonder how he recognized the Supervisor, nor was he surprised to see him completely unchanged. That was almost the only thing that had turned out as he had expected.

"I have been waiting for you," said Karellen.

23

"IN THE EARLY DAYS," said Karellen, "it was safe for us to go among them. But they no longer needed us: our work was done when we had gathered them together and given them a continent of their own. Watch."

The wall in front of Jan disappeared. Instead he was looking down from a height of a few hundred meters on to a pleasantly wooded country. The illusion was so perfect that he fought a momentary giddiness.

"This is five years later, when the second phase had begun."

There were figures moving below, and the camera swooped down upon them like a bird of prey.

"This will distress you," said Karellen. "But remember that your standards no longer apply. You are not watching human children."

Yet that was the immediate impression that came to Jan's mind, and no amount of logic could dispel it. They might have been savages, engaged in some complex ritual dance. They were naked and filthy, with matted hair obscuring their eyes. As far as Jan could tell, they were of all ages from five to fifteen, yet they all moved with the same speed, precision, and complete indifference to their surroundings.

Then Jan saw their faces. He swallowed hard, and forced himself not to turn away. They were emptier than the faces of the dead, for even a corpse has some record carved by time's chisel upon its features, to speak when the lips themselves are dumb. There was no more emotion or feeling here than in the face of a snake or an insect. The Overlords themselves were more human than this.

"You are searching for something that is no longer there," said Karellen. "Remember—they have no more identity than the cells in your own body. But linked together, they are something much greater than you."

"Why do they keep moving like this?"

"We called it the Long Dance," replied Karellen. "They never sleep, you know, and this lasted almost a year. Three hundred million of them, moving in a controlled pattern over a whole continent. We've analyzed that pattern endlessly, but it means nothing, perhaps because we can see only the physical part of it—the small portion that's here on Earth. Possibly what we have called the Overmind is still training them, molding them into one unit before it can wholly absorb them into its being."

"But how did they manage about food? And what happened if they hit obstructions, like trees, or cliffs, or water?"

"Water made no difference: they could not drown. When they encountered obstacles, they sometimes damaged themselves, but they never noticed it. As for food—well, there was all the fruit and game they required. But now they have left that need behind, like so many others. For food is largely a source of energy, and they have learned to tap greater sources."

The scene flickered as if a heat haze had passed over it. When it cleared, the movement below had ceased.

"Watch again," said Karellen. "It is three years later."

The little figures, so helpless and pathetic if one did not know the truth, stood motionless in forest and glade and plain. The camera roamed restlessly from one to the other: already, thought Jan, their faces were merging into a common mold. He had once seen some photographs made by the superposition of dozens of prints, to give one "average" face. The result had been as empty, as void of character as this.

They seemed to be sleeping or entranced. Their eyes were tightly closed, and they showed no more awareness of their surroundings than did the trees under which they stood. What thoughts, Jan wondered, were echoing through the intricate network in which their minds were now no more—and yet no less—than the separate threads of some great tapestry? And a tapestry, he now realized, that covered many worlds and many races—and was growing still.

It happened with a swiftness that dazzled the eye and stunned the brain. At one moment Jan was looking down upon a beautiful, fertile country with nothing strange about it save the countless small statues scattered—yet not randomly—over its length and breadth. And then in an instant all the trees and grass, all the living creatures that had inhabited this land, flickered out of existence and were gone. There were left only the still lakes, the winding rivers, the rolling brown hills, now stripped of their green carpet—and the silent, indifferent figures who had wrought all this destruction.

"Why did they do it?" gasped Jan.

"Perhaps the presence of other minds disturbed them —even the rudimentary minds of plants and animals. One day, we believe, they may find the material world equally distracting. And then, who knows what will happen? Now you understand why we withdrew when we had done our duty. We are still trying to study them, but we never enter their land or even send our instruments there. All we dare do is to observe from space."

"That was many years ago," said Jan. "What has happened since?"

"Very little. They have never moved in all that time, and take no notice of day or night, summer or winter. They are still testing their powers; some rivers have changed their courses, and there is one that flows uphill. But they have done nothing that seems to have any purpose."

"And they have ignored you completely?"

"Yes, though that is not surprising. The—entity—of which they are part knows all about us. It does not seem to care if we attempt to study it. When it wishes us to leave, or has a new task for us elsewhere, it will make its desires very obvious. Until then, we will remain here so that our scientists can gather what knowledge they may."

So this, thought Jan, with a resignation that lay beyond all sadness, was the end of man. It was an end that no prophet had ever foreseen—an end that repudiated optimism and pessimism alike.

Yet it was fitting: it had the sublime inevitability of a great work of art. Jan had glimpsed the universe in all its awful immensity, and knew now that it was no place for man. He realized at last how vain, in the ultimate analysis, had been the dream that had lured him to the stars.

For the road to the stars was a road that forked in two directions, and neither led to a goal that took any account of human hopes or fears.

At the end of one path were the Overlords. They had preserved their individuality, their independent egos: they possessed self-awareness and the pronoun "I" had a meaning in their language. They had emotions, some at least of which were shared by humanity. But they were trapped, Jan realized now, in a cul-de-sac from which they could never escape. Their minds were ten—perhaps a hundred—times as powerful as men's. It made no difference in the final reckoning. They were equally helpless, equally overwhelmed by the unimaginable complexity of a galaxy of a hundred thousand million suns, and a cosmos of a hundred thousand million galaxies.

And at the end of the other path? There lay the Overmind, whatever it might be, bearing the same relation to man as man bore to amoeba. Potentially infinite, beyond mortality, how long had it been absorbing race after race as it spread across the stars? Did it too have desires, did it have goals it sensed dimly yet might never attain? Now it had drawn into its being all that the human race had ever achieved. This was not tragedy, but fulfillment. The billions of transient sparks of consciousness that had made up humanity would flicker no more like fireflies against the night. But they had not lived utterly in vain.

The last act, Jan knew, had still to come. It might occur tomorrow, or it might be centuries hence. Even the Overlords could not be certain.

He understood their purpose now, what they had done with man and why they still lingered upon Earth. Towards them he felt a great humility, as well as admiration for the inflexible patience that had kept them waiting here so long.

He never learned the full story of the strange symbiosis between the Overmind and its servants. According to Rashaverak, there had never been a time in his race's history when the Overmind was not there, though it had made no use of them until they had achieved a scientific civilization and could range through space to do its bidding.

"But why does it need you?" queried Jan. "With all its tremendous powers, surely it could do anything it pleased."

"No," said Rashaverak, "it has limits. In the past, we know, it has attempted to act directly upon the minds of other races, and to influence their cultural development. It's always failed, perhaps because the gulf is too great. We are the interpreters—the guardians. Or, to use one of your other metaphors, we till the field until the crop is ripe. The Overmind collects the harvest—and we move on to another task. This is the fifth race whose apotheosis we have watched. Each time we learn a little more."

"And you do not resent being used as a tool by the Overmind?"

"The arrangement has some advantages: besides, no one of intelligence resents the inevitable."

That proposition, Jan reflected wryly, had never been fully accepted by mankind. There were things beyond logic that the Overlords had never understood.

"It seems strange," said Jan, "that the Overmind chose you to do its work, if you have no trace of the paraphysical powers latent in mankind. How does it communicate with you and make its wishes known?"

"That is one question I cannot answer—and I cannot tell you the reason why I must keep the facts from you. One day, perhaps, you will know some of the truth."

Jan puzzled over this for a moment, but knew it was useless to follow this line of inquiry. He would have to change the subject and hope to pick up clues later.

"Tell me this, then," he said. "Here is something else you've never explained. When your race first came to Earth, back in the distant past, what went wrong? Why had you become the symbol of fear and evil to us?"

Rashaverak smiled. He did not do this as well as Karellen could, but it was a fair imitation.

"No one ever guessed, and you see now why we could never tell you. There was only one event that could have made such an impact upon humanity. And that event was not at the dawn of history, *but at its very end.*"

"What do you mean?" asked Jan.

"When our ships entered your skies a century and a half ago, that was the first meeting of our two races, though of course we had studied you from a distance. And yet you feared and recognized us, as we knew that you would. It was not precisely a memory. You have already had proof that time is more complex than your science ever imagined. For that memory was not of the past, but of the *future*—of those closing years when your race knew that everything was finished. We did what we could, but it was not an easy end. And because we were there, we became identified with your race's death. Yes, even while it was ten thousand years in the future! It was as if a distorted echo had reverberated round the closed circle of time, from the future to the past. Call it not a memory, but a premonition."

The idea was hard to grasp, and for a moment Jan wrestled with it in silence. Yet he should have been prepared; he had already received proof enough that cause and event could reverse their normal sequence.

There must be such a thing as racial memory, and that memory was somehow independent of time. To it, the future and the past were one. That was why, thousands of years ago, men had already glimpsed a distorted image of the Overlords, through a mist of fear and terror.

"Now I understand," said the last man.

The Last Man! Jan found it very hard to think of himself as that. When he had gone into space, he had accepted the possibility of eternal exile from the human race, and loneliness had not yet come upon him. As the years passed, the longing to see another human being might rise and overwhelm him, but for the present, the company of the Overlords prevented him from feeling utterly alone.

There had been men on Earth as little as ten years ago, but they had been degenerate survivors and Jan had lost nothing by missing them. For reasons which the Overlords could not explain, but which Jan suspected were largely psychological, there had been no children to replace those who had gone. *Homo sapiens* was extinct.

Perhaps, lost in one of the still-intact cities, was the manuscript of some latter-day Gibbon, recording the last days of the human race. If so, Jan was not sure that he would care to read it; Rashaverak had told him all he wished to know.

Those who had not destroyed themselves had sought oblivion in ever more feverish activities, in fierce and suicidal sports that were often indistinguishable from minor wars. As the population had swiftly fallen, the aging survivors had clustered together a defeated army closing its ranks as it made its last retreat.

That final act, before the curtain came down forever, must have been lit by flashes of heroism and devotion, darkened by savagery and selfishness. Whether it had ended in despair or resignation, Jan would never know.

There was plenty to occupy his mind. The Overlord base was about a kilometer from a deserted villa, and Jan spent months fitting this out with equipment he had taken from the nearest town, some thirty kilometers distant. He had flown there with Rashaverak, whose friendship, he suspected, was not completely altruistic. The Overlord psychologist was still studying the last specimen of *Homo sapiens*.

The town must have been evacuated before the end, for the houses and even many of the public services were still in good order. It would have taken little work to restart the generators, so that the wide streets glowed once more with the illusion of life. Jan toyed with the idea, then abandoned it as too morbid. The one thing he did not wish to do was to brood upon the past. There was everything here that he needed to maintain him for the rest of his life, but what he wanted most was an electronic piano and certain Bach transcriptions. He had never had as much time for music as he would have liked, and now he would make up for it. When he was not performing himself, he played tapes of the great symphonies and concertos, so that the villa was never silent. Music had become his talisman against the loneliness which, one day, must surely overwhelm him.

Often he would go for long walks on the hills, thinking of all that had happened in the few months since he had last seen Earth. He had never thought, when he said goodby to Sullivan eighty terrestrial years ago, that the last generation of mankind was already in the womb.

What a young fool he had been! Yet he was not sure that he regretted his action: had he stayed on Earth, he would have witnessed those closing years over which time had now drawn a veil. Instead, he had leapfrogged past them into the future, and had learned the answers to questions that no other man would ever know. His curiosity was almost satisfied, but sometimes he wondered why the Overlords were waiting, and what would happen when their patience was at last rewarded.

But most of the time, with a contented resignation that comes normally to a man only at the end of a long and busy life, he sat before the keyboard and filled the air with his beloved Bach. Perhaps he was deceiving himself, perhaps this was some merciful trick of the mind, but now it seemed to Jan that this was what he had always wished to do. His secret ambition had at last dared to emerge into the full light of consciousness.

Jan had always been a good pianist—and now he was the finest in the world.

24

IT WAS Rashaverak who brought Jan the news, but he had already guessed it. In the small hours of the morning a nightmare had awakened him, and he had not been able to regain sleep. He could not remember the dream, which was very strange, for he believed that all dreams could be recalled if one tried hard enough immediately after waking. All he could remember of this was that he had been a small boy again, on a vast and empty plain, listening to a great voice calling in an unknown language.

The dream had disturbed him: he wondered if it was the first onslaught of loneliness upon his mind. Restlessly, he walked out of the villa on to the neglected lawn.

A full moon bathed the scene with a golden light so brilliant that he could see perfectly. The immense, gleaming cylinder of Karellen's ship lay beyond the buildings of the Overlord base, towering above them and reducing them to man-made proportions. Jan looked at the ship, trying to recall the emotions it had once roused in him. There was a time when it had been an unattainable goal, a symbol of all that he had never really expected to achieve. And now it meant nothing.

How quiet and still it was! The Overlords, of course, would be as active as ever, but for the moment there was no sign of them. He might have been alone on Earth—as, indeed, in a very real sense he was. He glanced up at the Moon, seeking some familiar sight on which his thoughts could rest.

There were the ancient, well-remembered seas. He had been forty light-years into space, yet he had never walked on those silent, dusty plains less than two light-seconds away. For a moment he amused himself trying to locate the crater Tycho. When he did discover it, he was puzzled to find that gleaming speck further from the center line of the disc than he had thought. And it was then that he realized that the dark oval of the Mare Crisium was missing altogether.

The face that her satellite now turned towards the Earth was not the one that had looked down on the world since the dawn of life. The moon had begun to turn upon its axis.

This could mean only one thing. On the other side of the Earth, in the land that they had stripped so suddenly of life, *they* were emerging from their long trance. As a waking child may stretch its arms to greet the day, they too were flexing their muscles and playing with their new-found powers. . . .

"You have guessed correctly," said Rashaverak. "It is no longer safe for us to stay. They may ignore us still, but we cannot take the risk. We leave as soon as our equipment can be loaded—probably in two or three hours."

He looked up at the sky, as if afraid that some new miracle was about to blaze forth. But all was peaceful: the Moon had set, and only a few clouds rode high upon the west wind.

"It does not matter greatly if they tamper with the Moon," Rashaverak added, "but suppose they begin to interfere with the Sun? We shall leave instruments behind, of course, so that we can learn what happens."

"I shall stay," said Jan abruptly. "I have seen enough of the universe. There's only one thing that I'm curious about now—and that is the fate of my own planet."

Very gently, the ground trembled underfoot.

"I was expecting that," Jan continued. "If they alter

the Moon's spin, the angular momentum must go somewhere. So the Earth is slowing down. I don't know which puzzles me more—*how* they are doing it, or *why*."

"They are still playing," said Rashaverak. "What logic is there in the actions of a child? And in many ways the entity that your race has become is still a child. It is not yet ready to unite with the Overmind. But very soon it will be, and then you will have the Earth to yourself."

He did not complete the sentence, and Jan finished it for him.

"—if, of course, the Earth still exists."

"You realize that danger—and yet you will stay?"

"Yes. I have been home five—or is it six?—years now. Whatever happens, I'll have no complaints."

"We were hoping," began Rashaverak slowly, "that you would wish to stay. There is something that you can do for us. . . ."

The glare of the stardrive dwindled and died, somewhere out there beyond the orbit of Mars. Along that road, thought Jan, he alone had traveled, out of all the billions of human beings who had lived and died on Earth. And no one would ever travel it again.

The world was his. Everything he needed—all the material possessions anyone could ever desire—were his for the taking. But he was no longer interested. He feared neither the loneliness of the deserted planet, nor the presence that still rested here in the last moments before it went to seek its unknown heritage. In the inconceivable backwash of that departure, Jan did not expect that he and his problems would long survive.

That was well. He had done all that he had wished to do, and to drag out a pointless life on this empty world would have been an unbearable anticlimax. He could have left with the Overlords, but for what purpose? For he knew, as no one else had ever known, that Karellen spoke the truth when he had said: "The stars are not for Man."

He turned his back upon the night and walked through the vast entrance of the Overlord base. Its size affected him not in the least: sheer immensity no longer had any power over his mind. The lights were burning redly, driven by energies that could feed them for ages yet. On either side lay machines whose secrets he would never know, abandoned by the Overlords in their retreat. He went past them, and clambered awkwardly up the great steps until he had reached the control room.

The spirit of the Overlords still lingered here: their machines were still alive, doing the bidding of their now far-distant masters. What could he add, wondered Jan, to the information they were already hurling into space?

He climbed into the great chair and made himself as comfortable as he could. The microphone, already live, was waiting for him; something that was the equivalent of a TV camera must be watching, but he could not locate it.

Beyond the desk and its meaningless instrument panels, the wide windows looked out into the starry night, across a valley sleeping beneath a gibbous moon, and to the distant range of mountains. A river wound along the valley, glittering here and there as the moonlight struck upon some patch of troubled water. It was all so peaceful. It might have been thus at Man's birth as it was now at his ending.

Out there across unknown millions of kilometers of space, Karellen would be waiting. It was strange to think that the ship of the Overlords was racing away from Earth almost as swiftly as his signal could speed after it. Almost—but not quite. It would be a long chase, but his words would catch the Supervisor and he would have repaid the debt he owed.

How much of this, Jan wondered, had Karellen planned, and how much was masterful improvisation? Had the Supervisor deliberately let him escape into space, almost a century ago, so that he could return to play the role he was fulfilling now? No, that seemed too fantastic. But Jan was certain, now, that Karellen was involved in some vast and complicated plot. Even while he served it, he was studying the Overmind with all the instruments at his command. Jan suspected that it was not only scientific curiosity that inspired the Supervisor: perhaps the Over-lords had dreams of one day escaping from their peculiar bondage, when they had learned enough about the powers they served.

That Jan could add to that knowledge by what he was now doing seemed hard to believe. "Tell us what you see," Rashaverak had said. "The picture that reaches your eyes will be duplicated by our cameras. But the message that enters your brain may be very different, and it could tell us a great deal." Well, he would do his best.

"Still nothing to report," he began. "A few minutes ago I saw the trail of your ship disappear in the sky. The Moon is just past full, and almost half its familiar side has now turned away from Earth—but I suppose you already know that."

Jan paused, feeling slightly foolish. There was something incongruous, even faintly absurd, about what he was doing. Here was the climax of all history, yet he might have been a radio-commentator at a race-track or a boxing-ring. Then he shrugged his shoulders and put the thought aside. At all moments of greatness, he suspected, bathos had never been far away—and certainly he alone could sense its presence here.

"There have been three slight quakes in the last hour," he continued. "Their control of Earth's spin must be marvellous, but not quite perfect. . . . You know now, Karellen, I'm going to find it very hard to say anything your instruments haven't already told you. It might have helped if you'd given me some idea of what to expect, and warned me how long I may have to wait. If nothing happens, I'll report again in six hours, as we arranged. . . .

"Hello! They must have been waiting for you to leave. Something's starting to happen. The stars are becoming dimmer. It's as if a great cloud is coming up, very swiftly, over all the sky. But it isn't really a cloud. It seems to have some sort of structure—I can glimpse a hazy network of lines and bands that keep changing their positions. It's almost as if the stars are tangled in a ghostly spider's web.

"The whole network is beginning to glow, to pulse with light, exactly as if it were alive. And I suppose it is: or is it something as much beyond life as *that* is above the inorganic world?

"The glow seems to be shifting to one part of the sky —wait a minute while I move around to the other window.

"Yes—I might have guessed. There's a great burning column, like a tree of fire, reaching above the western horizon. It's a long way off, right round the world. I know where it springs from: *they're* on their way at last, to become part of the Overmind. Their probation is ended: they're leaving the last remnants of matter behind.

"As that fire spreads upwards from the Earth, I can see the network becoming firmer and less misty. In places it seems almost solid, yet the stars are still shining faintly through it.

"I've just realized. It's not exactly the same, but the thing I saw shooting up above your world, Karellen, was very much like this. Was that part of the Overmind? I suppose you hid the truth from me so that I would have no preconceived ideas—so that I'd be an unbiassed observer. I wish I knew what your cameras were showing you now, to compare it with what my mind imagines I'm seeing!

"Is this how it talks to you, Karellen, in colors and shapes like these? I remember the control screens on your ship and the patterns that went across them, speaking to you in some visual language which your eyes could read.

"Now it looks exactly like the curtains of the aurora, dancing and flickering across the stars. Why, that's what it really is, I'm sure—a great auroral storm. The whole landscape is lit up—it's brighter than day—reds and golds and greens are chasing each other across the sky—oh, it's beyond words, it doesn't seem fair that I'm the only one to see it—I never thought such colors—

"The storm's dying down, but the great misty network is still there. I think that aurora was only a by-product of whatever energies are being released up there on the frontier of space. . . .

"Just a minute: I've noticed something else. *My weight's decreasing.* What does that mean? I've dropped a pencil—it's falling slowly. Something's happened to gravity. There's a great wind coming up—I can see the trees tossing their branches down there in the valley.

"Of course—the atmosphere's escaping. Sticks and stones are rising into the sky, almost as if the Earth itself is trying to follow *them* out into space. There's a great cloud of dust, whipped up by the gale. It's becoming hard to see . . . perhaps it will clear in a moment, and I'll be able to find out what's happening.

"Yes—that's better. Everything moveable has been stripped away, the dust clouds have vanished. I wonder how long this building will stand? And it's getting hard to breathe—I must try to talk more slowly.

"I can see clearly again. That great burning column is still there, but it's constricting, narrowing; it looks like the funnel of a tornado, about to retract into the clouds. And—oh, this is hard to describe, but just then I felt a great wave of emotion sweep over me. It wasn't joy or sorrow; it was a sense of fulfillment, achievement. Did I imagine it? Or did it come from outside? I don't know.

"And now—*this* can't be all imagination—the world feels empty. Utterly empty. It's like listening to a radio set that's suddenly gone dead. And the sky is clear again—the misty web has gone. What world will it go to next, Karellen? And will you be there to serve it still?

"Strange: everything around me is unaltered. I don't know why, but somehow I'd thought that . . ."

Jan stopped. For a moment he struggled for words, then closed his eyes in an effort to regain control. There was no room for fear or panic now: he had a duty to perform—a duty to Man, and a duty to Karellen.

Slowly at first, like a man awakening from a dream, he began to speak.

"The buildings round me, the ground, the mountains—everything's like glass—*I can see through it.* Earth's dissolving. My weight has almost gone. You were right —they've finished playing with their toys.

"It's only a few seconds away. There go the mountains, like wisps of smoke. Good-by, Karellen, Rashaverak—I am sorry for you. Though I cannot understand it, I've seen what my race became. Everything we ever achieved has gone up there into the stars. Perhaps that's what the old religions were trying to say. But they got it all wrong: they thought mankind was so important, yet we're only one race in —do *you* know how many? Yet now we've become something that you could never be.

"There goes the river. No change in the sky, though. I can hardly breathe. Strange to see the Moon still shining up there. I'm glad they left it, but it will be lonely now—

"The light! From *beneath* me—inside the Earth—shining upward, through the rocks, the ground, everything—growing brighter, brighter, blinding—"

In a soundless concussion of light, Earth's core gave up its hoarded energies. For a little while the gravitational waves crossed and re-crossed the Solar System, disturbing ever so slightly the orbits of the planets. Then the Sun's remaining children pursued their ancient paths once more, as corks floating on a placid lake ride out the tiny ripples set in motion by a falling stone.

There was nothing left of Earth: *They* had leeched away the last atoms of its substance. It had nourished them, through the fierce moments of their inconceivable metamorphosis, as the food stored in a grain of wheat feeds the infant plant while it climbs towards the Sun.

Six thousand million kilometers beyond the orbit of Pluto, Karellen sat before a suddenly darkened screen. The record was complete, the mission ended; he was homeward bound for the world he had left so long ago. The weight of centuries was upon him, and a sadness that no logic could dispel. He did not mourn for Man: his sorrow was for his own race, forever barred from greatness by forces it could not overcome.

For all their achievements, thought Karellen, for all their mastery of the physical universe, his people were no better than a tribe that had passed its whole existence upon some flat and dusty plain. Far off were the mountains, where power and beauty dwelt, where the thunder sported above the glaciers and the air was clear and keen. There the sun still walked, transfiguring the peaks with glory, when all the land below was wrapped in darkness. And they could only watch and wonder; they could never scale those heights.

Yet, Karellen knew, they would hold fast until the end: they would await without despair whatever destiny was theirs. They would serve the Overmind because they had no choice, but even in that service they would not lose their souls.

The great control screen flared for a moment with somber, ruby light: without conscious effort, Karellen read the message of its changing patterns. The ship was leaving the frontiers of the Solar System: the energies that powered the stardrive were ebbing fast, but they had done their work.

Karellen raised his hand, and the picture changed once more. A single brilliant star glowed in the center of the screen: no one could have told, from this distance, that the Sun had ever possessed planets or that one of them had now been lost. For a long time Karellen stared back across that swiftly widening gulf, while many memories raced through his vast and labyrinthine mind. In silent farewell, he saluted the men he had known, whether they had hindered or helped him in his purpose.

No one dared disturb him or interrupt his thoughts: and presently he turned his back upon the dwindling Sun.

ARTHUR C. CLARKE

Arthur C. Clarke was born at Minehead, Somerset, England, in 1917 and is a graduate of King's College, London, where he obtained First Class Honors in Physics and Mathematics. He is past chairman of the British Interplanetary Society, a member of the Academy of Astronautics, the Royal Astronomical Society, and many other scientific organizations. During the War, as an RAF officer, he was in charge of the first radar talk-down ("G.C.A.") equipment during its experimental trials. His only *non*-s.f. novel, *Glide Path,* is based on this work.

Author of almost 50 books, in 1962 he went to New Delhi to receive the £1,000 Kalinga Prize for science writing from the Director-General of UNESCO. In 1962 he was awarded a gold medal of the Franklin Institute for having originated communications satellites in a technical paper published in 1945. This described in detail the geostationary satellite system now used by all commercial comsats.

Almost twenty million copies of his books have been printed in over 30 languages. An article on comsats in LIFE was awarded the Aviation-Space Writers' 1965 prize as the best aerospace reporting of the year in any medium, and in 1969 he won the AAAS—Westinghouse science writing prize. He shared an 'OSCAR' nomination with Stanley Kubrick in 1969 for '2001: A Space Odyssey,' and he has won the top science fiction awards, the

HUGO, NEBULA, and John W. Campbell Award —all three of which were won by his novel *Rendezvous with Rama*.

He has contributed to PLAYBOY, LOOK, TIME, READER'S DIGEST, HOLIDAY, HORIZON, and the NEW YORK TIMES, as well as the Observer, Sunday Times and Daily Telegraph Magazines.

For the past twenty years Mr. Clarke's hobby has been underwater exploration along the Great Barrier Reef of Australia and off the coast of Ceylon, where he has resided since 1956. Nine of his books have been concerned with this work, which has also been the subject of TV features. In 1961 his colleagues discovered a man-of-war which sank in 1702 off the coast of Ceylon with at least a ton of silver aboard: the account of its salvage is described in THE TREASURE OF THE GREAT REEF and INDIAN OCEAN TREASURE.

Mr. Clarke joined Walter Cronkite and Captain Wally Shirra on CBS TV during the Apollo 11, 12 and 15 missions. He has appeared with David Frost, Hugh Downs, Dick Cavett, Patrick Moore and many other radio and TV personalities.

In 1968 he was chosen to write the Epilogue to the Astronauts' own account of the Apollo Mission, FIRST ON THE MOON.

July 1974.

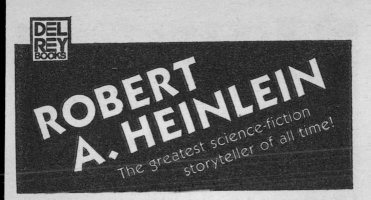